ALSO BY SOPHIE LARK

Brutal Birthright

Brutal Prince

Stolen Heir

Savage Lover

Bloody Heart

Broken Vow

Heavy Crown

Sinners Duet

There Are No Saints

There Is No Devil

STOLEN HEIR

SOPHIE LARK

Bloom *books*

Published by Bloom Books, an imprint of Sourcebooks
P.O. Box 4410, Naperville, Illinois 60567-4410
(630) 961-3900
sourcebooks.com

Originally self-published in 2022 by Sophie Lark.

Cataloging-in-Publication Data is on file with the Library of Congress.

Printed and bound in the United States of America.
LSC 10 9 8 7 6 5 4 3 2

This book is for my fairy-tale lovers.
For those who feel the call of the dark, the
monstrous, and the mysterious. For those who
know they could never be happy with Prince
Charming...and want to meet the Beast.

XOXO

Sophie Lark

SOUNDTRACK

1. "Blood in the Cut"—K.Flay
2. "Someone You Loved"—Lewis Capaldi
3. "Satin Birds"—Abel Korzeniowski
4. "Earned It"—The Weeknd
5. "Company"—Tinashe
6. "Bad Intentions"—Niykee Heaton
7. "War of Hearts"—Ruelle
8. "As Shadows Fall"—Peter Gundry
9. "Latch (acoustic)"—Sam Smith
10. "Castle"—Halsey
11. "Monsters"—Ruelle

Music is a big part of my writing process. If you start a song when you see a 🎵 while reading, the song matches the scene like a movie score.

Spotify   Apple Music

THE GALLOS

1

MIKOLAJ WILK

WARSAW, POLAND

On my way home from work, I stop and buy a bag of fresh *chrusciki* for Anna. Little spots of grease seep through the paper bag from the egg-and-cream pastries, dusted with powdered sugar to suit their name of "angel wings." She's writing her university entrance exams today. I already know we'll have something to celebrate. Anna is brilliant. I'm sure she'll pass with top marks.

We may be twins, but you'd never guess it. She has brown hair, while I'm blond as corn silk. She devours every book she can get her hands on, while I left school at fourteen.

I didn't have much choice about that. Someone had to pay the rent on our dismal little flat.

Our father had a good job at the Huta Warszawa Steelworks. He was a maintenance technician, bringing home a salary of almost six thousand zloty a month. Enough to keep us all in new shoes with a full fridge.

Until he was cooked like a lobster in a pot while working on a blast furnace. He isn't dead. Just so badly burned that he can barely work the buttons on the remote while he watches television all day long, holed up in his room.

Our mother left. I heard she married an accountant and moved to Kraków. I haven't heard from her since.

It doesn't matter. I make enough at the deli to keep us going for now. Someday Anna will be a professor of literature. Then we'll buy a little house somewhere other than here.

We've lived our whole lives in the Praga District, on the right bank of the Vistula River. Across the water, you can see the prosperous centers of business and finance. We live in a slum. Tall filthy rectangular brick buildings blocking out the sun. Empty factories from the communist era when this was the center of state-run industry. Now their windows are smashed and doors chained shut. Addicts break in to sleep on piles of rags and inject themselves with flesh-rotting Russian *krokodil*.

Anna and I will have a proper house with a garden and nobody above or below us, banging and shouting at all hours of the night.

I don't expect my sister home for several hours, so when I open the door to our flat and spot her schoolbag on the floor, I'm confused and surprised. Anna is scrupulously tidy. She doesn't dump her backpack on the floor, letting the books spill out. Some of her textbooks are muddy and wet. The same with her shoes, abandoned next to the bag.

I can hear water running in the bathroom. Also strange—Anna doesn't shower at night.

I drop the bag of pastries on the kitchen table and run to our one and only bathroom. I knock on the door, calling out for my sister.

There's no answer.

When I press my ear against the door, I hear her sobbing over the sound of the shower.

I ram my shoulder against the door, hearing the cheap wood splinter as the lock gives way. Then I force myself into the tiny bathroom.

Anna is sitting in the shower, still wearing her school clothes. Her blouse is almost torn off her body. The thin material only clings to her arms and waist.

She's covered in cuts and welts—all over her shoulders, arms, and back. I see dark bruises around her neck and the tops of her breasts. Even what look like bite marks.

Her face is worse. She has a black eye and a long gash down her right cheek. Blood leaks from her nose, dripping into the water pooled around her legs, diffusing like watercolor paint.

She can't look at me. After the first glance, she buries her face in her arms, sobbing.

"Who did this to you?" I demand, my voice shaking.

She presses her lips together and shakes her head, not wanting to tell me.

It isn't true that twins can read each other's minds. But I do know my sister. I know her very well. And I know who did this. I've seen the way they look at her whenever she leaves our flat. I see them leaning against their expensive cars, their arms folded, their sunglasses failing to conceal how they leer. Sometimes they even shout things at her, though she never turns her head or answers.

It was the *Braterstwo*. The Polish Mafia.

They think they can have whatever they want—expensive watches, gold chains, phones that cost more than I make in a month. Apparently, they decided they wanted my sister.

She doesn't want to tell me because she's afraid of what will happen.

I grab her by the shoulder and make her look at me. Her eyes are red, swollen, terrified.

"Which ones did it?" I hiss. "The one with the shaved head?"

She hesitates, then nods.

"The one with the dark beard?"

Another nod.

"The one with the leather jacket?"

Her face crumples.

He's the ringleader. I've seen how the others defer to him. I've seen how he stares at Anna most of all.

"I'll get them, Anna. Every last one of them will pay," I promise her.

Anna shakes her head, silent tears sliding down her battered cheeks. "No, Miko." She sobs. "They'll kill you."

"Not if I kill them first."

I leave her there in the shower. I go into my bedroom and pry up the floorboard under which I've hidden my metal lockbox. It has all my savings in it—the money intended to send Anna to school. She missed her exams. She won't be going this year.

I fold the bills into a wad and stuff them in my pocket. Then I leave the flat, running through the rain over to the pawnshop on Brzeska Street.

Jakub sits behind the counter, as he always does, reading a paperback with one half its cover torn off. Stoop-shouldered, balding, with bottle-cap glasses in thick plastic frames, Jakub blinks at me like an owl that woke up too early.

"How can I help you, Mikolaj?" he says in his raspy voice.

"I need a gun."

He gives a hoarse chuckle. "That would be illegal, my boy. What about a guitar or an Xbox instead?"

I fling the wad of bills down on his countertop. "Cut the shit. Show me what you have."

He looks down at the money, not touching it. After a moment, he comes around the counter, shuffling over to the front door. He turns the latch, locking it. Then he shuffles toward the back.

"This way," he says, without turning his head.

I follow him into the back of the store. This is where he lives—I see an old couch with stuffing spilling from the holes in the upholstery. A square television set. A tiny kitchen with a hot plate, which smells of burned coffee and cigarettes.

Jakub leads me over to a chest of drawers. He pulls open the top drawer, revealing a small selection of handguns. "Which one do you want?"

I don't know anything about guns. I've never held one in my life.

I look at the jumble of weapons: some carbon, some steel, some sleek, some practically ancient. One is all black, medium in size, modern and simple looking. It reminds me of the gun James Bond carries. I pick it up, surprised by how heavy it is in my hand.

"That's a Glock," Jakub says.

"I know," I reply, though I actually don't.

"It's a .45. You need ammo, too?"

"And a knife."

I see the look of amusement on his face. He thinks I'm playing commando. It doesn't matter—I don't want him to take me seriously. I don't want him warning anyone.

He gives me a Leatherneck combat knife in a polymer sheath. He shows me how to grip the sheath to pull the blade free, as if he's demonstrating for a child.

He doesn't ask what I want it for. He doesn't offer any change either.

I hide my weapons under my clothes and hurry back to the flat. I intend to check in on Anna before I track down those walking corpses who dared to put their hands on my sister.

When I unlock the front door once more, a strange chill creeps down my spine.

I don't know what it is exactly. Everything looks the same as before—the backpack is in the same spot in the hallway, my sister's sneakers right next to it. I can still hear the low chatter of the television in my father's room, a sound that runs day and night. I can even see its blue light leaking out from under his door.

But I don't hear the shower running anymore. And I don't hear my sister. I hope that means she's resting in her room.

That's what I expect. I expect her to be lying in her bed under the covers. Hopefully asleep. Yet, as I pass the bathroom door on my way to check on her, I hesitate.

There's a small sound coming from within. A steady dripping. Like a faucet not quite turned off.

The door is ajar—I splintered the frame forcing my way inside the first time. Now it won't close all the way.

I push the door open, and the bright fluorescent light momentarily dazzles my eyes.

My sister lies in the bathtub, staring up at the ceiling. Her eyes are wide and fixed, utterly dead. Her face is paler than chalk. One arm dangles over the side of the tub. A long gash runs from wrist to elbow, open like a garish smile.

The floor is coated in blood. It runs from the tub all the way to the edge of the tiles, right up to my feet. If I take a single step inside, I'll be walking on it.

Somehow, that paralyzes me. I want to run to Anna, but I don't want to walk through her blood. Foolishly, insanely, I feel like that would hurt her. Even though she's plainly dead.

Yet I have to reach her. I have to close her eyes. I can't stand the way she's staring up at the ceiling. There's no peace on her face—she looks just as terrified as she did before.

Stomach rolling and chest burning, I run over to her, my feet sliding on the slick tile. I gently lift her arm before putting it back inside the tub with her. Her skin is still warm, and for a second, I think there may be hope. Then I look at her face again and know how stupid I really am. Gently, I close her eyes.

Then I go into her room. I find her favorite blanket—the one with the moons and stars on it. I bring it into the bathroom and cover her body with it. There's water in the tub. It soaks the blanket. It doesn't matter—I just want to cover her so no one else can look at her. Not anymore.

I go back in my own room. I sit on the floor, next to the empty cash box I haven't yet returned to its hiding place under the floorboards.

The depth of my guilt and sorrow is unbearable. I literally can't bear it. I feel like it's tearing away pieces of my flesh, pound by pound, until I'll be nothing but a skeleton—bare-bones, without muscle, nerve, or heart.

That heart is calcifying inside me. When I first saw Anna's

body, my heart beat so hard that I thought it would burst. Now it's contracting slower and slower, weaker and weaker.

I've never spent one whole day away from my sister. She's been my closest friend, the only person I truly cared about. Anna is better than me in every way. She's smarter, kinder, happier.

I often felt that when we formed in the womb, our characteristics were split in two parts. She got the better part of us, but as long as she was close by, we could share her goodness. Now she's gone, and all that light has gone with her.

All that's left are the qualities that lived in me: focus, determination…and rage.

It's my fault she's dead. I should have stayed here with her. I should have watched her, cared for her—that's what she would have done.

I'll never forgive myself for that mistake.

But if I allow myself to feel the guilt, I'll put that gun to my head and end it all right now. I can't let that happen. I have to avenge Anna. I promised her that.

I take every ounce of emotion remaining and lock it deep inside myself. By sheer force of will, I refuse to feel anything. Anything at all.

All that's left is my objective.

I don't execute it at once. If I try, I'll get myself killed without achieving my goal.

Instead, I spend the next few weeks stalking my prey. I find out where they work. Where they live. Which strip clubs and restaurants and nightclubs and brothels they frequent.

Their names are Abel Nowak, Bartek Adamowicz, and Iwan Zielinski. Abel is the youngest. He's tall, lanky, and sickly looking, with a shaved head—a nod to his neo-Nazi ideology. He went to the same school as me once upon a time, two years ahead of me.

Bartek has a thick black beard. He appears to be in charge of the streetwalkers in my neighborhood because he's always lurking on the corner at night, making sure the girls hand their earnings over to him without giving away so much as a free conversation to the men seeking their company.

Iwan is the boss of all three. Or the sub-boss, I should say. I know who sits above him. I don't care. Those three will pay for what they did. And it won't be quick or painless.

I track down Abel first. That's easy to do because he frequents the Piwo Klub, as do several of our mutual friends. I find him sitting at the bar, laughing and drinking, while my sister has been lying in the ground for seventeen days.

I watch him get drunker and drunker.

Then I stick a scribbled sign to the bathroom door: *Zepsuta Toaleta.* Broken toilet.

I wait in the alleyway. Ten minutes later, Abel comes out to take a leak. He unbuttons his tight jeans before aiming his stream of piss against the brick wall.

He has no hair to grab, so I wrap my forearm around his forehead and jerk his head back. I cut his throat from ear to ear.

The combat knife is sharp; I'm surprised how hard I have to saw to make the cut. Abel tries to scream. It's impossible—I've severed his vocal cords, and blood is flooding down his throat. He only makes a strangled gurgling sound.

I let him fall to the filthy concrete on his back so he can look up at me.

"That's for Anna, you diseased prick." I spit in his face and leave him there, still writhing and drowning in his own blood.

Then I go home to my apartment. I sit in Anna's room, on her bed, which has been stripped to the mattress. I see her favorite books on the shelf next to her bed, their spines creased because she read them over and over. *The Little Prince, The Bell Jar, Anna Karenina, Persuasion, The Hobbit, Anne of Green Gables, Alice in Wonderland, The Good Earth.* I look around at the postcards pinned to her walls— the Colosseum, Eiffel Tower, Statue of Liberty, Taj Mahal. Places she dreamed of visiting but will never see now.

I just killed a man. I should feel something: guilt, horror. Or, at the very least, a sense of justice. But I feel nothing. I'm a black hole inside. I can take in anything without any emotion escaping.

I had no fear as I approached Abel. If my heart won't beat over that, it won't beat for anything.

One week later, I go after Bartek. I doubt he'll be expecting me—Abel has too many enemies for them to guess who killed him. They probably won't think of my sister at all. I doubt she's the first girl the *Braterstwo* attacked. And I haven't breathed a word to anyone about my desire for revenge.

I follow Bartek to his girlfriend's flat. From what I hear, she used to work the street corner herself before being upgraded to his mistress. I buy a red cap and a pizza, then knock on her door.

Bartek opens it, shirtless and lazy, smelling like sex. "We didn't order any pizza." He grunts, about to shut the door in my face.

"Well, I can't take it back," I tell him. "So you might as well keep it." I hold up the box, wafting its tantalizing scent of pepperoni and cheese.

Bartek looks at it, tempted. "I'm not paying for it," he warns me.

"That's fine." I hold it out, looking him right in the eye. He doesn't show the slightest sign of recognition. He's probably forgotten about Anna already, let alone wondered if she had a brother.

As soon as his hands are full of the pizza box, I pull my gun and shoot him three times in the chest. He drops to his knees, his face comically surprised.

Once his bulk is out of the way, I realize his girlfriend was standing directly behind him. She's short, blond, and curvy, wearing cheap lace lingerie. She claps a hand to her mouth, about to scream.

She's already seen my face.

I shoot her, too, without hesitation.

She tumbles over. I don't have a glance to spare for her. I'm looking down at Bartek, watching the color fade from his skin as he bleeds out on the floor. I must have hit his lungs. His breath whistles, then stops.

I spit on him, too, before turning and walking away.

Maybe I shouldn't have left Iwan for last. He may be the most difficult. If he's at all intelligent, he'll put two and two together and guess someone has a grudge.

But that's the only way I can do it—the only way I can feel the full weight of catharsis.

So I wait two more weeks, searching for him.

Sure enough, he's lying low. Like an animal, he senses someone is hunting him, even if he doesn't know exactly who.

He surrounds himself with other gangsters. He's always watching as he goes in and out of his flashy car and when he takes his tribute from the low-level dealers of the neighborhood.

I'm watching, too. I'm only sixteen years old. I'm skinny, half-grown, wearing my deli apron under my coat. I look like every other kid in Praga—poor, underfed, and pale from lack of sunlight. I'm a nobody to him. Just like Anna was. He would never suspect me.

Finally, I spot him leaving his apartment alone. He's carrying a black duffel bag. I don't know what's in the bag, but I'm afraid he may be planning to leave town.

I chase him, impatient and a little reckless. It's been forty-one days since Anna died. Each one has been an agony of emptiness. Missing the only person who meant anything to me. The only spot of brightness in my shit life.

I watch Iwan walking ahead of me, trim in his black leather jacket. He's not an ugly man. In fact, most women would probably consider him handsome—dark hair, constant five-o'clock shadow, square jaw, eyes just a little too close together. With his money and connections, I'm sure he never lacks for female attention.

I've watched him enter and leave nightclubs with girls on his arm. Brothels, too. He didn't attack my sister for sex. He wanted to hurt her. He wanted to torment her.

Iwan cuts through an alleyway, then enters the back of a derelict building via an unlocked metal door. I lurk in the alley to see if he'll reemerge. He does not.

I should wait. That's what I've been doing.

But I'm tired of waiting. This ends tonight.

I crack open the door and slip inside. It's dark in the warehouse, and there's the distant dripping of a leaky roof. It smells dank and moldy. The air is at least ten degrees colder than outside.

The warehouse is full of the skeletal remains of rusted equipment. It might have been a textile factory once, or light assembly. It's difficult to tell in the gloom. I don't see Iwan anywhere.

Nor do I see the person who hits me from behind.

Blinding pain explodes in the back of my skull. I fall forward onto my hands and knees. The light snaps on, and I realize I'm surrounded by a half dozen men. Iwan is at the forefront, still carrying his duffel bag. He drops it on the ground next to him.

I'm hauled to my feet by two other men, my arms pinned behind my back. They search me roughly before finding the gun. They hand it to Iwan.

"Were you planning to shoot me in the back with this?" he snarls.

Holding the gun by the barrel, he cracks me across the jaw with the stock. The pain is explosive. I taste blood in my mouth; one of my teeth feels loose.

I'm probably about to die. Yet I don't feel afraid. All I can feel is rage that I won't be able to kill Iwan first.

"Who do you work for?" Iwan demands. "Who sent you?"

I spit a mouthful of blood onto the ground, spattering his shoe. Iwan bares his teeth and raises the gun to hit me again.

"Wait." A man steps forward. He's maybe fifty years old, medium height, pale eyes, deep pitted scars on the sides of his face—as if he had been hit with buckshot or had severe acne at one point in his life. The moment he speaks, every eye in the room fixes on him with an expectant silence that shows he's the real boss here, not Iwan Zielinski.

"Do you know who I am?" he says in his gravelly voice.

I nod. This is Tymon Zajac. More commonly known as

Rzeźnik—the Butcher. I didn't know for certain that Iwan worked for him, but I could have guessed it. In Warsaw, all lines flow toward the Butcher.

He stands in front of me, eye to eye—his are bleached of color by age and perhaps all the things they've seen. They cut into me.

I don't drop my gaze. I feel no fear. I don't care what this man does to me.

"How old are you, boy?"

"Sixteen."

"Who do you work for?"

"I work at Delikatesy Świeży. I make sandwiches and clean tables."

His mouth tightens. He gives me a hard stare as he tries to determine if I'm joking. "You work at the deli."

"Yes."

"Did you kill Nowak and Adamowicz?"

"Yes," I say unflinchingly.

Again, he's surprised. He didn't expect me to admit it. "Who helped you?"

"No one."

Now he does look angry. He turns his fury on his own men. He says, "A busboy stalked and killed two of my soldiers, all on his own?"

It's a rhetorical question. No one dares answer.

He faces me once more. "You meant to kill Zielinski tonight?"

"Yes."

"Why?"

There's the slightest flicker of fear on Iwan's broad face. "Boss, why are we—" he starts.

Zajac holds up a hand to silence him. His eyes are still fixed on me, waiting for my response.

My mouth is swollen from the blow of the gun, but I speak my words clearly. "Your men raped my sister on her way to her university entrance exams. She was sixteen years old. She was a good girl—kind, gentle, innocent. She wasn't part of your world. There was no reason to hurt her."

Zajac's eyes narrow. "If you wanted restitution—"

"There is no restitution," I say bitterly. "She killed herself."

There's no sympathy in Zajac's pale eyes—only calculation. He weighs my words, considering the situation.

Then he looks at Iwan once more.

"Is this true?"

Iwan licks his lips, hesitating. I can see the struggle between his desire to lie and his fear of his boss. At last he says, "It wasn't my fault. She—"

The Butcher shoots him right between the eyes. The bullet disappears into Iwan's skull, leaving a dark round hole between his eyebrows. His eyes roll back, and he falls to his knees before toppling over.

A carousel of thoughts spins in my head. First, relief that Anna's revenge is complete. Second, disappointment that it was Zajac who pulled the trigger. Third, the realization that it's my turn to die. Fourth, the understanding that I don't care. Not even a little bit.

"Thank you," I say to the Butcher.

He looks me up and down, head to toe. He takes in my torn jeans, my filthy sneakers, my unwashed hair, and my lanky frame. He sighs. "What do you make at the deli?"

"Eight hundred zloty a week," I say.

He lets out a wheezing sigh—the closest thing to a laugh I'll ever hear him make.

"You don't work there anymore," he says. "You work for me now. Understand?"

I don't understand at all. But I nod.

"Still," he says grimly. "You killed two of my men. That can't go unpunished."

He nods toward one of his soldiers. The man unzips the duffel bag lying next to Iwan's body. He pulls out a machete as long as my arm. The blade is dark with age, the edge sharpened razor fine. The soldier hands the machete to his boss.

The Butcher walks over to an old worktable. The top is splintered, and it's missing a leg, but it still stands upright.

"Hold out your hand," he tells me.

His men have let go of my arms. I'm free to walk over to the table. Free to put my hand flat on its surface, fingers spread wide.

I feel a strange sense of unreality, like I'm watching myself do this from three feet outside my body.

Zajac raises the cleaver. Then he brings it whistling down, splitting my pinky in half, right below the first knuckle. This hurts less than the blow from the gun. It only burns, like I dipped my fingertip in flame.

Zajac picks up the little piece of flesh that was once attached to my body. He throws it on top of Iwan's corpse.

"There," the Butcher says. "All debts are paid."

TEN YEARS LATER

2
NESSA GRIFFIN

CHICAGO

I'm driving over to Lake City Ballet through streets lined with double rows of maple trees, their branches so thick that they almost form an arch overhead. The leaves are deep crimson, drifting down to form crunching drifts in the gutters.

I love Chicago in the fall. Winter is awful, but I won't complain as long as I get to see these brilliant reds, oranges, and yellows a few weeks longer.

I just visited Aida at her new apartment close to Navy Pier. It's such a cool place—it used to be an old church. You can still see the original bare brick walls in the kitchen, and huge old wooden beams run across the ceiling like whale ribs. She's even got a stained glass window in her bedroom. When we sat on her bed, the sunlight came pouring through, coloring our skin in rainbow hues.

We were eating popcorn and clementines, watching the sixth *Harry Potter* movie on her laptop. Aida loves fantasy. I've come to like it, too, from all the things she's shown me. But I still can't believe she's brave enough to eat in bed. My brother is very fastidious.

"Where's Cal?" I asked her nervously.

"At work."

My brother just became the newest alderman of the Forty-Third

Ward. That's in addition to his position as scion of Chicago's most successful Mafia family.

It always gives me a strange feeling when I think of us that way—as Irish Mafia. I've never known anything else. To me, my father, brother, sister, and mother are the people who love me and take care of me. I don't think of them as criminals with blood on their hands.

I'm the youngest in the family. They try to hide their crimes from me. I'm not part of the business, not the way my older siblings are. Callum is my father's right hand. Riona is head legal counsel. Even my mother is heavily involved in the mechanics of our business.

Then there's me: the baby. Spoiled, sheltered, protected.

Sometimes I think they want to keep me that way so at least one part of the family stays pure and innocent.

It puts me in a strange position.

I don't want to do anything wrong—I can't even crush a bug, and I can't tell a lie to save my life. If I even try, my face gets beet red, and I start sweating and stammering, and I feel like I'm going to throw up.

On the other hand, sometimes I feel lonely. Like I don't belong with the rest of them. Like I'm not really part of my own family.

At least Cal married somebody awesome. Aida and I clicked from the start. We're not alike—she's bold and funny and never takes shit from anyone. Especially not my brother. At first, it seemed like they'd kill each other. Now I can't imagine Cal with anybody else.

I wish they would have kept living with us longer, but I get that they want their own space. Unfortunately for them, I intend to keep visiting pretty much every day.

It makes me feel guilty that I don't have the same relationship with my own sister. Riona's just so…intense. She definitely picked the right line of work—arguing is an Olympic sport for her. Paying her to do it is like paying a duck to swim. I want us to be close the way other sisters are, but I always feel like she's barely tolerating me. Like she thinks I'm stupid.

Sometimes I feel stupid. But not today. Today I'm driving over to the ballet theater to see the programs they've printed for our newest show. It's called *Bliss*. I helped choreograph half the dances, and the idea of actually seeing them performed on the stage makes me so excited, I can barely breathe.

My mother put me in ballet classes when I was three years old. I took horseback riding and tennis and cello lessons, too, but it was dancing that stuck. I walked everywhere on my toes, with strains of *The Rite of Spring* and the *Pulcinella* Suite floating through my head.

I loved it like I loved breathing. And I was good, too. Very good. The problem is there's a difference between being good and being great. A lot of people are good. Only a handful are great. Though two people can spend the same thousands of hours giving their blood, sweat, and tears, the chasm between talent and genius is as wide as the Grand Canyon. Unfortunately, I found myself on the wrong side.

I didn't want to admit it. I thought if I dieted more, worked harder, I could still be a prima ballerina. But by the time I graduated high school, I realized I wasn't even the best ballerina in Chicago, let alone on a national scale. I'd be lucky to secure a position as an apprentice with a major dance company, let alone move up to a core member.

Still, I took a corps de ballet spot with Lake City Ballet while attending classes at Loyola. I wanted to keep dancing while I got my degree.

The director and head choreographer is Jackson Wright. He's a bit of an ass—what director isn't, I guess. *Director* and *dictator* seem to be synonymous in this industry. Still, the man is brilliant.

Lake City Ballet is contemporary, experimental. They put on all sorts of insane shows, like one done entirely in black light and florescent body paint and another with no music at all, only drums.

Our upcoming show is centered on joy—which is perfect for me since I'm about the most cheerful person you could meet. Not much gets me down.

Maybe that's why Jackson let me do so much of the choreography. He's been letting me do bits and pieces ever since he realized I have a knack for it. This is the first time I've composed entire dances all on my own.

I can't wait to see it come alive with makeup and costumes and lights. My own thoughts made flesh on the stage. I'm picturing my family sitting right in the front row, amazed that I could be the sculptor and not just the clay. Actually impressed with me for once!

I'm practically skipping into the studio. There's a conditioning class going on in Room One and technique in Room Two. I'm hit with the familiar blend of feet thumping on hardwood floors, the live pianist keeping time, and the mingled scents of sweat, perfume, and floor wax. It smells like home.

The air is thick with the heat of all these bodies. I take off my jacket, heading straight to Jackson's office.

His door is half-open. I knock gently on the frame, waiting for his terse "come in," before I enter.

He's sitting behind his desk, looking through a messy stack of paper. His office is a disaster—stuffed full of framed photographs, posters of past performances, disorganized folders, and even bits and pieces of costumes in the initial design phase. Jackson controls everything about the shows, down to the last tutu.

He's a little taller than me, fit and lean from a strict vegan diet. He's got a thick shock of black hair with a few streaks of gray at the temples. He's extremely vain about his hair, always running his hands through it while he talks. His skin is tan, his face narrow, his eyes large and dark and expressive. Plenty of the dancers have a crush on him, both male and female.

"Nessa," he says, looking up from his papers. "To what do I owe the pleasure?"

"Isabel told me the programs were in!" I say, trying not to grin too hard. Isabel is the head costume designer. She can hand sew at machine speeds while simultaneously shouting directions at all her assistants. She's got a sharp tongue and a warm heart. I like to think of her as my dance mom.

"Oh, right. Over there," Jackson says, jerking his head toward a cardboard box stuffed full of programs set on a folding chair.

I scurry over before lifting out the topmost bundle and slipping off the elastic band so I can take a program.

The cover image is beautiful—it's Angelique, one of our principals, dressed in a red silk gown. She's leaping through the air with one leg at an impossible angle over her head, her foot perfectly arched like a bow.

I open the program and scan through the list of dances, then down to the credits. I'm expecting to see my name—in fact, I intended to ask Jackson if I could take this home to show my parents.

Instead, I see…absolutely nothing. Jackson Wright is listed as head choreographer, Kelly Paul as second. There's no mention of me at all.

"What?" Jackson says testily, noting the stunned expression on my face.

"It's just…I think they forgot to put me as one of the choreographers," I say tentatively. By *they*, I mean whoever designed the program. It must be an accidental omission.

"No," Jackson says carelessly. "They didn't forget."

I look up at him, my mouth a little O of surprise. "What…what do you mean?"

"They didn't forget," he repeats. "You're not credited."

My heart flutters against my chest wall like a moth against a window. My natural inclination is to nod, say *okay*, and leave. I hate confrontation. But I know if I do that, I'll hate myself even more later. I have to understand what's happening here.

"Why am I not credited?" I ask, trying to keep my voice as calm and unaccusing as possible.

Jackson gives a sigh of annoyance, putting down the papers he was perusing, which become lost in the mess on his desk.

"You're not a choreographer here, Nessa," he says, as if he's explaining that one and one makes two. "You're a corps member. Just because you threw a few ideas in the ring—"

"I created four of the dances!" I blurt, my face burning. I know I sound like a child, but I can't help myself.

Jackson stands from his desk. He comes over to me and puts his arm around my shoulder. I think he's trying to comfort me, but then I realize he's steering me toward the door.

"Here's the thing, Nessa," he says. "You put in some work. But your work is not that original. It's simplistic. The parts of the performance that bring it alive, that make it sing, are from me. So you'd only be embarrassing yourself, trying to insist on credit that you don't deserve."

My throat is so swollen with embarrassment that I can't speak. I'm desperately trying to hold back the tears burning my eyes.

"Thanks for stopping by," he says as we reach the doorway. "Keep the program if you like."

I didn't even realize it was still clutched in my hand, wrinkled from how hard I'm squeezing it.

Jackson pushes me out of his office. He closes his door with a gentle *snick*, leaving me alone in the hallway.

I'm standing there stunned, silent tears running down my face. God, I feel like a fool.

Not wanting anyone else to see me, I stumble back down the hallway, heading for the front doors.

Before I can reach them, I'm intercepted by Serena Breglio. She's a corps member, like me. She stepped out of the conditioning class to visit the water fountain in the hall.

She stops short when she sees me, drawing her blond eyebrows together in concern. "Nessa! What's wrong?"

"Nothing." I shake my head. "It's nothing. I was just…just being stupid." I wipe my cheeks with the backs of my hands, trying to compose myself.

Serena casts a suspicious glance back at Jackson's closed door. "Did he do something?" she demands.

"No."

"Are you sure?"

"Very sure."

"Well, have a hug at least," she says, wrapping an arm around my shoulders. "Sorry, I'm sweaty."

That doesn't bother me at all. Sweat, blisters, broken toenails... they're all as common as bobby pins around here.

Serena's a classic California blond. She's got a lean, athletic frame, and somehow manages to maintain her tan even in the Midwest. She looks like she should be on a surfboard, not pointe shoes. But she's good enough that she might move up to a demi-soloist position any day now.

She's as competitive as they come in the studio and a sweetheart outside it. I don't mind her seeing me like this. I know she won't gossip to the other girls.

She asks, "Are you coming out with us tonight?"

"Where are you going?"

"There's a new club that just opened up. It's called Jungle."

I hesitate.

I'm not really supposed to go places like that. Especially not without telling my parents or my brother. But if I tell them, they won't want me to go. Or they'll send one of their bodyguards along to monitor me—somebody like Jack Du Pont, who'll sit in the corner glowering at me, scaring away anybody who might ask me to dance. It's embarrassing, and it makes my friends feel weird.

"I don't know..."

"Oh, come on." Serena squeezes my shoulders. "Marnie's going, too. Come with us, have a drink. You can be home by eleven."

"All right," I say, feeling rebellious just by agreeing. "Let's do it."

"Yes!" Serena pumps her fist. "I better get back in there before Madame Brodeur gives me shit. You gonna wait out here?"

I shake my head. "I'll be at the café next door."

"Perfect," Serena says. "Order me a scone."

3
MIKO

CHICAGO

I'M SITTING IN MY OFFICE AT THE BACK OF THE CLUB, MARKING down numbers in my ledger.

I've got two nightclubs running now, as well as three strip clubs. They're all profitable, even this one that I only opened a few weeks ago. But that's not their real purpose. They're mostly for washing money.

Any industry with cash payments is a good receptacle. Laundromats, used car dealerships, taxi services, restaurants…they all serve as a basket in which to dump legitimate profits, as well as the illegal money earned through drugs, guns, larceny, and streetwalkers.

In the old days, you could open an empty storefront without even bothering to stock it with equipment. Al Capone had a storefront like that, right here in Chicago. His business card said *Used Furniture Dealer*. Now forensic accounting has gotten a lot more sophisticated. You need an actual thriving business.

The goal is to get your dirty money into the bank. You do it slow and steady, with daily deposits mixing dirty money and clean. It's best if your illegal cash makes up only 10 or 15 percent of the total.

You've got to be careful because banks are fucking rats. If they notice your little pizza parlor is suddenly doing a million dollars in business, or if they see your profits far exceed the checks you're writing to distributors, they're going to report you to the IRS.

But once the money is in the system, then you can send it anywhere. Offshore tax havens, large-scale real estate, brokerage accounts…

My assets are in the eight figures if you add them all. Looking at me, you'd never know it. I keep a low profile, and I force my men to do the same. You get lazy, sloppy, and flashy, and you draw the wrong kind of attention.

I run the Chicago *Braterstwo* now with my brother, Jonas. He's my brother by covenant, not by blood. We're the adopted sons of Tymon Zajac. For ten years, I worked for Tymon. He taught me, trained me, and mentored me.

My biological father died in Warsaw. I don't know where his gravestone sits. I don't care. I'll never set foot in Poland again. I don't even like to think about it.

Tymon brought me here, to America. He told me we'd build an empire larger than the entire wealth of our homeland. I believed him. His dream became my dream. It gave me something to live for.

For a time, we thrived. We began to take over this city, block by block.

But we're not the only gangsters in Chicago.

We found ourselves in conflict with the Colombians, the Russians, the Italians, and the Irish.

We crushed the Colombians, taking over their drug-running pipeline. That's when the money really started flowing in, funding our other operations.

Then the DOJ did us a favor cracking down on the arms trafficking run by the Russian *Bratva*.

Which left us free to attack the Italians, specifically the Gallo family. But Enzo Gallo wasn't as old and complacent as he seemed. His sons put three of our men in the ground, buried under the foundations of their high-rise on Oak Street.

Before we could strike back, the Gallos formed an unexpected alliance with the Griffins, Irish Mafia royalty at the pinnacle of crime in Chicago. The Gallos married their only daughter to Callum, the Griffins' only son.

It was extremely unexpected. Like an alliance between Israel and Palestine or between cats and dogs.

That was, perhaps, when Tymon made a mistake. He wasn't a man prone to mistakes. But in that moment, he acted rashly.

When Aida Gallo and Callum Griffin came poking around one of our clubs, we drugged them and brought them back to an old slaughterhouse on the west side of the city.

It was an impulsive decision, not planned out. Done on Tymon's orders—still, I blame myself for what happened.

I had an AR trained on them both. I should have gunned them down without hesitation, then and there.

Instead, they escaped down a drainage pipe.

It was a humiliating mistake. I knelt in front of Tymon, expecting him to mete out punishment. In ten years, I had never failed him so badly.

He ordered the rest of the men out of the room.

I closed my eyes, thinking he would bring his machete down on the back of my neck. That's justice in our world.

Instead, I felt his hand resting on my shoulder—heavy but without anger.

I looked up into his face.

In all the time I'd known Tymon, I had never seen him show hesitation or weakness. Suddenly, he looked tired. He was only fifty-eight years old but had been through a dozen lifetimes of blood and toil and struggle.

"Mikolaj," he said. "You're my son and my heir. I know you'll never fail me again."

I had long since lost the ability to feel anything like love. But I felt the fire of a loyalty stronger than love. Tymon had spared my life twice. He would never need to do it a third time.

I was reinvigorated. I planned to work with my father to crush the Italians and the Irish. To take our place once and for all as the rulers of the city.

Instead, a week later, Dante Gallo murdered Tymon. Dante gunned the Butcher down, leaving him to bleed out in the gutter.

I've yet to take my revenge. It shames me every day that passes.

I have two factors to consider:

First, my men. The Griffins and the Gallos combined are a powerful force. They command the loyalty of dozens of Irish and Italian families. If I attack them directly, I can't hope to succeed. Not yet anyway.

Second, I want them to suffer. I could kill Callum or Dante. But what would that accomplish? I want to break the entire empire down. I want to drive the two families apart. Then I want to pick off their members one by one.

To do that, I need to find their weak point. Their vulnerability.

I've been watching and waiting. Letting them think the *Braterstwo* are defeated, that they cut the head off the snake when they killed Tymon.

In the meantime, I run my business. I keep my territory secure. And I amass more money and power by the day.

There's a knock on my door. Jonas enters without waiting, carrying a crate of Żubrówka, a Polish vodka. He pulls out one of the bottles, showing me the bright green label and the single blade of bison grass swimming in the pale amber liquor.

"Just in time." He grins. "We were about to run out."

Jonas has a broad frame packed with muscle and thick black hair that he combs straight back from his forehead. His eyes are so dark that you can't tell the pupil from the iris, and his eyebrows are straight slashes that go up at the outer edges like Spock. His personality is the opposite of Vulcan, however. Jonas isn't logical. He's impulsive—quick to laugh and quick to brawl. He doesn't think things through. Which is why I'm the boss instead of him.

It's what Tymon wanted. Not that it matters—now that my adoptive father is dead, I won't be second to anyone ever again.

"What's the total from liquor sales this week?" I ask Jonas.

"Fifty-seven thousand," he replies proudly.

That's up 12 percent from the week before.

"Good." I nod.

"There's one thing, though," Jonas says, frowning.

"Hold on…" I tap the shoulder of the girl currently kneeling between my legs, sucking my cock. Her name is Petra. She's one of our bartenders—one of our best, actually. She's as skilled with her mouth as she is with her hands. It's a pleasant accompaniment to the tedious task of balancing the books. But I don't usually come. As hard as she works, my cock only seems half-alive, like the rest of me.

I tell her, "You can leave."

Petra stands from behind the desk, brushing off the knees of her tight black pants. She's wearing a corset top, half unlaced to show her generous cleavage. Her lipstick is smeared around her mouth.

Jonas smirks, realizing we weren't alone in the room. He eyes Petra's breasts, then her ass as she leaves the office. Not like he hasn't seen it all before.

"How is she?" he says. "I haven't had the pleasure yet."

"She's fine," I say shortly. "What did you want to tell me?"

Jonas turns serious again, getting back to business. "I think one of the bartenders is stealing from us."

"How do you know?"

"I've been weighing the bottles. We're short thirty-eight ounces."

"Are they heavy pouring?"

"No. I put regulators on the nozzles."

"Then they're either giving drinks to friends or pocketing the cash."

"Somebody is," Jonas agrees.

"I'll watch them tonight."

"Perfect," Jonas says, smirking once more and folding his arms across his chest.

"What?" I ask him, annoyed.

"You gonna put your cock back in your pants?"

I look down at my cock, still smeared with Petra's lipstick. I'd already forgotten about the truncated blow job. I tuck myself back in my trousers, scowling. "Happy now?"

"Sure," Jonas says.

We head out onto the floor together.

The night is just getting into full swing—guests lined up at the bar, the dance floor crowded, every booth full. I look around at the bustling space, and I see money, money, money: waitresses stuffing cash into their aprons, handing patrons drinks marked up 400 percent; bartenders swiping credit cards again and again, each swipe another infinitesimal addition to the wealth of the *Braterstwo*.

The walls are covered with grass paper, the booths upholstered in rich emerald velvet. The lights are a dim watery green, with patterned shadows that make it appear as if the patrons are walking through tall grass.

This club is indeed a jungle, and I'm its king. The customers pay homage to me without even knowing it as I drain their wallets drink by drink.

I position myself at the corner of the dance floor, pretending to watch the clientele. Really, I have my eyes on my own employees. In particular, on the bartenders.

There are four behind the counter of the main bar: Petra, Monique, Bronson, and Chaz. All are fast and flashy workers, hired for skill and sex appeal. I'm not ruling out the women, but I already suspect the men. Petra and Monique make a staggering number of tips from the lonely businessmen in the area. Bronson and Chaz do pretty damn well for themselves, too, but in my experience, masculine greed won't allow a man to be satisfied with three hundred a night.

A good bartender is like a juggler and a magician all in one. They're chatting with the customer while simultaneously flipping glasses, agitating shakers, and pouring twelve shots in a row. They make money disappear and alcohol rain down. They're always doing ten things at once.

It takes a practiced eye to see what they're really up to.

In twenty-eight minutes, I've spotted the thief.

It isn't Bronson, with the bulging muscles and frat boy charm. He slips a free drink to a giggling blond but still rings it in, using his own tips to cover it.

No, it's Chaz who's the tricky little fuck. Chaz with the silver rings, hipster beard, and man bun.

That egotistic little shit has two separate scams running at the same time. First, he's taking payments from three or four customers at once, carrying the cash over to the till and pretending to ring it all in. But as his fingers fly over the screen, I see he's only ringing in nine out of ten drinks, counting on the volume of transactions to hide what he's doing from anybody watching.

Second—something Jonas hasn't even caught—Chaz has a bottle of Crown Royal he's snuck into the building. It's a top-shelf liquor, eighteen dollars a pop. Any time a customer orders it, Chaz pours from his own bottle that he's set on the shelf in place of my liquor. Then he takes the entire payment and drops it directly in his tip jar.

In the time I'm watching, he steals about seventy-six dollars. By my rough calculations, that means he's skimming over nine hundred dollars a night.

I motion to Jonas, calling him over.

"It's Chaz," I tell him.

Jonas looks over at Chaz and his shit-eating grin as he pops the top off four bottles of Heineken before sliding them across the bar to a quartet of rowdy college girls. Jonas's face darkens. He takes a step forward, like he's going to grab Chaz by the shirt and haul him over the bar right then and there.

"Not yet." I lay a hand on Jonas's chest. "Let him finish his shift. We don't want to be shorthanded tonight. Grab him on his way out."

Jonas grunts and nods. A scuffle breaks out over by the bathrooms, and Jonas heads in that direction to make sure the bouncers break it up.

I lean back against the pillar at the corner of the dance floor, my arms folded in front of my chest. The satisfaction of catching the thief is already fading. My mind is turning back, as it always does, to the nagging problem of the Griffins and the Gallos.

Right at that moment, a girl walks into the club.

I see a hundred gorgeous women every night, dolled up in their tight dresses and heels, faces painted, hair freshly coiffed, skin dusted with glitter.

This girl catches my eye because she's the opposite of that. Young, fresh-faced. So cleanly scrubbed that she almost glows. Her light-brown hair is pulled back in a simple ponytail. Her eyes are wide and innocent. She hasn't tried to cover the spattering of freckles across her nose.

She's wearing a lightweight wraparound sweater, and under that is a pale pink bodysuit, almost the same color as her skin. Odd attire for a nightclub. Her friends are dressed in the usual crop tops and minidresses.

As soon I see her, I get a rush of adrenaline. My muscles tighten like coiled springs, and I feel my pupils dilating. I imagine I can smell her perfume, light and sweet, over the scent of smoke, alcohol, and sweat.

It's the reaction of a predator when it sights its prey.

Because I recognize this girl.

It's Nessa Griffin. The cherished baby girl of the Irish Mafia. Their little darling. She wandered into my club like an innocent gazelle. Foolish. Lost. Ripe for the taking.

It's like a sign from heaven. But I don't believe in heaven. Let's call it a sign from the devil, then.

I watch her as she weaves her way through the club with her friends. They order drinks from frat boy Bronson. He flirts as hard as he can as he mixes their martinis. Even though his attention is directed more at Nessa's blond friend, Nessa still blushes and can't meet his eye.

Nessa takes her melon martini and sips it awkwardly, unable to keep from making a face even though it's mostly juice. She only drinks a quarter of it before setting it back on the bar.

The blond is still giggling up at Bronson. The other friend has struck up a conversation with a skinny nerdy-looking guy. Nessa gazes around the room, shyly curious.

I'm staring at her openly. I don't look away when our eyes meet. I watch her expression to see if she knows who I am.

Her cheeks turn pink, deeper than the color of her top. She looks away, then sneaks a glance back in my direction to see if I'm still staring. When she sees that I am, she spins all the way around to put her back to me, taking another hasty gulp of her drink.

She's totally ignorant. She doesn't know who I am. This is just the behavior of an awkward girl who prefers to hide in the middle of her more confident friends.

I stride back toward my office, but I'm intercepted by Jonas right before I reach the door.

"Where are you going?" he asks, noting my hurry.

"You've got the floor tonight. I have something else to attend to."

"What about Chaz?"

I pause. I was looking forward to seeing that slimy little fucker's face when he realized he was caught. His smug smile fading away, replaced by fear, then abject terror. I was going to make him beg and plead and piss himself before I took my payment out of his hide.

But now I have bigger fish to fry.

"Take him down to the basement at the end of the night," I say to Jonas. "Break his hands. Then dump him off back at his flat."

"What about the money?"

"I'm sure it already went straight up his nose."

There's no way that little shit dared steal from me just to put the cash into a savings account. He's got a habit.

Jonas nods and heads back out into the club.

I enter my office and rifle through the top drawer of my desk. I pull out a GPS tracking device about the size, shape, and color of a penny. I slip it into my pocket. Then I head back out on the floor.

It only takes me a moment to spot Nessa Griffin. She's dancing with her friends, swaying to a remix of "Roses." I'm not the only one who's watching her now. She draws the eye of men and women alike, surprisingly sensual as she dances. She seems to have forgotten her shyness, lost in the music.

It's all too easy to sneak up behind her and slip the tracker into her purse. She's so oblivious that I even let my fingers trail through the ponytail hanging down her back. Her hair is fine and silky, cool to the touch. Now I really can smell her perfume, light and clean: scents of lily, orchid, and plum.

I walk away before she notices a thing.

Now I'll know everywhere she goes.

I'll follow her. Stalk her. And take her at my leisure.

4

NESSA

I'VE BARELY BEEN TO ANY NIGHTCLUBS BEFORE. ACTUALLY, I'M NOT even old enough to get inside. Serena gives me her sister's expired ID, which really looks nothing like me except that we both have brown hair. The bouncer gives it only a cursory glance before waving us in.

As soon as we're through the door, it's like we've stepped into another world. The light is dim and flickering, and the music pounds against my skin with palpable force. I know this place just opened, but it has a sort of old-school imperialist look, like it was made for British colonialists exported to India. The dark wood and weathered silver sconces and deep green velvet look like they came out of an old library.

I only wish I'd brought a change of clothes like the other girls did because they look as sexy and cool as every other person in this place, while I just…don't.

I don't even know what to order when we head over to the bar. I get the same thing as Serena, which turns out to be a watermelon martini with a twist of lime peel floating in the glass.

Even the bartender is insanely hot. I feel like the employees must all moonlight as models because every one of them looks like they get their exercise walking up and down runways.

Serena's loving it. She's leaning her elbows on the bar, grinning up at the bartender, asking him how many girls' numbers he gets every night.

"Not enough," he says, winking. "I've definitely got room for one more in my phone."

I take a sip of my drink. It's sickly sweet, but I can still taste the bite of alcohol underneath. It makes me gag a little. I don't know how my brother drinks whiskey straight—it all tastes like paint thinner to me.

I don't want to get too tipsy, so I set my drink back on the bar, looking around the club.

I love people watching.

If I could just sit in the corner, totally invisible, and watch people walk by all night long, I wouldn't mind that at all. I like trying to guess who's a couple and who's not, who's celebrating their last day of exams and who came here with workmates. I love seeing people's gestures and expressions, the way they dance and talk and laugh.

I don't like attention myself. So, when I see a man leaning against a pillar next to the dance floor, staring right at me, his gaze hits me like a slap. I drop my eyes, pretending to be super interested in my own fingernails, until I think he's probably moved on to something else.

When I glance up again, he's still staring. He's tall, slimly built, with hair so blond, it's almost white. He's sharp-featured and pale. He looks like he hasn't eaten or slept in a long time, his cheeks hollow and dark smudges under his eyes. He's quite beautiful—like a starving angel. But there's no kindness or friendliness in his face.

I turn all the way around back to the bar, grabbing my drink once more. I make conversation with Marnie, determined not to look over at the strange man anymore.

Once we've all finished our drinks, it's time to dance. You'd think we'd get sick of it with all the practicing we do, but dancing at the club is completely different. There's no technique to it. It's the only time we can just flail around without having to think about it.

The more we dance, the sillier we get. We do the Humpty Dance and the Cabbage Patch, then the Renegade and the Triangle. Marnie tries to convince the DJ to play Lizzo, but he says he's not allowed; he has to stick to the set list.

In her bid to continue flirting with the hunky bartender, Serena goes back for several more drinks, until she's too loopy to dance anymore. Marnie and I bring her water, and we all crowd into a booth to rest for a minute.

"So are you gonna tell me why you were so upset earlier?" Serena demands, lounging in the corner of the booth.

"Oh." I shake my head. "It's stupid. I thought I'd be credited for the dances I choreographed for *Bliss*."

"Why aren't you credited?" Marnie asks. She's tall and skinny, with a cute little gap in her front teeth. She's a great artist, and sometimes works on the sets as well as dancing in the corps.

"I don't know. Jackson probably changed most of what I did."

"No, he didn't." Marnie shakes her head. "I just watched the duet last night. It's the same as how you made it."

"Oh."

Now I feel worse than ever. Is my work really so bad that Jackson thought I simply didn't deserve credit? But if that's the case, why did he even use it in the show?

"He's stealing from you," Serena says in disgust. "He's such an asshole."

"What are you going to do about it?" Marnie asks.

"What can I do? He's a god in the dance world." I grimace. "I'm nobody."

Marnie makes a sympathetic face. She knows it's true.

Serena is fiercer. "That's bullshit! You can't let him get away with that."

"What am I going to do? Report him to the Supreme Court of Ballet? There's no higher power here."

"Well, you know those nasty green smoothies he keeps in the

fridge?" Serena says. "You could drop a couple of laxatives in there. At the very least."

She breaks down in giggles, definitely more than a little drunk.

Her helpless laughter makes me laugh, and Marnie does, too. Soon we're all snorting and giggling until tears run down our cheeks.

"Knock it off!" Marnie says. "You're gonna get us all kicked out."

"No way," Serena says. "That bartender and I are like this now."

She tries to hold up her first and second finger intertwined, but she's too uncoordinated to make anything but a peace sign. Which makes Marnie and me laugh all the harder.

"I better get you home, you idiot," Marnie says.

Marnie and Serena share a flat over on Magnolia Avenue. It's only a five-minute Uber ride away.

"You wanna share a car?" Marnie asks me.

"I've got to go the other way. I left my Jeep at the studio."

"You can't walk alone," Serena says, trying to compose herself and be serious for a second.

"It's only a couple of blocks," I assure her.

I've only had the one drink, so I figure I'm good to walk back to Lake City Ballet.

We part ways at the door, Marnie helping to support Serena while they wait for their Uber, and me heading off down Lowell.

Even though it's late, Chicago is too busy a city for the streets to ever be truly empty. Plenty of cars are driving by, and the roads are lit by the high-rises and the old-fashioned streetlamps. A couple of teenagers on skateboards zip past me, shouting something I can't make out.

However, as I turn down Greenview, the sidewalks become more deserted. It's chilly. I wrap my arms around myself, walking quickly. My purse bounces against my hip; I've got the strap slung across my body so nobody will try to grab it. I wonder if I should take out my keys—I have a little canister of pepper spray attached to my key chain just in case. It's six years old, though, so who knows if it still works.

I don't know why I'm feeling paranoid all of a sudden. My skin feels prickly and stretched, my heart rate picking up more than the brisk walk deserves.

Maybe it's just my imagination, but I think I hear footsteps behind me. They seem a little too quick, like the person is trying to catch up to me.

Pausing at the corner of Greenview and Henderson, I sneak a glance over my shoulder.

There's definitely a man about a hundred yards back. He's wearing a sweatshirt, his hands stuffed in the pockets and the hood pulled up. His head is down, so I can't see his face.

He's probably just headed home, same as me. Still, I cross the road and start walking even faster. I don't want to keep looking back to see if he's gaining on me. I feel the urge to start running.

I see Lake City Ballet up ahead, my white Jeep still parked out front. The rest of the lot is deserted. Everybody's long since gone home.

I slip my hand into my purse, feeling for my keys as I walk. I want to have them ready to open the car door. I feel my phone, my ChapStick, a coin...no keys, though. What the hell? It's not even a large purse.

The dance studio is locked and dark.

I know the door code. All the dancers know it since we're allowed to come practice whenever we like.

When I'm a half block away, I break into a run. I sprint toward the studio, uncertain whether the pounding footsteps I hear belong to me or somebody following me.

I reach the door, madly trying to punch in the code: 1905. The year Anna Pavlova first performed "The Dying Swan." Jackson is a little obsessed.

My fingers fumble over the keypad. I punch the numbers in wrong twice in a row before the lock finally clicks.

I shove the door closed behind me before turning the latch and pressing my forehead against the glass, peering out into the darkness. My heart is racing, my hands sweaty on the handle. I expect to see some maniac charging toward me, brandishing a knife.

Instead, I see…nothing at all.

There's nobody on the sidewalk. Nobody following me. The person in the hoodie probably turned down another street without me even noticing.

I'm such an idiot. I've always had a wild imagination. When I was little, I had the craziest nightmares, and I was always sure they were real, no matter how impossible it might be for my sister to turn into a tiger or for me to find a dozen severed heads in our fridge.

I sink to the floor, looking through my purse for my keys once more. There they are—in the little side pocket where they always reside. I was just too panicked to feel them.

I check my phone as well. No texts or messages from my parents, even though it's after midnight.

It's funny. They're so overprotective. But they're also so busy that they haven't even noticed I'm gone.

Oh well. I'm at the studio, and I'm the furthest thing from tired after ten thousand volts of adrenaline ran through my veins. I might as well practice a while.

So I head upstairs to my favorite room. It's the smallest of the studios. The floor is so springy, it's almost like dancing on a trampoline.

I strip off my jeans and sweater, leaving only the leotard underneath. Then I set my phone into the dock and find my favorite playlist. It starts with "Someone You Loved" by Lewis Capaldi. I warm up on the barre as the lilting piano intro begins.

5
MIKO

I STAND AT THE EDGE OF THE PARKING LOT, JUST OUT OF SIGHT, laughing softly to myself.

Little Nessa Griffin spooks easy.

Watching her sprint toward the studio gave me a thrill so sweet, I could almost taste it. I could have caught her if I wanted to. But I have no intention of taking her tonight.

That would be too easy to trace back to me, after she only just left my club.

When I make Nessa disappear, it will be like dropping a stone in the ocean. There won't be a single ripple to show where she's gone.

I wait to see if she's going to come back out and get in her car, but she stays inside the studio. After a minute, a second-floor light flicks on, and she walks into a tiny practice room.

I can see her perfectly. She doesn't realize that the illuminated room is like a light box suspended above the street. I can see every last detail as if it were a diorama in my hands.

I watch as Nessa strips off her sweater and jeans, a revealing skintight bodysuit underneath. It's pale pink, so sheer and tight that I can see the outline of her breasts and ribs, her navel, and her ass when she turns.

I didn't know she was a dancer. I should have guessed—she and her friends all have that look. Nessa is skinny. Too skinny, with long legs and arms. There's a little muscle, too—on the balls of her calves and in her shoulders and back. Her neck is long and slim like the stalk of a flower.

She pulls her hair free of its elastic, letting it spill down around her shoulders. Then she twists it up in a bun on the very top of her head to secure it in place once more. She doesn't bother with shoes, taking her position barefoot at the wooden bar that runs the length of the mirror. She faces herself, her back to me. I can still see her in double—the actual, real Nessa and her reflection.

I watch as she bends and stretches, warming up. She's flexible. Her joints look loose and rubbery.

I wish I could hear the music she's playing. Classical or modern? Fast or slow?

Once she's warmed up, she starts twirling across the floor. I don't know the names of any dance moves, except maybe a pirouette. I don't even know if she's good.

All I know is it's beautiful. She looks effortless, weightless, a leaf in the wind.

I'm watching her with awe. The way a hunter would watch a doe that walks into a clearing. Nessa is lovely. Innocent. Perfectly at peace in her natural environment.

I'll send my arrow straight into her heart. That's my right, as the hunter.

For over an hour, I watch as she dances tirelessly.

She's still going at it when I walk back to my club. Maybe she'll stay there all night. I'll know if she does because the tracker is still in her purse.

I follow Nessa Griffin all week long. Sometimes driving. Sometimes walking. Sometimes sitting at a table in the same restaurant.

She never notices me. And she never seems to sense she's being followed after that first night.

I see where she goes to school, where she shops. I see where she lives, though I was already more than familiar with the Griffins' mansion on the lake.

I even watch her visit her sister-in-law several times. It pleases me to know that they're close. I want to punish the Griffins *and* the Gallos. I want to set them against one another. It won't work unless they all feel the loss of Nessa Griffin.

After a week, I feel quite certain that Nessa will suit my purposes.

So it's time to make my move.

6
NESSA

I MISS MY BROTHER. I'M HAPPY THAT HE'S SO HAPPY WITH AIDA. And I know it was time for him to get his own place. But our house is so much worse without him at the breakfast table.

For one thing, he used to keep Riona in line.

When I come downstairs, she's got folders and papers spread around her in such a wide radius that I have to eat at the very corner of the table.

"What are you working on?" I ask her, grabbing a slice of crispy bacon and taking a bite.

We have a chef who makes every meal look like one those TV commercials where you've got orange juice, milk, fruit, toast, pancakes, bacon, and sausages all perfectly arranged like normal people actually eat all that in one sitting.

We're spoiled; I'm well aware of it. But I'm not going to complain about it. I like having my meals prepared for me. And I love living in a big bright modern house, with its sprawling green grounds and a perfect view of the lake.

The only thing I don't love is how grouchy my sister is first thing in the morning.

She's already wearing her business attire, her red hair pulled up in a glass-smooth chignon, a mug of black coffee in front of her. She's poring over some brief, making color-coded notes in pencil.

When I speak to her, she sets down the red pencil and fixes me with an annoyed stare.

"What?" she says tartly.

"I was just asking what you were working on."

"I'm not working on anything now. Because you interrupted me."

"Sorry." I wince. "What is it, though?"

Riona sighs and fixes me with a look that plainly says she doesn't think I'm going to understand what she's about to tell me. I try to look extremely intelligent in return.

My sister would be beautiful if she ever smiled. She's got skin like marble, gorgeous green eyes, and lips as red as her hair. Unfortunately, she also has the temperament of a pit bull. And not a nice pit bull—the kind that's trained to go right for the throat in every encounter.

"You're aware that we own an investment firm?" she says.

"Yes." *No.*

"One of the ways we predict trends in publicly traded companies is via geolocation data pulled from smartphone apps. We purchase the data in bulk, then analyze it using algorithms. However, under the new privacy and security laws, some of our past data purchases are being scrutinized. So I'm in charge of liaising with the SEC to make sure…"

She sees my expression of complete noncomprehension. "Never mind," she says, picking up her pencil again.

"No, th-that sounds really…I mean, it's super important, so it's good y-you're…" I'm stammering like an idiot.

"It's fine." Riona cuts me off. "You don't have to understand it. It's my job, not yours."

She doesn't say it, but the unspoken addendum is that I don't have a job in the Griffin empire.

"Well, good talking to you," I say.

Riona doesn't respond. She's already fully immersed in her work again.

I grab one more strip of bacon for the road.

As I'm picking up my backpack, my mother comes into the kitchen. Her blond bob is brushed so smooth that it almost looks like a wig, though I know it isn't. She's wearing a Chanel suit, my grandmother's diamond ring, and the Patek Philippe watch my father bought her for her last birthday. Which means she's probably going to a charity board meeting or accompanying Dad on some business lunch.

My father follows closely after her, dressed in a perfectly tailored three-piece suit, his horn-rimmed glasses giving him a professorial air. His graying hair is still thick and wavy. He's handsome and trim. My parents married young—they don't look fifty, though that was the birthday that earned my mother's watch.

My mother kisses the air next to my cheek, careful not to smudge her lipstick. "Off to school?" she says.

"Yeah. Statistics, then Russian lit."

"Don't forget we're going to dinner with the Fosters tonight."

I stifle a groan. The Fosters have twin daughters my age, and they're both equally awful. "Do I have to come?"

"Of course," my father says. "You want to see Emma and Olivia, don't you?"

"Yes." *No.*

"Make sure you're home by six, then," my mother says.

I shuffle out to my car, trying to think of something to be cheerful about today. Statistics? No. Dinner? Definitely not. Ugh, I miss driving to school with Aida. She finished the last of her classes over the summer, while I've still got three years left. I don't even know what I'm majoring in. I'm taking a bit of business, a bit of psychology. It's all interesting enough, but none of it sets my heart on fire.

The truth is I want to do something in the arts. I loved, loved, loved choreographing those dances. I thought they were good! Then Jackson took all my hopes and crumpled them up like day-old newspaper.

Maybe he's right. How can I make great art when I've barely experienced anything at all? I've been sheltered and babied my whole life. Art comes from suffering—or, at the very least, adventure. Jack London had to go to the Klondike and lose all his front teeth to scurvy before he could write *The Call of the Wild*.

Instead of going to the Klondike, I drive over to Loyola, a lovely redbrick campus right on the water. I park my Jeep and head to class. I sit through statistics, which is about as interesting as Riona's legal work, and then Russian literature, which is a little better because we're currently reading *Doctor Zhivago*. I've watched the movie with my mother nine times over. We both have a crush on Omar Sharif.

That helps me follow along much better than I did with *Fathers and Sons*. I may even get an A, though it'll be my first one this semester.

After a break for lunch, I sit through one more class, behavioral psychology, and then I'm free. At least until dinnertime.

I retrieve the Jeep and head off campus, wondering if I've got time to sneak in a quick conditioning class at Lake City Ballet before I've got to go home and shower. I'd rather be late. Whatever it takes to cut a little time off dinner with the Fosters…

I've barely pulled onto the main road before my steering wheel begins to judder and shake. The engine makes an awful grinding sound and smoke pours out from under the hood.

I pull over as quickly as I can before putting the car into park.

I switch off the engine, hoping the whole thing doesn't burst into flames. I've only had this car for three years, and it was brand-new when I got it. It hasn't had so much as a flat tire before.

I fumble for my phone, thinking I better call my brother, or one of the house staff, or AAA.

Before I've dialed anybody, a black Land Rover pulls up behind me. A man climbs out of the driver's side. He's got black hair, stubble, and a broad build. He looks intimidating, but his tone is friendly as he says, "Something wrong with the engine?"

"I guess so…" I open my car door and climb out. "I don't know anything about cars. I was just about to call someone."

"Let me take a look," the man offers. "I might be able to save you a tow if it's an easy fix."

I'm about to tell him not to go to any trouble. The smoke and the smell are so bad that I can't imagine I'll be driving away from this. No point in him getting his hands all greasy for nothing. But he's already popping the hood, careful not to singe his fingers on the overheated metal.

He leans back so the smoke doesn't billow right into his face, then peers in at the engine once it clears. "Oh, there's the problem… your engine seized up. Here, take a look."

I have no idea what I'll be looking at, but I obediently walk over and peek inside like I'm going to suddenly understand car mechanics.

"See?" He pulls the dipstick out to show me. I recognize that at least because I've seen Jack Du Pont changing the oil on all the cars in our garage.

"How can it be out of oil?" I ask.

Jack does all the maintenance. Does oil get used up if you drive around too much?

"Someone must have drained it," the man says. "It's bone-dry."

"Like a prank?" I say, mystified.

"More like a ruse," the man replies.

That's a strange answer.

I realize I'm standing quite close to this stranger who appeared the instant my car broke down. Almost like he'd been driving right behind me, just waiting for it to happen…

Something sharp bites my arm.

I look down. A syringe is embedded in my flesh, the plunger pushed all the way down.

I look up into the man's eyes, so dark that they appear almost black, no separation between pupil and iris. He's staring at me with anticipation.

Distantly, I hear myself say, "Why did you do that?"

The sound of the cars rushing by becomes dull and slow. The man's eyes are dark smears in a peach blur. All the bones dissolve in my body. I get floppy as a fish, tumbling sideways. If the man weren't closing his arms tightly around me, I'd fall right into the road.

7
MIKO

Six months ago, anonymously and through a discreet broker, I bought one of the biggest Gilded Age mansions in Chicago. It's located on the north end of the city in a densely wooded lot.

You'd hardly know you were in Chicago at all. The trees are so thick and the stone walls around the property are so high, barely any sunlight filters in through the windows. Even the walled garden is full of shade-loving plants that can stand the dim light and silence.

It's called the Baron's House, because it was built for beer baron Karl Schulte, in the German Baroque style. It's all weathered gray stone, black iron railings, and ornate sculptural reliefs in the shape of scrolls, medallions, and two hulking male figures that hold up the portico on their shoulders.

I bought it thinking it would be a refuge. A place to go when I want solitude.

Now I realize it makes the perfect prison.

Once you pass through the iron gates, you might as well have disappeared.

I'm going to make Nessa Griffin disappear. From the moment Jonas brings her to me, not another soul will see her face. No spies, no witnesses. Her family can tear the city down brick by brick, and they won't find a trace of her.

Picturing their panic makes me smile for the first time in a long time. The Griffins and the Gallos have so many enemies, they won't know who snatched her. The members of the *Braterstwo* are their worst and most recent foes, but in their arrogance, they think they destroyed us by killing Tymon. They're so fucking myopic, I doubt they even know my name.

That's exactly how I like it. I'm the virus that will invade their system unseen and unnoticed. They won't realize what's happening until they're coughing up blood.

I hear a car pulling into the yard and feel a spike of anticipation. I'm actually looking forward to this.

My footsteps ring on the bare stone of the lobby. I'm down the steps and beside the Land Rover before Jonas has even exited the car.

He hauls his bulk out of the front seat, looking pleased with himself. "It went perfectly. I had Andrei take the Jeep to the chop shop. He shorted out the GPS first, so they won't be able to track it past where it broke down. Then he had the whole thing dismantled and crushed. They won't find so much as a headlight."

"You have her purse?"

"Right here." He reaches into the front seat and pulls out the purse, a simple leather satchel, the same one she carried at the club. Lucky for me, it's the only purse she's been using while I've been tracking her all week. If she'd been a typical spoiled socialite with a dozen designer handbags, that would have been very inconvenient. But it wouldn't have stopped me.

"I threw her phone in a dumpster in Norwood," Jonas says.

"Good." I nod. "Let's get her upstairs."

Jonas opens the rear door. Nessa Griffin is passed out on the back seat. Her arm dangles limply, her eyes twitching behind closed lids. She's dreaming about something.

Jonas takes her feet, and I take her head, carrying her inside the house. Her body hangs awkwardly between us. After a moment I say, "I'll do it," and scoop her up in my arms instead.

Even though she's deadweight, it's not a heavy load. I can carry her up the stairs easily. Actually, it's alarming how fragile she is. Too skinny, her collarbones showing through her skin, hollow and birdlike. She's pale from the drugs, her skin almost translucent.

She'll have the whole east wing to herself. Jonas's rooms are on the ground floor, as are Andrei's and Marcel's. I live in the west wing.

The only other person who comes into this house is Klara Hetman, our housekeeper. I have no concerns about her discretion. She's Jonas's cousin from Bolesławiec. Even if she could speak English, she knows better than to risk my wrath. I could send her back to that shithole with a snap of my fingers. Or put her six feet under.

I carry Nessa into her new room. I bought this house furnished. The bed is an ancient four-poster made of dark wood, with a dusty crimson canopy. I lay her on top of the covers, her head on the pillow.

Jonas followed me up. He's standing in the doorway, his eyes roaming over Nessa's limp, helpless body. He grins lecherously. "You want me to help undress her?"

"No," I snap. "You can leave."

"All right." He turns around and ambles away, back down the hallway.

I wait until he's gone, and then I look down at Nessa's pale face again.

Her eyebrows are contracted, giving her a plaintive look even with her eyes closed. Her eyebrows are much darker than her hair.

I pull off her sneakers before dropping them on the floor next to the bed. Underneath, she's wearing those little socks that only cover half the foot so they don't show over the tops of her shoes. I strip off the socks, revealing slim little feet that are beat to shit. She's got bruises, blisters, calluses, and Band-Aids on several toes. Still, she's painted her toenails pink, an attempt at beautification so pointless that it almost makes me laugh.

She's still wearing jeans and a zip-up hoodie.

The drugs Jonas gave her will keep her knocked out for hours.

I could strip her naked if I wanted to. She wouldn't feel a thing. It might be amusing to do it, just so she'd wake up that way, without any idea of what happened to her.

My fingers linger over her breastbone, grazing the zipper of her sweatshirt.

I let my hand drop by my side.

She'll be terrified enough. No need to make her hysterical.

Instead, I pull a blanket over her body.

It's already getting dark in her room. The windows are leaded glass, almost impossible to break. Even if she could open them, she's up on the third floor with no way to climb down. Then there are the stone walls, the cameras, and the perimeter sensors.

Still, as an added precaution, I pick up the ankle monitor I've been keeping on the nightstand next to her bed. I close it around her ankle, snapping it shut. It's smash proof, waterproof, and has to be opened with a code that only I know. It's slim and light, but as tenacious as a manacle.

I leave the room, locking her door from the outside.

Then I slip the key into my pocket.

No one is going in there without my permission.

8
NESSA

I wake in a dark room, on a strange bed.

The first thing I notice is the dusty, ancient smell. It smells like old wood. Dried rose petals. Ash. Musty drapes.

My head feels swollen and heavy. I'm so tired that I want to go right back to sleep. But a nagging voice in my brain tells me that I've got to get up.

I sit up, making the blanket puddle around my waist. Just that movement sets my head spinning. I lean forward, hands pressed against my temples, trying to steady myself.

When my vision clears, I look around, blinking and trying to make out the shape of the room.

Even though the windows are uncovered, barely enough moonlight filters in for me to see anything. I'm sitting in a four-poster bed in what appears to be a huge bedroom. Several massive pieces of furniture are set against the walls, each one the size of a half-grown elephant—a wardrobe, a vanity, and something farther off that might be a writing desk. Also, there's a gaping hole large enough to stand in that I think is a fireplace. It looks like a cave. A cave that could have anything inside.

Flickers of memory float in my brain like sparks around a campfire. A steering wheel shuddering under my hands. A flash of sunlight as I climbed out of the car. A black-haired man with a sympathetic expression that didn't quite extend to his eyes.

My heart starts racing. I'm in an unknown house, brought here by an unknown man.

I've been fucking kidnapped!

This realization isn't quite as foreign to me as it might be to a normal girl. I'm a Mafia daughter. While I may sail through sunlit seas, I'm all too aware of the sharks swimming right below the water. There's an undercurrent of danger at all times—overheard in conversations as I walk past my father's office, hinted at in the strain lines on my parents' faces.

Deep down, I guess I always knew something crazy might happen to me. I've never felt entirely safe, no matter how sheltered I seem.

Still, theory and reality are two different things. I'm not wrapped in my parents' arms anymore. I'm in the house of an enemy. I don't know who he is—but I know *what* he is. These men are brutal, violent, and without compassion. Whatever they do to me, it'll be ugly.

I have to get out of here.

Right now.

I slip out from under the covers, intending to run.

As soon as my feet hit the floor, I realize I'm missing my shoes and socks.

It doesn't matter. Unless the floor is made of broken glass, I can run away barefoot.

When I try to take my first step, my knees crumple, and I fall forward onto my palms. My head is a balloon barely tethered to my shoulders. My stomach flips in nauseating loops.

Vomit rises in my throat. I swallow it back down, my eyes stinging with tears. I don't have time to puke or cry. I just need to leave.

I creep across the room toward the door. It feels like I'm traveling the length of a football field. I'm crawling across an antique rug, then for a stretch of time over bare hardwood.

At last, I reach the door. Only then does it occur to me that I'm probably locked inside. But to my surprise, the knob turns easily under my hand.

I pull myself upright using the door handle, giving myself another minute for the room to stop spinning. I take slow, deep breaths. This time my knees stay steady, and I manage to walk. I slip out into a long dark hallway.

The house is utterly silent. There's no light and no sign of any other people. This place is so old and creepy that a ghost could pop out of the walls any second. I feel like I'm in a horror movie, in the part where the girl wanders around like an idiot and the whole audience covers their eyes, knowing something awful is about to happen.

I can't really be alone.

I'm not stupid enough to think someone went to all the trouble of kidnapping me only to leave me completely unattended. They could be hiding all around me. They could be watching me on camera right now.

I don't understand this game.

Is my kidnapper a cat playing with their food before they eat it?

It doesn't matter. My only other option is staying in my room, and I'm not going to do that.

I creep down the hallway, searching for the most likely route out of this place.

It's nerve-racking to walk past so many empty doorways.

This place is huge, bigger than my parents' house by far. Not nearly as well maintained, though. The carpet in the hallway is threadbare and lumpy; I have to shuffle my feet along so I don't trip. The windows are thick with dust, and the paintings on the walls have been knocked askew. It's hard to make out the subjects in the dark, but I think some of them are mythological. I see a long oil painting of a convoluted labyrinth, a Minotaur lurking in the center.

Finally, I come to a wide curving staircase leading to the lower level. I peer down, but I don't see any light in that direction. God, it's disorienting walking through a strange place in the dark. I'm losing my sense of time and direction. Every sound is amplified, which only confuses me more. I can't tell if the creaks and groans I hear are a person or only the settling of the house.

I hurry down the staircase, trailing my fingertips along the banister. My head is clearing by the minute. It does seem unlikely that I'll escape this easily, but maybe it's possible. Maybe they miscalculated whatever fucked-up drug they gave me and they expect me to sleep all night. Maybe they're just incompetent. I might have been snatched by amateurs or by crazy people who don't think things through.

I cling to my optimism so fear doesn't overwhelm me.

Once I'm down the stairs, I hunt for the front door, lost in a rabbit warren of rooms. Old architects didn't care for open floor plans. I'm wandering through libraries and sitting rooms and billiard rooms and god knows what else. Several times I bump into an end table or the back of a couch, and I once almost knock over a standing lamp, barely catching its pole before it hits the ground.

With each minute that passes, my nerves become increasingly frayed. What the hell is this place, and why am I here?

At last, I catch a glimpse of the same cool, pale outdoor light I saw from my window. Moon or stars. I hurry in that direction, through a glass conservatory packed with tropical plants. The thick foliage hangs from the ceiling. The pots are so tightly clustered that I have to push my way through the leaves, feeling like I'm already outside.

I've almost reached the back door when a voice says, "Finally awake."

I stop dead in my tracks.

I can see the glass door in front of me. If I run, I could probably get there before this person can grab me.

However, I'm at the back of the house. I'd only be running into a yard—if the door is unlocked at all.

With slow shallow breaths, I turn to face my captor.

I'm so dazed and terrified that I almost expect to see fangs and claws. A literal monster.

Instead, I see a man sitting on a bench. He's slim, pale, and casually dressed. His hair is so blond that it's almost white, on the long side and swept back from his face. His sharp features only appear more so in this light—high cheekbones, razor-fine jaw, dark shadows under his eyes. Beneath his black T-shirt are full sleeves of tattoos on both arms, all the way down the backs of his hands, then rising over his neck to his chin. His glittering eyes are two shards of shattered glass.

I recognize him at once.

It's the man from the nightclub. The one who was staring at me.

"Who are you?" I ask.

"Who do you think I am?"

"I have no idea."

He sighs and stands from the bench. Involuntarily, I take a step backward.

He's taller than I expected. He may be lean, but his shoulders are broad, and he moves with a grace I recognize. This is a person in control of their body. Someone who can move quickly and without hesitation.

"I'm disappointed in you, Nessa…" His voice is low and clear and carefully enunciated, with a hint of an accent I can't quite place. "I knew you were sheltered. But I didn't think you were stupid."

His insult cuts me like a lash. Maybe it's the expression on his face, his lip curled up in revulsion. Or maybe it's the fact I'm already keyed up tight with terror.

I don't usually have a temper. Actually, I can be a bit of a pushover.

My brain decides that now is the moment to finally get snippy. Right when it could get me killed.

"I'm sorry," I snap. "Am I not meeting your expectations as a hostage? Please, enlighten me as to how perceptive you'd be if somebody drugged you and plopped you in the middle of some creepy haunted mansion?"

As soon as I say it, I regret it. He takes another step toward me, his eyes ferocious and cold, his shoulders rigid with anger.

"Well," he hisses softly, "I'd probably be smart enough not to antagonize my captor."

My legs shake beneath me. I take another few steps until I feel the cool glass door against my back. My hand gropes blindly for the doorknob.

"Come on now, Nessa," he says, his eyes boring down into mine as he draws closer. "You can't be completely ignorant of what goes on in your family?"

He knows my name. He sent the man with the black hair to kidnap me—which means that guy works for him as a soldier. His accent is subtle and unusual—nothing I recognize like French of German. It could be Eastern European. He has that look—the high cheekbones, the fair skin, and the hair. Russian?

Four months ago, my family had a run-in with a Polish gangster. Someone called the Butcher. Nobody told me about it, of course. Aida mentioned it later, in passing. Her oldest brother killed him. That was the end of it.

Or so I thought.

"You work for the Butcher," I say, my voice coming out in a squeak.

He's right in front of my face now, towering over me. I can almost feel the heat radiating off his skin. Waves of loathing pour out of him as he looks down at me with those ice-blue eyes.

This man hates me. He hates me like I've never been hated in my life. I think he could cheerfully peel the flesh off my bones with his fingernails.

"His name was Tymon Zajac," he spits, each word clipped as if by shears. "He was my father. And you killed him."

He means my family killed him.

But in our world, the sins of the family are visited on all who share the same blood.

I find the door handle at last, scrambling to turn it behind my back.

It's fixed in place like a lump of solid metal.

I'm locked in with this beast.

9
MIKO

THE GIRL IS TERRIFIED. SHE'S SHAKING SO HARD THAT HER TEETH click together.

She scrambles wildly behind her for the door handle. When she finds it at last, she tries to wrench it open to flee out into the back garden. The door is locked. She's got nowhere to go, unless she wants to fling herself through solid glass.

Her pulse jumps in her throat beneath the thin, delicate skin. I can taste the adrenaline in her breath. Her fear is salt on a dish—it only makes this moment more delicious.

I expect her to start crying. This girl obviously has no spine. She's weak, babyish—the spoiled princess of American royalty. She'll beg me not to hurt her. I'll store each and every plea in my mind so I can relay them to her family members when I kill them.

Instead, she takes a deep breath and straightens her shoulders. She closes her eyes for a moment, her lips parting as she lets out a long sigh. Those big green eyes open again looking right up into my face, wide and frightened, but resolute.

"I didn't kill your father," she says. "But I know how people like you think. There's no reasoning with you. I'm not going to cower and beg—you'd probably just enjoy it. So do what you have to do."

She lifts her chin, her cheeks flushed pink.

She thinks she's brave.

She thinks she could stay strong if I wanted to torture her. If I wanted to break her bones, one by one.

I've made grown men scream for their mothers. I can only imagine what I could make her do, given enough time.

Sure enough, as soon as I lift my right hand, she flinches, scared of a blow to the face.

But I have no intention of hitting her. Not yet.

Instead, I rest my fingertips against that soft pink cheek lightly dusted with freckles. It takes every ounce of self-control I possess to resist digging my fingers deep into her flesh.

I stroke my thumb across her lips. I can feel them trembling.

"If only it were that easy, my little ballerina…"

Her eyes widen, a shiver running all the way down her slim frame. It scares her that I know this fact about her. I know what she does, and I know what she loves.

This girl has no idea how easy she is to read. She's never learned to put up walls, to protect herself. She's as vulnerable as a bed of tulips. I intend to stomp through her garden, ripping the blossoms from the ground one by one.

"I didn't bring you here to kill you quickly," I tell her, my voice tender, caressing. I touch the edge of her jaw, delicate as a bird's wing. "Your suffering will be long and slow. You will be the blade I use to cut your family again and again and again. Only when they're weak and desperate and full of misery, only then will I allow them to die. And you'll watch it all, little ballerina. Because this is a tragedy—and the swan princess only perishes in the final act."

Tears fill her eyes before slipping silently down her cheeks. Her lips tremble with disgust.

She looks at me and sees a monster out of a nightmare.

And she's absolutely right.

In the time I worked for Zajac, I did unspeakable things. I've blackmailed, stolen, beaten, tortured, and murdered people. I did it all without conscience or remorse.

All that was good inside me died ten years ago. The last shred of the boy I used to be was tied to Zajac—he was the only family I had left. Now he's gone, and there's no humanity inside me at all. I feel nothing anymore but need. I need money. Power. And above all, revenge.

There's no good or bad, no right or wrong. Only my goals and the things that stand in the way of those goals.

Nessa shakes her head slowly, making the tears flow all the faster. "I'm not going to help you hurt the people I love. No matter what you do to me."

"You won't have a choice," I say, a smile curving the corners of my mouth. "I told you. This is a tragedy—your fate is already set."

Her body stiffens. For a moment I see that spark of rebellion flare in those wide eyes. I think she might pluck up the courage to try to hit me.

But she isn't quite that foolish.

Quietly, she says, "This isn't fate. You're just an evil man trying to play god."

She lets go of the doorknob and stands up straight, though it brings us even closer together.

Nessa says, "You don't know what kind of story we're in any more than I do."

I could strangle her right now. That would extinguish the defiance in those eyes. That would show her that whatever sort of story this may be, it isn't one with a happy ending.

But then I'd deny myself the bitter pleasures I've waited for during all these months.

Softly, I say, "Why don't you tell me who I should kill first? Your mother? Your father? What about Aida Gallo? After all, it's her brother who shot Tymon..."

With each family member I name, Nessa's body jerks like I've hit her. I think I know the one who will hurt her most...

"Or what about your big brother, Callum? He thought he was

too good to work with us. Now he's got a big fancy office in city hall. It's so easy to find him there. Or I could visit his apartment on Erie Street…"

"No!" Nessa cries, unable to stop herself.

God, this is too easy. It's barely any fun at all.

"Here are the rules for the present," I tell her. "If you try to escape, I'll punish you. If you try to hurt yourself, I'll punish you. If you refuse any of my orders…well, you get the idea. Now quit your sniveling and get back to your room."

Nessa looks pale and sick.

She was defiant when she thought it was only her life on the line. But when I named her brother and sister-in-law, it stripped away her resistance in an instant.

I'm starting to regret picking her for this little game. I don't think she's going to put up much of a fight.

Sure enough, as soon as I step back to give her space to pass, she meekly runs back in the direction of her room. Without even a final retort to salvage her dignity.

I pull out my phone so I can access the cameras mounted in every corner of this house.

I watch as she climbs the stairs, then flees down the long hallway to the guest suite at the end of the east wing. She pushes her door closed and collapses on the ancient four-poster bed, sobbing into her pillow.

I sit back down on the bench so I can watch her cry. She cries for an hour before finally falling back asleep.

I don't feel guilt or pleasure watching her.

I don't feel anything at all.

10
NESSA

I SPEND THE NEXT FOUR DAYS LOCKED IN THAT ROOM.

What at first seemed like a huge space soon begins to feel horribly claustrophobic.

The only time my door opens is when the housemaid brings me a tray of food three times a day. She's about thirty years old, with dark hair, almond-shaped eyes, and a Cupid's bow mouth. She wears an old-fashioned maid's uniform, complete with thick dark tights, a long skirt, and an apron. She gives me a polite nod when she drops off the new tray and picks up the old one.

I try to talk to her, but I don't think she speaks English. Or she's been instructed not to answer me. Once or twice she gives me a sympathetic look, particularly as I become more disheveled and irate, but I'm under no illusions that she's going to help me. Why should she risk her job or even her life for a stranger?

I spend a lot of time looking out the window. The windows are six feet high, tall and rectangular, with arched tops and beveled glass striped with strips of lead. They don't open. Even if they did, there are three very tall stories down to the ground.

The windows are set in stone walls more than a foot thick. It's like being locked in the tower of a castle.

I have my own bathroom at least, so I can pee and shower and brush my teeth.

The first time I walked in there and saw a hairbrush, a comb, a toothbrush, and some floss lined up next to the sink, all brand-new and untouched, it gave me a shiver of dread. My abduction was planned far ahead of time. I can only imagine what other plots are spinning in my captor's deranged mind.

I still don't know his name. I was so horrified when we met that I didn't even ask him.

In my mind, I've been calling him the Beast. Because that's what he is to me—a rabid dog that lost its master. Now he's trying to bite anyone he can reach.

I don't eat any of the food on the trays.

At first, it's because my stomach is churning with stress and I don't have any appetite.

By the second day, it's become a form of protest.

I have no intention of playing along with the Beast's psychopathic plot. I won't be his little pet locked up in this room. If he thinks he's going to keep me here for weeks or months, only to kill me in the end, I'd rather starve just to ruin his plans.

I still drink water out of the bathroom sink—I don't have quite enough nerve to face the torture of dehydration. But I'm pretty confident I can go a long time without eating. Calorie restriction and ballet go hand in hand. I know what it's like to feel hungry, and I'm used to ignoring it.

It makes me tired. But that's fine. I don't have anything to do in this damned room anyway. There are no books. No paper in the writing desk. The main way to spend my time is window gazing.

I have no barre, but I can still practice *ronds de jambe a terre*, pliés, tendus, dégagés, frappés, adagios, and even grand battements. I don't dare practice any serious jumps or cross-floor exercises because of the ancient rugs on the floor. I don't want to trip and sprain an ankle.

The rest of the time, I sit in the window seat, looking down at the walled garden. I see fountains, statues, gazebos, and pretty bench seats. It's all overgrown—apparently the Beast doesn't pay for a gardener. But the asters are blooming, and the snapdragons, and the Russian sage. The purple blooms are brilliant against the red leaves. The longer I'm trapped inside, the more desperate I am to sit down there smelling the flowers and the grass, instead of being locked in this dim and dusty room.

By the fourth day, the maid tries to encourage me to eat. She gestures at the tray of tomato soup and bacon sandwiches, saying something in Polish.

I shake my head. "No thanks. I'm not hungry."

I want to ask her for books, but the stubborn part of me won't ask my captors for anything. Instead, I try to remember the best parts of all my favorite novels, especially the ones I loved when I was little. The walled garden reminds me of *The Secret Garden*. I think about Mary Lennox. She was only a child, but she already had an iron will. She wouldn't cave over a bowl of soup, no matter how good it smelled. She'd throw it against the wall.

On the fifth day, the maid doesn't bring me any breakfast or lunch. Instead, she arrives in the afternoon carrying a green silk dress in a garment bag. She starts filling the huge claw-foot tub with hot water, gesturing for me to get undressed.

"Absolutely not." I cross my arms over my chest.

I've been putting on my same dirty clothes after every shower, refusing to wear anything out of the wardrobe.

The maid sighs and leaves the room before returning a few minutes later with a burly black-haired man at her side.

I recognize him. He's the asshole who pretended like he was going to fix my car, then jabbed me in the arm instead. The thought of him putting those big, meaty hairy hands on me while I was unconscious makes my skin crawl.

I don't like his smile when he sees me again. His teeth are too square and too white. He looks like a ventriloquist's dummy.

"Get undressed," he orders.

"Why?"

"Because the boss says so." He grunts.

When someone tells me to do something, I feel this impulse to obey. That's what I'm used to doing, at home and at the dance studio. I follow orders.

Not here. Not with these people.

I wrap my arms tight around my body and shake my head. "Unlike you, I don't answer to your boss."

The maid shoots me a warning look. I can tell from the distance she keeps between herself and the black-haired man that she doesn't like this guy either. She's trying to tell me not to mess with him, that his veneer of civility only runs so deep.

I could have guessed that for myself. As much as I dislike the Beast, he at least appeared intelligent. This guy is a goon through and through, with his caveman brow and bad-tempered scowl. Stupid people are not creative. They always resort to violence.

"Here's the thing," the goon says, frowning at me. "Klara here is supposed to help bathe you and get you dressed. If you won't let her do that, then it'll be up to me to strip you naked and soap you down with my bare hands. And I won't be as gentle about it as Klara. So it's in your best interest to cooperate."

The idea of this overgrown ape attacking me with a bar of soap is more than I can stand.

"Fine!" I snap. "I'll take a bath. But only if you leave."

"You don't get to set terms." The ape laughs, shaking his oversize head at me. "I'm supposed to supervise."

God, I want to puke just from the smug expression on his face. He's not watching me get in that tub—not voluntarily anyway. What would Mary Lennox do?

"If you try to make me put that dress on, I'll rip it to shreds," I tell him calmly.

"We've got lots of dresses," the ape says, as if he doesn't care.

I see the flicker of annoyance on his face, though. His instructions were to make me wear *that* dress, not just any dress.

"Go away, and Klara can help me get ready," I insist.

The smug smile fades off his face. Instead of an ape, he looks like a sulky toddler. "Fine," he says shortly. "You better hurry up, though."

With that attempt to salvage his dignity, he stomps back out into the hall.

Klara looks relieved that the confrontation ended that easily. She gestures toward the bathtub, which is now full almost to the brim with steaming water. She's scented it with some kind of oil—almond or coconut.

At least I know her name now.

"Klara?" I say.

She nods.

"Nessa." I touch my own chest.

She nods again. She already knew that.

"What's his name?" I point toward the door where the ape just disappeared.

She hesitates a moment, then says, "Jonas."

"Jonas is a dick," I mutter.

Klara doesn't answer, but I think I see the tiniest of smiles tugging at her lips. If she understands me, then she definitely agrees.

"What about your boss?" I ask her. "What's his name?"

An even longer pause, during which I don't think she's going to answer. Then, at last, Klara whispers, "Mikolaj."

She says it like the name of the devil. Like she wants to cross herself afterward.

It's obvious she's a lot more afraid of him than she is of Jonas.

She points to the bath again and says, "*Wejdź proszę.*" I don't know a single word of Polish, but I'm assuming that means "get in, please" or "hurry, please."

"All right," I say.

I strip off my sweatshirt and jeans, which were getting kind of gross, then unhook my bra and step out of my panties.

Klara looks at my naked body. Like most Europeans, she's not embarrassed by nudity. "*Piękna figura*," she says.

I'm assuming *figura* means "figure." Hopefully *piękna* means "pretty" and not "gangly" or "horrifying."

I've always liked languages. My parents taught me Gaeilge as a child, and I took French and Latin in school. Unfortunately, Polish is a Slavic language, so it doesn't share many words. I'm curious if I can get Klara to speak, to see if I can catch the gist of it.

I know she's not supposed to talk to me. But she is supposed to get me dressed. The more I pester her, the more she relents so I'll cooperate with the bathing and the hair washing. Soon I've learned the words for soap (*mydło*), shampoo (*szampon*), washcloth (*myjka*), bathtub (*wanna*), dress (*suknia*), and window (*okno*).

Despite herself, Klara seems impressed that I can remember it all. It becomes a game, one she's enjoying almost as much as I am. She's smiling by the end, showing a row of pretty white teeth, and even laughing at my poor pronunciation when I try to repeat the words back to her.

I doubt she gets much in the way of pleasant interaction with Jonas and the others. The only people I've seen around this place are hulking, surly tattooed men. And of course, the Beast, who's apparently called Mikolaj, though I find it hard to imagine him having an actual mother and father who would give him a real human name.

He claims the Butcher is his father.

I suppose that's possible. After all, my father is a gangster. But I don't trust anything Mikolaj says. Lying comes easier than breathing to men like him.

Klara insists on not only washing me but shaving every inch of me below the eyebrows. I consider putting up a fight about this, but I go along with it, if only because she's finally talking to me; I don't want that to stop. I do make her tell me the words for razor and shaving cream and towel as she dries me off.

Once I've got the towel wrapped firmly around my body, she sits me in a chair and starts brushing my hair.

My hair has gotten too long lately. Since I wear it up in a bun or a ponytail every day, I hadn't really noticed. It's almost down to the small of my back, thick and wavy and taking forever to dry as Klara tirelessly works the blow dryer and the paddle brush.

She's good at that, as she seems to be at everything.

"Did you work at a salon?" I ask her.

She quirks an eyebrow at me, not understanding the question.

"Salon? Spa?" I say, pointing between her and the blow dryer.

After a moment, her pretty face lights up in understanding, but she shakes her head. "*Nie,*" she says. *No.*

When she's finished with my hair, Klara does my makeup, then helps me step into the green dress and a pair of strappy gold sandals. The material of the dress is so thin and light that I still feel naked after she zips it up. Indeed, I am naked underneath, the clinging material not allowing for so much as a thong.

Klara sets gold earrings into my ears, then steps back to admire the effect.

It's only then that I stop to wonder what, exactly, I'm getting dressed up for. I was so caught up in the bizarre process that I forgot to worry about the purpose of it all.

"Where am I going?"

Klara shakes her head, either not understanding or not permitted to say.

I'm ready to step foot outside my room for the first time in nearly a week.

I can't help my excitement. This is how pathetically constricted my sense of freedom has become—stepping out into the rest of the house is like traveling to China.

I hate that I'm escorted by Jonas, who's sulking over the fact he didn't get to watch me take a bath. He tries to grab my arm. I shake him off, snapping, "I can walk just fine on my own!"

He snarls at me, and I shrink back, a kitten that takes a swipe at a big dog and then immediately regrets it.

Still, it worked. He lets me walk down the hallway on my own, stalking ahead so fast that I can barely keep up in the spindly sandals.

Why in the hell did they dress me up like this? Where am I going?

I can only hope they didn't go to all this trouble just to make a pretty corpse out of me.

It's evening again. The house is lit by electric lights so faint and yellowed that they might as well be candlelight.

I've yet to see the interior of the mansion in full daylight. It may not be much brighter than it is now. The narrow windows and thick stone walls don't allow much sunlight to intrude, particularly when the house seems to be set in the middle of a tiny forest.

I don't even know if we're still in the city. God, we could be in a whole different country for all I know. I don't think so, however. The Irish Mob, the Italian Mafia, the Polish *Braterstwo*, the Russian *Bratva*—they're all warring for control of Chicago as they have been for generations. Sprinkle in a hundred other gangs and cohorts, locally grown and foreign, with fortunes rising and falling, and the balance of power bending and shifting…

Nobody leaves. Nobody gives up the fight.

The Beast wants his revenge, and he wants the city, too. He wouldn't take me far away. Because then he'd be too far from Chicago himself.

I bet we're still within an hour of the city. Maybe inside Chicago itself. There are plenty of old mansions—I could be in any of them.

And if I am still in Chicago…then my family will find me, I'm sure of it. They'll never stop hunting. They'll bring me home.

Hope is a butterfly fluttering inside my chest. Fragile but alive.

It buoys me up as Jonas silently leads me through the double doors of the grand dining room.

A long table fills the space, the kind that could feast a king and his entire court. Nobody sits at the dozens of chairs on either side. There's just one man at the head: the Beast.

All the platters of food are clustered at that end. Roasted chicken stuffed with lemon, white filet of sole, braised vegetables, beet salad, fluffy piles of mashed potatoes dripping melted butter, crusty brown bread, and creamy mushroom soup. With goblets of dark red wine.

Two places have been laid: one for him and one for me.

The food is untouched. Mikolaj waits for me.

He's wearing a long-sleeved shirt, charcoal gray, with the sleeves pushed up to the elbows, showing his tattooed forearms. His tattoos rise up his neck, intricate and dark like a high collar. The smooth skin of his face and hands is ghostly pale by contrast.

His expression is wolflike—hungry and malevolent. His eyes are a wolf's eyes, blue and wintry. They pull me in against my will. I meet his gaze, look away, then have to look back again. We're the only two people in the room. Jonas left.

"Sit," Mikolaj says sharply. He indicates the seat right next to him.

I'd prefer to be much farther down the table.

It's pointless to argue, however—with a snap of his fingers, he could call back his bodyguard. Jonas would shove me in whatever chair the Beast demands. He could tie me to it, and there's not a thing I could do to stop him.

As soon I sink onto the cushioned seat, my nostrils fill with the warm and tantalizing scent of the food. Saliva floods my mouth. I almost got over being hungry. Now, all in an instant, I'm weak and dizzy, desperate to eat.

Mikolaj sees it.

"Go ahead," he says.

My tongue darts out to moisten my lips. "I'm not hungry," I lie weakly.

Mikolaj makes an irritated sound. "Don't be ridiculous. I know you haven't eaten in days."

I swallow hard. "And I'm not going to. I don't want your food. I want to go home."

He barks out a laugh. "You're not going home. Ever."

Oh my god.

No, I don't believe that. I can't believe it.

I'm not staying here, and I'm not eating his food.

I twist my hands into a knot in my lap. "Then I guess I'll starve," I say softly.

The Beast spears a piece of roast beef with a set of pointed tongs. He lays it on his plate, picks up his knife and fork, and saws off a bite. He places it in his mouth, staring at me while he slowly chews and swallows.

"Do you think I care if you starve?" he asks conversationally. "I want you to suffer, little ballerina. On my terms, not yours. If you continue to refuse your meals, I'll tie you to your bed and shove a feeding tube down your throat. You won't die until I allow it. At the perfect moment, orchestrated by me."

I really am faint. My plan seems more foolish by the minute. What does it benefit me to be tied to the bed? What good does it do to starve? It's just making me weaker. Even if I had an opportunity to escape, I'd be too drained to take advantage of it.

I twist my hands tighter and tighter.

I don't want to give in to him. But I don't know what else I can do. He's put me in a trap. Every move I make only tightens the noose.

At last, I whisper, "I'll eat."

"Good." He nods. "Start with some broth so you don't throw it all up again."

"On one condition."

He scoffs. "You don't set conditions."

"It's nothing onerous."

Mikolaj waits to hear it, perhaps out of simple curiosity.

"I'm bored in my room. I'd like to go into the library and down to the garden. You've got this thing on my ankle. And cameras, and guards. I won't try to escape."

I don't really expect him to agree. Why should he? He told me he wants me to suffer. Why would he allow me any entertainment?

To my surprise, he considers the proposal. "You'll eat, and shower, and put on clean clothes every day?"

"Yes." I nod too eagerly.

The silence stretches, his pale blue eyes panes of glass in an empty house. He's so cold, yet everywhere he looks, my skin burns.

He says, "You can go around the house and garden. Everywhere but the west wing."

I don't ask him what's in the west wing. That's probably where his own rooms are located. Or where he keeps the severed heads of his victims, mounted on the wall like hunting trophies. I wouldn't put anything past him.

Mikolaj ladles the beef broth into my bowl, his movements smooth and precise. The palms of his hands are mesmerizing, pale and smooth, one of the only patches of skin on his body not completely covered in dense tattoos.

"There," he says. "Eat."

I spoon the broth into my mouth. It is, without a doubt, the most delicious thing I've ever tasted. Rich, buttery, expertly seasoned. I want to lift the bowl and drink it all.

"Slow," he warns me. "You'll make yourself sick."

Once I've eaten half the soup, I take a sip of the wine. That's delicious, too, tart and fragrant. I only take the one sip because I barely ever drink, and I don't want to lose my wits around the Beast. I'm not stupid enough to think he brought me down here just to feed me.

He's silent until we've both finished eating. Almost everything on the table is still untouched. I could only handle the soup and a little bread. He ate the beef with a small serving of vegetables. No wonder he's so lean. Maybe he doesn't like human food. Maybe he prefers drinking warm blood.

When he's finished, he pushes his plate to the side and leans his chin in the palm of his hand, fixing me with his icy stare. "What do you know about your family's business?"

I was feeling warm and happy from the influx of food, but I immediately close up again like a clam hit with a blast of cold water.

"Nothing," I tell him, setting down my spoon. "I don't know anything. And if I did, I wouldn't tell you."

"Why not?" His eyes gleam with amusement. He finds this funny for some inscrutable reason.

"Because you'd try to use it to hurt them."

He purses his lips in mock concern. "Doesn't it bother you that they don't include you?"

I press my lips together, not wanting to dignify that with a response. But I find myself blurting, "You don't know anything about us."

"I know your brother will inherit your father's position. Your sister will do her level best to keep everyone out of jail. What about you, Nessa? Where do you fit in? I suppose they had a marriage arranged for you, like they did for your brother. Maybe to one of the Gallos... They have three sons, don't they? You and Aida could have been sisters twice over."

His words chill my flesh worse than his gaze. How does he know so much about us?

"I don't...I'm not... There isn't any marriage pact," I say, looking down at my fingers. They're twisted so tight that they've gone pale and bloodless like a pile of worms in my lap.

I shouldn't have said that. He doesn't need any more information than he's already got.

Mikolaj chuckles. "That's too bad. You're very pretty."

I can feel my cheeks flaming, and I hate it. I hate that I'm shy and easily embarrassed. If Aida or Riona were here, they'd throw this wine right in his face. They wouldn't feel frightened and confused, fighting just to keep from crying.

I bite my lip so hard that I taste blood, mingled with the remains of the wine.

I look up at his face, which is unlike any face I've seen before—beautiful, brittle, terrifying, cruel. His thin lips look like they were drawn in ink. His eyes burn right through me.

It's so hard to find my voice.

"What about you?" I gulp. "Mikolaj, isn't it? I suppose you came from Poland, looking for the American Dream? No wife to bring along to your dreary old mansion, though. Women don't like to sleep with snakes."

I intended to offend him, but he only gives me a cold smile. "Don't worry. I never lack for female company."

I make a face. I can't deny that he is handsome, in a stark and terrifying sort of way. But I can't imagine wanting to get within ten feet of someone so vicious.

Unfortunately, I'm well within that radius, and soon I'll be closer.

Because now that we've eaten, Mikolaj expects further entertainment.

He leads me out of the dining room into the adjoining space. It's an actual ballroom with a polished parquet floor and a vast chandelier hanging from the center of the ceiling. The roof is painted deep navy with speckled spots of gold for stars. The walls are gold, the curtains dark blue velvet.

It's the only room I've seen so far that I'd actually call pretty—the rest of the house is too gothic and depressing. However, I can't enjoy it because music is playing, and Mikolaj apparently expects me to dance.

Before I can get away, he's grabbed my right hand in his, catching me around the waist with his left. He pulls me against his body with arms stronger than steel. He really is fast—and an irritatingly good dancer.

♫ *Satin Birds–Abel Korzeniowski*

He whirls me around the empty ballroom, his strides long and smooth.

I don't want to look at him. I don't want to talk to him. But I can't stop myself from asking, "How do you know how to dance?"

"It's a waltz," he says. "It hasn't changed much in two hundred years."

"Were you around when they invented it?" I say rudely.

Mikolaj just smiles and forces me to twirl before dipping me.

I recognize the song playing: it's "Satin Birds" by Abel Korzeniowski. Melancholy and haunting, but actually quite a beautiful song. One of my favorites, before this moment.

I don't like to think that an animal like this actually has good taste in music.

I hate how easily our bodies move in tandem. Dancing is second nature to me. I can't help following his lead, swift and smooth. Nor can I help the surge of pleasure that bubbles up inside me. It's wonderful to have so much space to move after five days of helpless captivity.

I find myself forgetting whose hand is sliding down my bare back, whose fingers are twined in mine. I forget that I'm locked in the arms of my worst enemy, that I can feel the heat radiating out of his body into mine.

Instead, I close my eyes and fly across the floor, spinning on the axis of his hand, dipping over the steel bar of his thigh. I want to dance so badly that I don't care where I am or who I'm with. This is the only way to escape right now—by losing myself in this moment, recklessly and irrevocably.

The starred ceiling whirls over my head. My heart beats faster and faster, having lost its stamina after a week of lethargy. The green silk gown flows around my body, barely touching my skin.

It's only when his fingers trail down my throat, running down to the bare flesh between my breasts, that my eyes pop open. I jerk upright, stopping dead on the spot.

I'm panting and sweating. His thigh is pressed between mine. I'm painfully aware of how thin this dress really is, no sort of barrier at all between us.

I yank myself out of his arms, stumbling over the hem of the gown. The thin silk tears with a sound like a shot. "Let go of me!"

"I thought you liked dancing." Mikolaj mocks me. "You seemed to be enjoying yourself."

"Don't touch me!" I cry, trying to sound as furious as I feel. My voice is naturally soft. It always comes out too gentle, even when I'm at my angriest. It makes me feel like a petulant child.

That's how Mikolaj treats me, rolling his eyes at my sudden change of mood. He was toying with me. As soon as I stop playing along, he has no more use for me.

He says, "Our evening's at an end. Go back to your room."

God, he's so infuriating!

I don't want to stay here with him, but I also don't want to be sent to bed. I don't want to be locked in there again, bored and alone. As much as I despise the Beast, this is the longest conversation I've had all week.

"Wait! What about my family?"

"What about them?" he says in a bored tone.

"Are they worried about me?"

He smiles without a hint of happiness—a smile of pure malice. "They're losing their fucking minds."

I can only imagine.

They would have noticed the very first night I failed to come home. I'm sure they tried to call my phone hundreds of times. They'd have called my friends, too. Sent their men to visit Loyola and Lake City Ballet, trying to retrace my steps. They probably hunted the streets for my Jeep. I wonder if they found it by the side of the road.

Did they call the police, too? We never call the police if we can help it. We make nice with the commissioner at parties, but we don't involve cops in our business any more than Mikolaj does.

This is the only time I've seen him smile—thinking of how terrified and anxious my family must be. It makes me want to run over and scratch his ice-chip eyes out of his head.

I can't believe I let him dance with me. My skin burns with disgust every place he touched me.

Still, I can't keep myself from begging. "Could you at least tell them I'm safe? Please."

I'm begging him with my eyes, my face, even my hands clasped in front of me.

If he has any soul, any at all, he'll see the pain in my face.

But he has nothing inside him.

He just laughs, shaking his head. "Not a chance. That would spoil all the fun."

11
MIKO

For five days I watch the Griffins tear the city apart looking for Nessa. My men report back to me how the Griffins threaten, bribe, and search, without finding a shred of evidence.

Only five people know where Nessa is hidden: Jonas, Andrei, Marcel, Klara, and me. Out of my dozens of soldiers, only the most trusted have any idea what I'm up to. I've warned each of them that if they whisper a word of it, even a hint to a friend or lover, I'll put a bullet in the back of their skull.

I'm thrilled to see that the Gallos are equally frantic to find Nessa. Dante, Nero, and Sebastian Gallo are all hunting for her, and Aida Gallo most of all. It's almost touching how two families who were mortal enemies just months ago are now united in their desperation to find the youngest of their number.

Or it would be touching if their alliance weren't the exact thing I'm determined to crack.

I drink it in. I love that they have no idea if she's alive or dead, no clue where she might have disappeared. Not knowing is the torture. Death can be accepted. But this…it will gnaw at them. Drive them into chaos.

Meanwhile, Nessa Griffin goes mad with boredom. I watch her via the cameras in her room. I see her pacing her cage like an animal in a zoo.

The starvation is a problem. She was already skinny to begin with—she doesn't have the fat stores to withstand weeks of hunger. I can't allow her to fuck up my plans with her petulant protests.

So I order Klara to get Nessa dressed for dinner. I intend to tempt her with food, and if that fails, to forcibly stuff it down her throat.

I wanted to see her in person again anyway. As a figure on my phone screen, she amuses me, but that can't compare to the exquisite bouquet of fear and fury she provides in the flesh.

When Jonas drags her into the formal dining room, I see that Klara has done her job a little too well. I've only seen Nessa in dance attire or school clothes, her hair pulled back and her face freshly scrubbed. Dressed to impress, Nessa Griffin is fucking stunning.

A few days without food have made her willowier than ever. The green silk dress clings to her frame, showing her every breath, down to the sudden intake of air when she spots me waiting for her.

Her light-brown hair floats around her shoulders in waves, longer and thicker than I expected it to be. It reflects the light just like the silk dress, just like her glowing skin and her big green eyes. Every bit of her is luminescent.

But incredibly fragile. The thinness of her neck, her arms, and her fingers is frightening. I could snap those birdlike bones without even trying. I can see her collarbones and her shoulder blades when she turns. The only parts of her with curves are those big, soft trembling lips.

I'm glad to see that while Klara has painted Nessa's face, she's left those lips bare. Pale pink like a ballet slipper. A raw and innocent color. I wonder if her nipples are the same shade underneath that dress.

I can still see the pale brown freckles scattered across her cheeks and the bridge of her nose. They're sweet and childish, in contrast to the surprisingly dark eyebrows that animate her face like punctuation marks. Her eyebrows swoop up like bird's wings when she's surprised and contract plaintively when she's distressed.

Even dressed like this, at her most mature and glamorous, Nessa looks incredibly young. She's fresh and youthful, in contrast to this house where everything is old and dusty.

I don't find her innocence attractive. In fact, I find it infuriating.

How dare she walk through life like a glass sculpture begging to be smashed? She's a burden on everyone around her—impossible to protect, impossible to keep intact.

The sooner I start the process of dismantling her, the better off everyone will be.

So I make her sit down. I make her eat.

She tries to strike her ridiculous bargain with me, and I allow it. I don't care if she wanders around the house. She really can't escape, not with the monitor around her ankle. It tracks her at all times, everywhere she goes. If she tries to break it, if it stops reading her pulse through her skin for even an instant, I'll be alerted.

I'm curious to see where she'll go, what she'll do. I've grown bored of watching her inside her room.

Buoying her up with this tiny victory will only give her further to fall. And if she actually starts to trust me a little, if she thinks I can be reasoned with…all the better.

Constant cruelty isn't how you worm your way inside someone's head. It's the mix of good and bad, give and take, that fucks with them. Unpredictability makes them desperate to please.

After we've eaten, I take Nessa into the ballroom. I've watched her dance several times now—at Jungle, at Lake City Ballet, and trapped in her room, in the space next to the four-poster bed.

Dancing transforms her. The girl who blushes and can't meet my eye is not the same one who lets herself go under the influence of music.

It's like watching a possession. As soon as I take her in my arms, her stiff and fragile body becomes as loose and liquid as the material of her dress. The music surges through her until she's thrumming with too much energy for one tiny frame. She's vibrating under my hands. Her eyes glaze over, and she doesn't seem to notice me at all anymore, other than as an apparatus to move her across the room.

It makes me almost jealous. She's disappeared somewhere that I can't reach her. She's feeling something I can't feel.

I whirl her around faster and faster. I'm good at dancing in the way that I'm good at everything—quick and coordinated. It's how I work and how I fight. How I fuck, even.

But I don't get pleasure out of it like Nessa does. Her eyes close and her lips part. Her face bears an expression usually reserved for sexual climax. Her body presses against mine, hot and damp with sweat. I feel her heartbeat through the thin silk. Her nipples stiffen against my chest.

I dip her backward, exposing the delicate column of her throat. I don't know if I want to kiss her or bite her—or wrap my hands around her neck and squeeze. I want to do something to yank her back from wherever she's gone. To force her attention back to me.

Usually, I'm irritated by women's attention. I hate their neediness, their clinging hands. I use them for release while making it very clear there will be no conversation, no affection, and definitely no love.

I haven't kissed a woman in years.

Yet here I am, looking down at Nessa's closed eyes and parted lips, thinking of how easily I could crush that delicate mouth under mine, forcing my tongue between those lips, tasting her sweetness like the nectar of a flower.

Instead, I touch the ivory column of her throat. I run my fingertips down her breastbone, feeling skin so soft, it might have been born yesterday.

Her eyes snap open. She tears herself away from me, an expression of horror on her face.

Now she's looking at me. Now she's seeing me—with complete revulsion.

"Don't touch me!" she cries.

I feel a bitter stab of satisfaction, seeing her wrenched back down so abruptly. She thinks she can float up to heaven whenever she likes? I'll drag her all the way down to hell with me.

"Go back to your room."

I take pleasure in dismissing her at my will. She's my prisoner, and she better not forget it. I may be giving her the run of the house, but that doesn't change our dynamic. She eats when I say. She wears what I say. She comes when I say, and she goes when I say.

She's only too happy to leave. She flees, the hem of the green silk dress flowing behind her like a cape.

Once she's gone, I expect to return to my usual state of apathy. Nessa is just a blip on my radar—a momentary jolt that disappears again just as quickly.

Not tonight. Her scent lingers in my nostrils—sweet almond and red wine. My fingertips still feel the softness of her skin.

Even after I pour myself a drink and gulp it down, I still feel agitated and aroused. My cock is uncomfortably stiff against my leg, remembering the feeling of Nessa's slim thigh pressed against it, only my trousers and a millimeter of silk between us.

I leave the house and drive over to Jungle, weaving through the nighttime traffic. I drive a Tesla because it's the perfect stealth wealth car. It looks like just another black sedan and draws no attention from the cops, despite costing me $168,000 fully loaded. The acceleration is like a drop off a roller coaster. My stomach lurches as I whip around the corner, utterly silent.

I park behind the club and enter through the back door, nodding to the bouncer as I pass.

I head straight for the main bar, pushing through the crush of drunken patrons. Petra is slammed with drink orders. She abandons them when I jerk my head toward my office, telling her to follow me.

She's wearing a bikini-style top that barely contains her tits and cutoff shorts that expose the bottom half of her ass. She's got that septum piercing I detest, as well as the ones in her ears, eyebrow, and belly button. I couldn't give a shit about any of it. She could be wearing a gorilla suit, and I wouldn't care, as long as it provided access to the part of her I need.

"I didn't think you were coming in tonight," she purrs, following me into the office.

"I wasn't," I say shortly.

I close the door behind us and yank down the front of her top, making her tits spill out. Usually, I like watching them bounce around while I fuck her, but tonight the sight of all that flesh just seems...excessive.

I flip her around and bend her over the desk instead. The backside isn't any better. Her spongy ass is turning me off in a way it didn't before, the same with the gamey scent of her sweat and her heavy perfume, which doesn't cover up the fact she's been smoking. None of that bothered me. Now it suddenly does.

My cock hasn't caught up with my brain, however. It's still raging from earlier, springing free of my pants and jabbing between Petra's ass cheeks.

"You're ready to go," she remarks in a pleased tone.

Sometimes it takes a while for her to get me "ready to go." Sometimes I'm not ready at all, even after thirty minutes of her sucking my cock, and I send her away without finishing.

Tonight, I've got enough pent-up aggression to fuck the entire lineup of the Dallas Cowboys cheerleaders. Without any foreplay, I slide on a condom, and I ram my cock into Petra from behind, fucking her into the desk. Every thrust makes the desk jolt against the floor. It sends ripples across the flesh of Petra's ample ass.

She's moaning and urging me on, as vocal as a porn star. About as creative as one too—her cries of "Oh! Oh! That's it! Harder!" sound scripted. Plus, they're getting louder by the minute.

"Shut up," I growl, gripping her hips and trying to focus.

Petra sinks into sullen silence.

I close my eyes, trying to recapture that sense of anxious arousal that brought me over here, that desperate need for release.

Instead, I remember the feeling of my hand on Nessa's bare back, sandwiched between her warm skin and her cool, silky hair. I remember how gracefully she moved across the floor, as if her feet weren't even touching the ground. I picture the pleasure on her face, her eyes closed, her lips parted…

I explode inside Petra, filling the condom with an excessive load of come. I grip the base of it as I withdraw, not wanting to risk spilling a single drop of it inside her. I've seen the way Petra drains men dry of tips—I don't even want to know the price she'd demand for an abortion.

Petra stands and pulls on her shorts, a smug smile on her face. That's the fastest she's ever made me come, so she's feeling pretty proud of herself.

"You must have been missing me," she says, playfully drumming her fingers on my chest.

I step out of her reach, dropping the condom in the trash. "Not even a little bit."

Her smile falls off her face, and she scowls at me, one tit still hanging out of her top. It looks lopsided and udderish, and it makes me feel queasy.

"You know, you should be nicer to me," she says angrily. "I get plenty of offers from other guys. And from other bars, too."

I should never have fucked her more than once. It gives women the wrong idea. Makes them think you came back to them out of something more than convenience.

"This is over," I tell her. "You can keep working here or not."

She stares at me in shock, mouth hanging open. "What?"

"You heard me. If you want to stay, get back behind the bar. And fix your top."

I hold open the door for her, not out of chivalry but to get her to leave faster.

I can tell she wants to scream at me, but she's not stupid enough to do it. She storms out without putting her breast back where it belongs. Oh well. The customers will enjoy it.

I sink into my chair, feeling moody and discontented.

Fucking Petra didn't give me the release I craved. In fact, I feel worse than ever—stressed and unsatisfied.

I head back out into the club, kicking a group of obnoxious finance types out of a VIP booth so I can sit there myself. I have the waitress bring me a bottle of Magnum Grey Goose, chilled, and I slug down a triple shot.

Not ten minutes later, something fantastic happens: Callum Griffin walks through my door. He's dressed in a stylish dark suit as per usual. But he's not looking nearly as well-groomed. His face is unshaven, his hair in need of a cut. Dark bags hang under his eyes.

The last time I saw him up close, he was strung up from a meat hook while Zajac went to work on him. He doesn't look much better tonight. Torture of the mind is as effective as torture of the body.

I know he doesn't have a weapon on him, having come through the metal detectors at the door. Still, I hope he's stupid enough to attack me. I'd love to show him his escape from the slaughterhouse was nothing more than a fluke.

His eyes sweep around the room. As soon as they land on me, he strides toward me, knocking several people out of his path with his shoulders.

He towers over me, his hands clenched into fists. I stay right where I am, not giving him the courtesy of standing to meet him face-to-face.

"Where is she?" he demands.

I take a long sip of my drink. "Where is who?" I say blandly.

Callum's face is rigid with rage, his shoulders like stone. I can tell he wants to jump on me. He may only be held back by the fact Simon has just appeared at my side, drawn by the clear signs of impending confrontation. Simon raises an eyebrow, asking if he should intercede. I lift an index finger off my glass, telling him to wait.

Spitting out each word as if it's painful, Callum says, "I know you have Nessa. I want her back—*now*."

Lazily, I swirl the ice cubes in my glass. The music is too loud to hear the sound they make clinking together.

Keeping the bored expression fixed on my face, I say, "I really have no idea what you're talking about."

The club is dark, but not too dark to see the pulse jumping in the corner of Callum's jaw. He wants to hit me more than he's ever wanted anything in his life. His struggle to deny that impulse is beautiful to behold.

"If you hurt her," he hisses, "if you so much as break one of her nails…"

"Now, now, Alderman," I say. "Threatening one of your constituents in a public place can't be good for your approval rating. You don't want a scandal so soon after your election."

I can tell he wants to rage and threaten, to try to break my neck. But none of that will help him.

So, with Herculean effort, he regains his control. He even tries to humble himself. Of course, for an arrogant prick like Callum Griffin, humility is shallow and short.

"What do you want?" he growls. "What will it take to get her back?"

There are so many answers I could give him.

Your empire.

Your money.

Your life.

He'll pay it all, and he still won't get Nessa back. She's mine now. Why should I ever let her go?

"I wish I could help you." I take a last sip of my drink.

Then I set down the glass and rise to my feet so Callum and I are exactly eye to eye. He has a little weight on me, but I'm faster. I could cut his throat right now, quicker than blinking.

That would be too easy and too unsatisfying.

"There was a time when we could have helped each other," I tell him. "My father came to you like you're coming to me now. Do you remember what you said to him?"

Callum's jaw jerks as he grinds his teeth together, biting back everything he wants to say.

At last, he mutters, "I turned down his bid for a property."

"Not quite. You said, 'What could you possibly offer me?' I'm afraid we're on the other side of the coin now. What do you have to offer me, Griffin? Nothing. Nothing at all. So get the fuck out of my club."

Callum lunges at me but is wrenched back by Simon and Olie, my two biggest bouncers. Watching Callum Griffin dragged out of Jungle and tossed out on the street, while dozens of club goers gawk and record the whole thing on their phones, is one of the most delicious moments of my life.

I sit back in the booth, finally feeling that sense of catharsis I've been searching for.

12
NESSA

ENCOUNTERS WITH MIKOLAJ LEAVE ME FEELING RAW AND FRAYED. His ferocious blue eyes seem to strip off my skin, leaving every nerve exposed. Then he pokes and prods at all my most sensitive places until I can't bear it another moment.

He terrifies me.

And yet he's not completely repulsive, not in the way he should be.

My eyes are drawn to him, and I can't look away. Every inch of his face is burned into my mind, from the sweep of his pale blond hair against his right cheek, to the dent in the center of his upper lip, to the tense set of his shoulders.

When he took my hand to dance, I was surprised how warm his fingers felt closing around mine. I guess I expected them to be clammy or covered in scales. Instead, I saw slim, strong artistic hands. Clean nails, cut short. And only one strange thing: he was missing half the pinky on his left hand.

Mikolaj isn't the only one with a missing finger. One of the other guards is likewise missing part of a pinky—the dark, handsome one, whose name might be Marcel. I noticed it when he was smoking below my window. He offered Klara a cigarette with the damaged hand. She shook her head and hurried back inside the house.

I've been around enough gangsters to know such things are done as punishment. The Yakuza does it. The Russians, too. They also remove tattoos when a soldier is demoted or brand him with a mark of dishonor.

I haven't gotten close enough to Mikolaj to see what his tattoos represent. He has so many. They must mean something to him.

I'm curious, and I don't want to be. I hate how he draws me in like hypnosis. I'm humiliated by how easily I agreed to dance with him. He used the thing I love the most to get at me. When I came back to reality, I couldn't believe how easily I'd lost myself.

This man is my enemy. I can't forget that for an instant.

He hates me. It blazes out of his face every time he looks at me.

This will sound incredibly sheltered, but no one has ever hated me before—not like this. I sailed through school with plenty of friends. I've never been bullied or even insulted—at least not to my face. I've never had anyone look at me with loathing, like I'm an insect, like I'm a pile of burning trash.

I try to be cheerful and kind. I can't stand conflict. My need to be loved is practically pathological.

I find myself squirming under Mikolaj's gaze, trying to think of a way to prove that I don't deserve his contempt. I'm compelled to reason with him, even when I know how impossible and pointless that would be.

It's pathetic.

I wish I were brave and confident. I wish I didn't care what anyone thought.

I've always been surrounded by people who love me. My parents, my older brother—even Riona, who may be prickly but still cares about me, deep down. Our house staff spoiled and adored me.

Now it's all been ripped away, and what am I without it? A weak and frightened girl who is so deeply, deeply lonely that I'd sit down to dinner with my own kidnapper again, just to have someone to talk to.

It's sick.

I have to find a way of surviving here. Some way to distract myself.

———————

The next morning, as soon as I wake up, I'm determined to start exploring the house.

I've barely sat up in bed before Klara brings in my breakfast tray. She has a hopeful, expectant look on her face. Someone must have told her I agreed to eat.

True to my word, I come sit at the little breakfast table over by the window. Klara sets the food in front of me before laying a linen napkin in my lap.

It smells phenomenal. I'm even hungrier than I was last night. I rip into the bacon and fried eggs, then shovel up mouthfuls of diced potatoes.

My stomach is a bear fresh out of hibernation. It wants everything, absolutely everything, inside it.

Klara is so pleased to see me stuffing potatoes in my mouth that she continues her Polish lessons, naming everything on the tray.

I'm starting to pick up some of the bridge words as well—for example, when she points to the coffee and says, "*To się nazywa kawa*," I'm pretty sure it means "that's called coffee."

In fact, the more comfortable Klara gets, the more she starts directing full sentences at me just out of friendliness, not expecting me to understand her.

As she pulls open the heavy crimson drapes, she says, "*Jaki Piękny dzień*," which I think is something like "It's a beautiful day" or maybe "It's sunny today." I'll figure it out as I hear more.

I notice Klara isn't missing any bits of her fingers, and she doesn't have any tattoos like Mikolaj's men—none that are visible anyway. I don't think she's *Braterstwo* herself. She just works for them.

I'm not stupid enough to think that means she's on my side. Klara is kind but we're still strangers. I can't expect her to help me.

I do expect to leave this room today, however. Mikolaj promised that if I kept eating, I could wander the rest of the house. Everywhere but the west wing.

After I finish, I tell Klara, "I want to go outside today."

Klara nods but points toward the bathroom first.

Right. I'm supposed to shower and change clothes.

The bedroom contains the giant claw-foot tub that Klara used to bathe me last night. The bathroom is much more modern, with a standing glass shower and double sinks. I rinse off quickly, then pick a clean outfit from the chest of drawers.

I pull out a white T-shirt and gray sweat shorts, like something you'd be assigned to wear in gym class. There are fancier clothes, but I don't want to draw attention, especially from Mikolaj's men.

Klara picks my dirty clothes off the floor, wrinkling her nose because they've gotten pretty filthy over the past few days, even though I haven't worn them out of the room.

"*Umyję je,*" she says.

I'm hoping that means "I need to wash these," not "I'm chucking these in the trash."

"Don't throw them away!" I beg her. "I need that bodysuit. For dancing."

I point to the leotard and do a quick first to second position with my arms, to show her that I want to wear it when I practice.

Klara nods. "*Rozumiem.*" *I understand.*

Klara insists on blow-drying my hair again and styling it. She does a sort of half-up, half-down thing with braids around the crown of the head. It looks nice but takes way too long when I'm impatient to start exploring. She tries to paint my face again, but I push away the makeup bag. I never agreed to put on a full face every day.

I hop off the chair, determined to get out of this room. As I pad toward the door in sock-clad feet, I almost expect it to be locked again. It opens easily. I'm able to walk out in the hallway, unescorted.

This time I peer into every room as I pass.

There are dozens of rooms, each with its own odd purpose. I

see a music room with a giant Steinway in its center, the lid partially raised, the legs elaborately carved with flora and marquetry. The next room contains several old easels and a wall of framed landscapes, which might have been painted by a previous occupant. Then three or four more bedrooms, each decorated in a different jewel tone. Mine is the red room, while the others are done in shades of emerald, sapphire, and golden yellow. Then there are several sitting rooms and studies and a small library.

Most of the rooms still have the original wallpaper, peeling in some spots and water damaged in others. The majority of the furniture is original too—elaborate cabinets, upholstered armchairs and chaises, mother-of-pearl end tables, gilded mirrors, and Tiffany lamps.

My mother would kill to walk around in here. Our house is modern, but she loves historical decor. I'm sure she could tell me the names of the furniture designers and probably the painters of the art on the walls.

Thinking about my mom makes my heart clench. I can almost feel her fingers tucking a stray piece of hair behind my ear. What is she doing right now? Is she thinking about me, too? Is she afraid? Is she crying? Does she know I'm still alive because mothers somehow always know?

I shake my head to clear it.

I can't do this. I can't wallow in self-pity. I have to explore the house and grounds. I have to make some kind of plan.

So I go through every room. Though I mean to be strategic, soon I'm lost in aesthetics once more.

I don't like to admit it, but this place is fascinating. I could spend hours in each of the rooms. The interiors are intricate, with layer after layer of pattern: painted friezes and woven rugs, murals and doorframe. There isn't a single mirror or cupboard that isn't carved and ornamented in some way.

I almost don't look out the windows at all. When I do, I notice something very interesting: through the towering oaks and maples and the even taller ash trees, I spy the corner of a building. A skyscraper. It's not one I know by sight—nothing as distinctive as the Tribune Tower or the Willis Tower. But I'm quite certain I'm still in Chicago.

That knowledge gives me hope. Hope that my family will track me down before too many more days slip away.

Or I could escape.

I know I have this damned bracelet around my ankle. But it's not invincible, and neither is the Beast. If I can get off the grounds, I'll be right in the city. I'll be able to get to a phone or a police station.

With that thought in mind, I head down the staircase once more to the main floor. I want to explore the grounds.

I find my way back to the formal dining room and the ballroom. I don't go inside either, having seen them well enough last night. Across from the ballroom is the grand lobby and the front door, which is twelve feet high and looks like it requires a winch to open. It's locked and latched—no going out that way.

I see Jonas walking toward the billiard room, and I duck into the nearest niche, not wanting him to see me. I've already passed two other soldiers. They ignored me, obviously instructed that I'm allowed to walk around the house.

I don't think Jonas would be so courteous. He seems to enjoy harassing me almost as much as his boss does.

Once he's passed by, I find my way back to the glassed-in conservatory. It's much hotter by day than by night. Still, my skin chills as I pass the bench where Mikolaj was sitting. It's empty now. I'm alone, unless he's hiding somewhere in all these plants.

Unlike that night, the back door is unlocked. I can turn the knob and step outside for the first time in a week.

The fresh air feels like 100 percent pure oxygen. It rushes into my lungs, clean and fragrant, giving me an instant high. I'd gotten used to the dusty dankness of the house. Now I'm intoxicated by the breeze on my face and the grass under my feet. I strip off my socks so I can walk around barefoot, feeling the springy earth against my arches and toes.

I'm inside a walled garden. I've been to famous gardens in England and France—even they couldn't match the pure density of this place. It's thickly green everywhere I look. The stone walls are covered in ivy and clematis, the flower beds carpeted with blooms. Shaggy hedges, rosebushes, and maple trees crowd together, with barely space to walk down the cobbled paths. I hear water flowing over fountains. I know from the top-down view out my window that this garden contains dozens of sculptures and baths hidden in the labyrinth of plants.

I want to spend the rest of the day out here, drowning in the scent of the flowers and the droning of the bees. But first I'll grab a book from the library so I can read outdoors.

I head back inside, still barefoot because I abandoned my socks on the lawn.

I take a wrong turn by the kitchen and have to double back, looking for the large library on the ground floor. As I'm passing the billiard room, I hear the low clipped voice of the Beast. He's talking to Jonas, speaking in Polish. They're sprinkling in words and phrases in English, as people will do when a sentence is easier to say in one language than another.

"*Jak długo będziesz czekać?*" Jonas says.

"*Tak długo, jak mi się podoba,*" the Beast replies lazily.

"*Mogą śledzić cię tutaj.*"

"The fuck they will!" Mikolaj snaps. He then lets out a torrent of Polish in which he is clearly telling Jonas off.

I creep closer to the doorway. I can't understand most of what they're saying, but Mikolaj sounds so pissed that I'm almost certain he's talking about my family.

"*Dobrze szefie,*" Jonas says, chastened. "*Przykro mi.*"

I know what that means. *Okay, boss. My apologies.*

Then Jonas says, "What about the Russians? *Oni chcą spotkania.*"

The Beast starts to answer. He says a couple of sentences in Polish, then pauses abruptly. In English, he says, "I'm not familiar with Irish customs, but I think listening in doorways is considered rude worldwide."

It feels like the temperature dropped twenty degrees. Both Mikolaj and Jonas stand silent in the billiard room. They're waiting for me to answer.

I'd like to fade into the wallpaper. Unfortunately, that's not an option.

I swallow hard, stepping into the doorway where they can see me.

"You know I can tell *exactly* where you are in the house at all times," the Beast says, fixing me with his malevolent stare.

Right. This damned ankle monitor. I hate how it's always clattering around on my foot, digging into me when I try to sleep.

Jonas seems caught between his desire to smirk at me and his discomfort at the dressing-down he just got from Mikolaj. His smug nature wins out. Cocking an eyebrow, he says, "Only been out of your room a few hours, and you're already getting in trouble. I told Miko we shouldn't let you out."

Mikolaj throws Jonas a sharp look, likely both annoyed at the intimation that his subordinate can "tell him" anything and irritated by the use of the nickname.

I wonder how he'd like my name for him.

Who am I kidding? He'd probably love it.

"What are you hoping to hear?" the Beast says mockingly. "The codes to my bank accounts? The password to the security system? I could tell you every secret I know, and you wouldn't be able to do anything about it."

I can feel my cheeks flushing pink.

He's right. I'm completely powerless. That's why he's letting me wander around his house.

"I'm surprised your parents didn't train you," Mikolaj says, drawing closer to me. He looks down at me, his face twisted with disdain. "They should have raised a wolf, not a little lamb. It almost seems cruel."

Even though I know it's intentional, and even though I'm fighting against it, his words burrow into my brain like barbs.

My brother, Callum, knows how to fight, how to shoot a gun. He was taught to be a leader, a planner, an executor.

I was sent to dance classes and tennis lessons.

Why didn't my parents consider what might happen if I ever left the safety of their arms? They brought me into a dark and dangerous world, and then they armed me with books, dresses, and ballet slippers…

It does seem intentional. And neglectful.

Of course, they never expected me to be kidnapped by a sociopath bent on revenge.

But maybe they should have.

"I wish you could fight back, *moja mała baletnica*." *My little ballerina.* "This would be so much more fun." Mikolaj looks down into my frightened face.

He cocks his head, a wolf trying to understand a mouse.

He smells like a wolf would smell—like the musk on a real fur coat. Like bare branches in the snow. Like bulrushes and bergamot.

He stares at me until I shrink under his gaze. Then he grows bored and turns away.

Without thinking, I cry out, "I don't think your father was much of a model! Cutting off his own son's finger!"

Mikolaj whips around again, his eyes narrowed to slits. "What did you say?" he hisses.

Now I'm sure I'm right.

"The Butcher cut off your pinky," I say. "I don't know why you're so determined to get revenge on his behalf if that's how he treated you."

In three steps, Mikolaj has crossed the space between us. I can't back up fast enough. My back hits the wall, and he's right in front of me, close enough to bite me, breathing down in my face.

"You think he should have coddled me and spoiled me?" He pins me against the wall with his fury. "He taught me every lesson worth knowing. He never spared me."

He holds up his hand so I can see the long flexible fingers— perfectly shaped, except for that pinky.

"This was my very first lesson. It taught me that there's always a price to pay. Your family needs to learn that. And so do you, *baletnica*."

Like a magic trick, a steel blade appears in his hand, taken from his pocket faster than I can blink. It slashes past my face, too quick for me to even put up my hands to protect myself.

I don't feel any pain.

I open my eyes. Mikolaj steps back, a long strip of my hair wrapped around his hand. He cut it right off.

I shriek, trying to feel where he took it from.

I know it's ridiculous, but it's deeply upsetting seeing those familiar light-brown strands draped over his palm. It feels like he stole a much more vital piece of me than hair.

I turn and run away, sprinting back upstairs. Jonas's and Mikolaj's laughter rings in my ears.

I sprint into my room and slam the door shut. As if Mikolaj cared to follow me. As if I could keep him out.

13
MIKO

As much as I've loved leaving the Griffins in torturous suspense, it's time to move on to the second phase of mental fuckery I have in store for them.

This part of the plan serves two purposes: First, I get the pleasure of extorting some cash from their coffers. Second, I can secure an alliance with a mutual enemy.

Kolya Kristoff is the head of the Chicago *Bratva*. The Russian Mafia isn't nearly as powerful in the Midwest as they are on the West Coast. In fact, they just lost a substantial portion of their assets when their previous boss got his ass thrown in prison on a twelve-year sentence. The Chicago PD snatched up eight million dollars of high-quality Russian weaponry, including compact SPP-1 pistols, which can shoot underwater, and Vityaz-SNs, the most modern version of the classic Kalashnikov.

I know this because one of those crates of beautifully oiled guns belonged to me, smuggled into Chicago but not yet handed over to my men.

The *Bratva* found themselves with no guns, no boss, and very little cash to pay back the clients who had already made down payments.

The *Bratva* owes me money. And they owe a lot of other people, too. They need cash. I need men.

We can help each other.

In a deliciously ironic twist, it's the Griffins and the Gallos who will pay the fee to secure the alliance against themselves.

They'll pay it in the form of a ransom of fourteen million dollars.

I picked that number because it's the amount the Griffins and the Gallos should be able to scrounge up without tedious delays. It will sting but not bankrupt them. They'll be willing to pay it, and it seems a fitting price for Nessa.

I include the stolen lock of hair inside the ransom note.

I'm certain her parents will recognize that distinctive light-brown shade and the softness of her natural, undyed hair. I think I could recognize it myself, wherever I might encounter it.

I rub it between my fingers and thumb before I drop it into the envelope. It feels like a silk tassel, as if it's very much still alive and growing even though it's been separated from its source.

The note is clear in its instructions:

> To prove we have Nessa, we've cut off a piece of her hair. If you fail to provide the ransom, the next package you receive will contain one of her fingers, then the rest of the hand. The last box will hold her head.

I wish I could see their faces as they agonize over that prospect.

It's fun to write, less fun to do. I enjoy torturing the Griffins and the Gallos, but I don't relish the idea of cutting bits and pieces off Nessa.

I doubt I'll have to follow through.

The two families have been hunting for Nessa across the city. They've paid thousands of dollars to informants, while beating and threatening many more. They raided two of my safe houses and got in a brawl with the bouncers at my club.

But they've found absolutely fucking nothing.

Because I'm not stupid enough to let some rat or some low-level soldier find out about my plans.

They suspect me while not even knowing for certain that I'm the one who took Nessa. Involving the Russians in the ransom will muddy the waters all the more.

I give the Griffins twenty-four hours to get the money together.

I provide a burner phone along with the ransom letter so I can tell them the drop point at the last minute. I have no interest in trying to contend with Dante Gallo's sniper rifle or a dozen of their men sequestered at ambush points, if I were stupid enough to give them advance notice of the location.

Still, I expect them to break the rules. They are gangsters after all. If I scratch their cultured surface, I'll find the grit underneath. They're just as willing as I am to do what it takes to get what they want. Or at least they think they are.

Jonas makes the call because he has no accent.

I can hear the tinny echo of Fergus Griffin responding. He's maintaining his politeness—he won't allow his temper to endanger his daughter. But I hear the rage simmering below the surface.

"Where do you want us to bring the money?" he says tightly.

"Graceland Cemetery," Jonas replies. "That's a thirteen-minute drive. I'll give you fifteen to be generous. Send two men in one car. Bring the phone. The Clark Street gate will be unlocked."

We're already waiting in the cemetery. I've got six of my men stationed at vantage points. Kolya Kristoff has brought four of his own.

Less than two minutes later, Andrei texts me to say that a black Lincoln Town Car has left the lakeside mansion with loyal lapdog Jack Du Pont driving and Callum Griffin in the passenger seat. As I expected, Marcel texts me a moment later, telling me that Dante and Nero Gallo have left their Old Town house. They're driving separate cars, presumably with several of their men along for the ride.

So predictable.

It doesn't matter. I've narrowed the funnel by unlocking a single cemetery gate. During the fall and winter months, the cemetery closes at 4:00 p.m. We've had plenty of time to capture the only two rent-a-cops patrolling the grounds and set our own men all around.

The Russians have even brought our hostage. She's bound hand and foot, dressed in the same clothes Nessa wore the day we kidnapped her—hoodie, jeans, and even her sneakers. A black cloth bag covers her head, the ends of her brown hair protruding underneath.

I look her over with a practiced eye.

"It's good," I say to Kolya.

Kolya grins, showing white teeth with pointed incisors. He's darker than the average Russian, with long narrow eyes below thick straight brows. Mongolian ancestry, probably. Some of the most ruthless *Bratva* are Tatars. He's young and confident—I doubt the Chicago *Bratva* will continue to flounder under his leadership. Which means he and I may soon be at odds again.

For now, we're allies. Happy to join forces against our common enemies.

"Where do you want her?" Kolya asks.

I point to the small temple at the edge of the lake. It looks like a miniature Parthenon. You can see all the way inside it through the gaps in the stone pillars.

"Put her in there."

I've chosen the cemetery for strategic reasons. It has only one proper entrance point, with high walls all around. It's 119 acres of winding paths through dense trees and stone monuments, large and crowded enough that it would be difficult for anyone to find us without specific directions.

Then, of course, there's the omnipresent reminder of death. The unspoken threat that the Griffins better cooperate if they don't want their youngest member to remain in the cemetery permanently.

Kolya will be the one collecting the ransom. He's agreed to this because he doesn't want the money out of his hands for a moment. It's his payment, in return for joining his forces to mine.

I've agreed to it because I'm only too happy to shift the Griffins' focus from my men to Kolya's. If anyone gets shot, I want it to be a Russian.

I fall back to a separate vantage point among the trees. We've all got earpieces; I can see and hear the exchange from here.

I don't give a shit that I'm walking over buried bodies in the dead of night. I don't believe in heaven nor hell, ghosts nor spirits. The dead are no danger because they don't exist anymore. I'm concerned with the living. Only they can get in my way.

Still, I'm not such a philistine that I can't recognize how beautiful this place is. Massive ancient oaks. Stone monuments built by some of the finest sculptors in Chicago.

There's one grave in particular that catches my eye because its statue is entirely enclosed in glass, like Snow White's coffin. I draw closer, wanting to make out the figure in the dark.

Inside the upright glass box sits a stone girl, life-size. She's wearing a dress, a sun hat dangling down her back by its strings. She's barefoot, holding an umbrella.

The inscription reads:

Inez Clark

1873–1880

Killed by Lightning While Playing in the Rain

I wonder if the glass box is meant to protect her statue from further storms.

I understand the sentiment. Too bad it's pointless. Once you've lost someone you love, there's no protecting them anymore.

My lookouts keep watch at every corner of the cemetery. They inform me when Callum Griffin arrives at the main gate and when the Gallo brothers drive up Evergreen Avenue a moment later, obviously intending to sneak over the back wall.

I signal for Jonas to call the burner phone. He'll direct Callum to the lake at the northeast end of the cemetery.

"Bring the money," Jonas orders. "You'd better fucking run. You've only got three minutes."

Keeping the time tight is essential. I want this finished before the Gallos find their way inside. And I want Callum too harried and winded to think clearly.

The lake is the most open part of the cemetery. The half-moon shines brightly down on the water, illuminating the sole figure of Kolya Kristoff. He's smoking a cigarette, exhaling the smoke upward to the sky as if he doesn't have a care in the world.

He barely looks up as Callum Griffin and Jack Du Pont come jogging down the path, each carrying two very heavy duffel bags in either hand. Even from where I'm standing under a willow tree, I can see the sweat running down their faces.

Callum nods to Jack. They drop the bags in front of Kolya's feet with a heavy thud. Kolya's white teeth flash again as he grins at the sound.

He nods to one of his men. The Russian lackey kneels, unzipping the bags and checking their contents.

"Clean bills, no trackers I assume," Kolya says.

"I'm not the fucking FBI," Callum replies disdainfully.

I can hear them clearly through my earpiece, Kolya a little louder than Callum.

Kolya's man rummages through the bags before holding up a standard-pressed gold bar for his boss's approval.

"That's not cash," Kolya remarks.

"You only gave us twenty-four hours," Callum says. "That's what I had on hand. Besides, a million in bills weighs seventeen pounds. You expect us to carry in two hundred and thirty-eight pounds?"

"Eh, you're big boys. You can handle it," Kolya sneers.

"It's all there," Callum barks impatiently. "Where's my sister?"

"Right behind you," Kolya says in his drawling tone.

Callum turns, spotting the slim ballerina figure of the girl in the temple, the bag still fixed over her head. "There better not be one fucking scratch on her," he threatens.

"She is in exactly the same condition as when I took her," Kolya promises.

"When *you* took her?" Callum hisses, "Don't you mean when Mikolaj did? Where is he anyway? I didn't take you for an errand boy, Kristoff."

Kolya shrugs, taking one last long pull off his cigarette. He flicks the butt into the lake, sending ripples running outward from the bank across the still water.

"This is the problem with you Irish," he says softly. "Surrounded by enemies and not afraid to make more. You should learn to be friendly."

"You don't make friends with termites when they burrow into your foundation," Callum says coldly.

My earpiece crackles as Andrei mutters, "Gallos are coming."

"Time to go," I say to Kolya.

He's frowning, spoiling for a fight with Callum. And he doesn't like taking orders from me.

But he wants the money. So he nods to his men, who pick up the duffel bags.

"We'll see each other soon," Kolya says to Callum.

"You're goddamned right we will," Callum snarls back.

The Russians take the ransom and jog off toward the main gate.

Callum nods to Jack Du Pont, silently ordering him to follow the Russians. Callum turns and runs in the opposite direction, toward the temple.

Quietly, I tell Marcel, "Jack Du Pont is headed your way. Let the Russians pass. Then cut his throat."

I watch Callum dash through the tall grass at the edge of the water, sprinting up to the temple.

I hear him as he calls out, "Nessa! I'm here! Are you okay?"

I hear the hoarseness in his voice and see his shoulders slump in relief as the girl turns blindly toward him, her hands still bound behind her back.

Dante and Nero Gallo arrive just in time to witness the reunion.

Dante's got his rifle on his shoulder. Nero's close behind, covering his back. They push their way through the trees on the opposite side of the temple.

We all watch as Callum pulls the black cloth bag off the girl's head. Exposing the terrified face of Serena Breglio.

Her newly dyed hair is limp around her shoulders. The Russians fucked that up—the brown is dark and muddy, but she was too far away for Callum to notice.

The Russians snatched her this afternoon, right outside her apartment on Magnolia Avenue. I gave them Nessa's clothes, which fit her perfectly. Ballet dancers all have that same physique.

Mascara tracks run down her cheeks from hours of tears. Serena tries to say something to Callum around the gag.

Callum's face is a mask of fury and disappointment. If he were a star, he'd go supernova.

He abandons the girl in the temple, not even bothering to untie her. Dante Gallo does it instead.

Callum sprints off toward the main gate, trying to chase the Russians.

I lift my rifle, watching the Gallo brothers through the sight.

I've got Dante right in my crosshairs. He's crouched over Serena, pulling the gag out of her mouth. His back is to me. I could put a bullet in the base of his neck, severing the spinal cord. He's the one who pulled the trigger on Tymon. I could end him right now.

But I've got other plans for Dante.

I lower my rifle, skirting the lake and following Callum Griffin instead.

I hear his howl as he discovers the body of his driver. They went to school together, or so I'm told. Marcel cut his throat, leaving Jack Du Pont to bleed out, slumped against a cross-shaped tombstone.

I guess Callum will be driving himself around from now on.

"You comin', boss?" Andrei says in my ear.

"Yes," I say. "On my way."

14
NESSA

All the men disappeared from the house today.

I don't know where they went. But I'm getting so used to the normal creaks and moans of the old mansion, I can tell when only that ambient sound remains, when all the footsteps, door banging, Polish conversation, and masculine chuckles are gone.

Klara is still here. I hear her vacuum cleaner running, and later I hear her singing down on the main level while she dusts. That's how I know for certain the Beast is gone—she wouldn't sing with him around.

They've stopped locking my door. I creep down to the main level to check the doors that lead out of the house. Those are locked and dead bolted, including the one through the conservatory out to the garden. I'm not getting out without a key.

It's what I expected. But it makes me wonder—where are the keys? All the men must have one. Klara, too, most likely.

I could sneak up on her while she's vacuuming. Hit her over the head with a vase.

I picture myself doing it, like a character in the movie. Knowing all along I never could.

I don't want to hurt Klara. She's been kind to me, as kind as she's allowed. She's taught me quite a bit of Polish. And she protects me from Jonas. I heard her arguing with him out in the hall, one night after I went to bed. He sounded drunk, slurring his responses. She was sharp and insistent. I don't know what he was trying to do, but she wouldn't let him into my room. She said, "*Powiem Mikolaj!*" which I'm pretty sure means "I'll tell Mikolaj."

If I escape while Klara is supposed to be guarding me, they may punish her. I know they cut off fingers willy-nilly around here. I can't let that happen to Klara.

So I head back to the east wing, thinking I'll find a new book in the library. I've been ransacking both the little reading room in my wing and the larger library on the main floor.

There are thousands of books for me to read: fiction and nonfiction, classics and contemporary novels. Most of the books are in English, but there are French novels, and German poetry, and a copy of *Don Quixote* in the original two-part Spanish set.

Someone here must be adding to the collection because there are plenty of Polish translations and native works like *Lalka* and *Choucas*, which I read in one of my literature courses.

I'm missing all my classes at school. All my dance classes, too. It's strange to think of my classmates walking around campus, studying and handing in assignments as usual, while I'm locked in suspended animation. It feels like I've been here for years, though it's only been two weeks.

If it goes on much longer, I won't be able to catch up. I'll fail the whole semester.

Of course, if the Beast kills me, it won't matter that I missed school.

I hunt through the smaller reading room, running my fingers down the dusty spines. *The Age of Innocence, 1984, Catch-22, The Doll*…

I pause. *The Doll* is the English translation of *Lalka*.

I pull it off the shelf, flipping through the pages. Then I tuck the little book under my arm and run back down to the main level, where I search the shelves for the original Polish version. There it is—the hardcover of *Lalka*, with its leather binding embossed in floral print. Now I have the same book in both languages.

My heart is racing from the run and the excitement of what I've found. I take the books back up to my room before lying on my bed to examine them. I set them side by side, opening each to the first chapter:

> Early in 1878, when the political world was concerned with the treaty of San Stefano, the election of a new Pope, and the chances of a European war, Warsaw businessmen and the intelligentsia who frequented a certain spot in the Krakowskie Przedmieście were no less keenly interested in the future of the haberdashery firm of J. Mincel and S. Wokulski.

There it is: the same paragraph in English and in Polish. I can read through sentence by sentence, comparing the two. It's not quite as good as a language textbook, but it's the next best thing. Pages and pages of sentences I can compare to learn vocabulary and syntax.

Polish is a damned hard language; I already know that from talking with Klara. Some of the sounds are so similar that I can barely distinguish them, like *ś* and *sz*. Not to mention its use of a case system and the near-opposite word order compared to English.

What I do have is infinite time to study.

I lie on my bed for most of the day, working my way through the first chapter of the book in both languages. Eventually, I stop, when my eyes are aching and my head is swimming.

Just as I'm closing the books, Klara comes into my room, carrying my dinner tray. I stuff the novels hastily under my pillow, in case she notices what I'm up to.

"*Dobry wieczór,*" I say. *Good evening.*

She gives me that short flash of a smile while she sets my tray on the table. "*Dobry wieczór,*" she replies, with much better pronunciation.

"Where is everyone?" I ask her in Polish. Actually, what I say is "*gdzie mężczyźni?*" or "*Where men?*" but let's use the intent of the sentence and ignore the fact I have the verbal complexity of a caveman.

Klara understands me well enough. She gives a quick glance toward the doorway like she thinks they might come home any second. Then she shakes her head, saying, "*Nie wiem.*" *I don't know.*

Maybe she really doesn't know. I doubt Mikolaj gives his maid a copy of his schedule. But Klara is smart. I bet she knows a lot more about what goes on around here than the men would expect. She just doesn't want to tell me. Because it's pointless. Because it will only get us in trouble.

I sit down in front of the tray, which as usual is loaded with far more food than I could actually eat. There's grilled rosemary chicken, lemon potatoes, sautéed Broccolini, fresh rolls, and a little side plate that looks like dessert.

The meals are always fantastic. I point to the tray, saying, "*Ty robisz?*" *You make?*

Klara nods. "*Tak.*" *Yes.*

Knowing Klara went to the trouble of cooking the meals makes me feel guilty for all the times I refused to eat.

"Your food is amazing," I tell her in English. "You should be a chef."

Klara shrugs, blushing. She hates when I compliment her.

"You remind me of Alfred," I tell her. "You know Alfred, from Batman? He's good at everything. Like you."

Klara smiles her Mona Lisa smile—inscrutable but, I hope, pleased.

"*Co to jest?*" I ask her, pointing to the dessert plate. It looks like a folded crepe, dusted with powdered sugar.

"*Nalesniki,*" she says.

I cut off a piece, though I haven't finished my dinner yet. It does taste like a crepe, with some kind of sweet cream cheese mixture inside. Actually, it's better than any crepe I've ever had—thicker and more flavorful.

"*Pyszne!*" I tell her enthusiastically. *Delicious!*

She grins. "*Mój ulubiony,*" she says. *My favorite.*

When I'm done eating, I look around for my bodysuit. I want to change clothes so I can practice dancing before bed.

I find the bodysuit washed and folded inside the chest of drawers. But I don't see any of my other clothes—the hoodie, jeans, or sneakers.

"*Gdzie są moje ubrania?*" I ask Klara.

Klara flushes, not meeting my eye. "*Jest dużo ubrań,*" she says, gesturing to the wardrobe and the chest of drawers. *There's plenty of clothing.*

How odd. Why did she take my clothes?

Well, it doesn't matter. It's the bodysuit I need the most.

I wish I had proper pointe shoes. Dancing barefoot is all right, but I can't practice everything I'd like. I need a better space for it, too.

Once I've changed clothes, I go poking around my wing, looking for a better dance room. Nobody comes into the east wing except me and Klara. I've come to see it as my own space, even though Mikolaj never actually said I could use the other rooms.

After examining all the spaces, I think the art room will be best. It has the most natural light and the least furniture in the way.

I spend about an hour rearranging it to suit my purpose. I drag all the chairs and tables to one side of the room, then roll up the ancient rugs, exposing the bare wood floors. I stack the easels and the loose canvases and put away all the spare art supplies, most of which are ruined anyway—tubes of dried paint, moldering brushes, and stubs of charcoal.

Now I've got plenty of space. But I'm still missing the most crucial thing of all.

I go downstairs to find Klara. She's in the kitchen, bleaching the countertops. She's wearing gloves to protect her hands, but I know her skin still gets raw from all the work she does around this place. It's not her fault it's still dusty and gloomy—it's just way too much work for one person. You'd need an army to keep this place clean. Especially at the rate idiots like Jonas mess it up again.

"Klara," I say from the doorway. "*Potrzebuję muzyki.*" *I need music.*

She straightens up, frowning a little.

I think she's annoyed that I interrupted her, but then I realize she's just thinking.

After a minute, she strips off her gloves, saying, "*Chodź ze mną.*" *Come with me.*

I follow her out of the kitchen, through the billiard room, then up a back staircase to a part of the house I haven't seen before. This area is plain and cramped—probably the servants' quarters once upon a time.

Klara takes me all the way up to the attic, which runs the length of the central portion of the house. It's a huge space, crowded with endless stacks of boxes and piles of old furniture. It also appears to house half the spiders in the state of Illinois. Sheets of old cobwebs hang from floor to ceiling. Klara pushes through them impatiently. I follow at a respectful distance, not wanting to meet an arachnid with that sort of work ethic.

Klara roots through the boxes. Hopefully she knows what she's looking for because we could spend a hundred years up here without coming to the end of it all. I see yellowed wedding dresses, stacks of old photographs, hand-knitted baby blankets, and worn leather shoes.

There's a whole box of gowns from the 1920s, beaded, feathered, and draped. They must be worth a fortune to the right person. They look like they should be displayed in a museum.

"Hold on," I say to Klara. "We've got to look at those."

She pauses in her search. I open the box of gowns instead, pulling them out of their tissue wrappings.

I can't believe how heavy and intricate the dresses are. They look hand sewn, each one representing hundreds of hours of labor. The materials are like nothing you'd find in a store nowadays.

"We have to try one on," I say to Klara.

She touches the fringed skirt of one of the gowns. I can tell she finds them as fascinating as I do, but she's not a rule breaker. The gowns are in this house, which means they belong to the Beast.

I don't give a damn whom they belong to. I'm putting one on.

I pull out a blue velvet gown with long floating butterfly sleeves. The deep V in the front goes down almost to the waist, where a jeweled belt sits. I put it on over my bodysuit, amazed at its weight. I feel like an empress. Like I should have a servant carrying my train.

Klara looks at the dress, wide-eyed. I can tell she wants to try one, too.

"Come on," I coax her. "No one will see us."

Biting her lip, she makes her choice. She quickly strips out of her maid's uniform. If there's any evidence that Mikolaj is a monster, it's the fact he makes her wear that awful thing day in and day out. It looks hot and uncomfortable.

Klara actually has a lovely figure underneath. She's fit and strong, probably from lifting and scrubbing all damn day.

She pulls out a long black gown with silver beading on the bodice. She steps into it, and I zip up the back. Then she turns around so I can admire the full effect.

It's absolutely gorgeous. The gown has a near-transparent bodice, thin black mesh with silver moons and stars embroidered across the breast. The drop waist is covered by a long dangling silver belt, like something you'd see on a medieval gown. With her black hair and dark eyes, Klara looks like an enchantress.

"Oh my god," I breathe. "You're so beautiful."

I pull Klara over to a dusty old mirror leaned against the wall. I brush it off with my hands so she can see her reflection clearly.

Klara stares at herself, equally entranced.

"*Kto to jest?*" she says softly. *Who is that?*

"It's you." I laugh. "You're magical."

My dress is pretty, but Klara's was made for her. Never did a piece of clothing fit someone so perfectly. It's like the seamstress looked a hundred years into the future for her muse.

"You have to keep it," I say to Klara. "Take it home with you. No one knows it's up here."

I say it in English, but Klara understands the gist. She shakes her head, struggling to undo the zipper.

"*Nie, nie,*" she says, pulling at the back. "*Zdejmij to.*" *Take it off.*

I help her unzip it before she tears the material. She steps out of the dress before swiftly folding it up and stowing it back in the box.

"*To nie dla mnie,*" she says, shaking her head. *It's not for me.*

I can tell that nothing I say will convince her.

It's tragic to think of that dress moldering up here in the attic with no one to use it or love it like Klara could. But I understand that she could never enjoy it, worrying that Mikolaj would find out. Where would she wear it anyway? As far as I can tell, she spends all her time here.

We put the dresses back in their box. Then Klara pulls on her uniform once more, itchier and hotter than ever by comparison to that gorgeous gown. She searches through a dozen more boxes until finally she finds the one she was looking for.

"*Tam!*" she says happily.

She drags out the box, thrusting it into my arms. It's heavy. I stagger under the weight. When she lifts the lid, I see dozens of slim, long spines in a riot of colors. It's a box of old records.

"Is there a record player?"

She nods. "*Na dół.*" *Downstairs.*

While I carry the records over to the old art room, Klara retrieves the turntable. She sets it up in the corner of the room, balanced on one of the little end tables I've shoved into the corner. The turntable is just as old as the vinyl, and even dustier. Klara has to clean it with a damp cloth. Even after she plugs it into the wall to prove the platter still spins, neither one of us is certain it will play.

I pull out one of the records, removing the vinyl from its protective sleeve. Klara places it carefully on the platter and sets the needle in place. There's an unpleasant static sound, then, to our joy and amazement, it begins to play "All I Have to Do Is Dream" by the Everly Brothers.

We both start laughing, faces and hands filthy with dust from the attic, but our smiles are as bright as ever.

"*Proszę bardzo. Muzyka,*" Klara says. *There you go. Music.*

"*Dziękuję Ci, Klara,*" I say. *Thank you, Klara.*

She smiles, shrugging her slim shoulders.

Once she leaves, I pore over the vinyl in the box. Most of it is from the '50s and '60s—not what I'd generally dance to, but miles better than silence.

There are also a few LPs of classical music, some by composers I've never heard of before. I play through the records, looking for one that suits my mood.

I usually lean toward cheerful, upbeat music. Taylor Swift has been my favorite singer for about a decade.

There's nothing like that in the box. A lot of it, I don't recognize at all.

One cover catches my eye: a single white rose on a black background. The composer's name is Egelsei.

I swap out the record before setting the needle in place.

The music is unlike anything I've heard before—haunting, dissonant...yet entrancing. It makes me think of this old mansion creaking in the night. Of Klara in her witchy gown, reflected in a dusty mirror. And of a girl, sitting at a long table lit by candlelight, facing a Beast.

It reminds me of fairy tales—dark and terrifying. But also tantalizing. Full of adventure, danger, and magic.

My favorite ballets have always been the ones based off fairy tales—*Cinderella, The Nutcracker, The Sleeping Beauty, The Tale of the Stone Flower, Swan Lake...*

I've always wished there were a ballet of my favorite fairy tale of all: Beauty and the Beast.

Why shouldn't there be?

I could make one.

I choreographed four songs for Jackson Wright.

I could make a whole ballet if I wanted to, start to finish. One that would be dark and gothic, frightening and beautiful, just like this house. I could take all my fear and fascination and pour it into a dance. It would be fucking beautiful. Realer than anything I've made before.

Jackson said my work lacked emotion. Maybe he was right. What had I ever felt before?

I've felt things now—all sorts of things. I've felt more emotions in these two weeks of captivity than in my whole life before.

Turning the volume up on the record player, I begin to choreograph my ballet.

15
MIKO

When I return home from the cemetery, I expect to find the mansion silent and dark.

Instead, as I walk through the main hall, I hear the distant sound of music in the east wing.

Nessa is not supposed to have music. She can't have a phone, a computer, or so much as a radio. Yet I hear the unmistakable sound of mingled piano and cello and the light thumps of her bare feet on the floor overhead.

Like a hook through a trout's mouth, it catches me and yanks me up the stairs before I've made the conscious decision to move. I follow the line of the sound, not to Nessa's room but to the salon where the baron's daughter used to exhibit her watercolors.

When I reach the open doorway, I stop and stare.

Nessa is dancing like I've never seen her dance before. She's spinning again and again, whipping her raised foot around the supporting leg, spreading her arms and then pulling them tight toward her body to spin her all the faster.

She looks like a figure skater, like the floor must be made of ice. I've never seen someone move so cleanly.

She's drenched in sweat. Her pale pink bodysuit is so wet that I can see every detail underneath as if she were completely naked. Her hair is coming loose from its tight bun, damp strands plastered to her face and neck.

Still she's spinning faster and faster, leaping across the floor, tumbling to the ground, rolling over, and jumping again.

I realize she's acting something out—some kind of scene. She seems like she's running away, looking back over her shoulder. Then she stops, returns to where she started, and dances the same thing over again.

She's practicing. No, that's not right—she's creating something. Refining it.

She's choreographing a dance.

She stops, starts over again.

This time she's doing a different part. This time she's the pursuer, chasing the unseen figure across the stage. It's supposed to be a duet—but because she's the only one here, she's acting out both parts.

I wish I could see what she's seeing inside her head.

I'm only catching bits and pieces of it. What I see is emotive, strung with intensity. But it's just a girl in an empty room—she's seeing a whole world around her.

It's mesmerizing. I watch her repeat this piece of the dance again and again, sometimes as the hunter, sometimes as the prey. Sometimes copying exactly what she did before, and sometimes altering it slightly.

The record ends, and we're both jolted back to reality.

Nessa is panting, exhausted.

I'm standing in the doorway without any idea of how much time has passed.

She looks up and sees me. Her body goes stiff, her hand flying to her mouth.

"Making yourself at home, I see," I say.

She's shoved all the furniture to the edge of the room and rolled up the rugs. She gazes guiltily at the bare floor.

"I needed space to dance." Her voice comes out in a croak. Her throat is dry because she's been dancing for so long.

"What was that?" I ask her.

"It's…something I'm making."

"What?"

"A ballet."

"I can see that," I say tersely. "What's it about?"

"It's a fairy tale," she whispers.

Of course it is. She's such a child.

But the dance wasn't childish. It was captivating.

The turntable is making that empty repetitive sound that means the tracks have run out. The needle skips over bare vinyl. I cross the room before lifting the tonearm and flipping the switch so the platter stops spinning.

"Where did you get this?"

"I…I found it," she says.

She's a terrible liar. Klara gave it to her, obviously. They were the only two people at home.

I suspected that Klara was becoming sympathetic to our prisoner. It's a conundrum I can't quite fix. I knew that anybody with a heart would find sweet little Nessa hard to ignore. But I can't trust any of my men to keep watch over her. She's too pretty. It's hard enough to get them to leave Klara alone, even when she wears her hideous uniform.

Innocent Nessa in leotards and gym shorts is a temptation too great to resist. I've had to bar my men from stepping foot in her room. Even then, I see them watching her everywhere she goes. Especially Jonas.

It makes me want to cut their balls off.

Nessa is my prisoner. No one touches her but me.

A clear droplet of sweat slides down her face, down the side of her throat, and then down her breastbone, disappearing into the space between her breasts.

My eyes follow. The translucent material of her bodysuit clings to her small round breasts. I can see the puckered areola and the pert little nipples pointing slightly upward. They're not pink like I guessed but light brown like the freckles on her cheeks. They're so sensitive that they stiffen right before my eyes, just from the heat of my gaze.

My eyes roam farther down. I can see the lines running down her taut stomach and the indent of her navel. Then, below that, the delta of her cunt and even the outline of her pussy lips, as wet with sweat as the rest of her body.

Most of all, I smell her scent. I smell her soap, her sweat. And even her sweet little pussy, musky and mild.

It makes me fucking ravenous.

My pupils have dilated so far that I can see every detail of her body: The tiny droplets of sweat above her lip. The flecks of brown in her green eyes. The goose bumps rising on her arms. The muscles trembling in her thighs.

I feel like I've been sleeping for a hundred years, and all at once, in this instant, I'm wide awake. My cock rages inside my pants, harder than I've ever felt it—stiff, pulsing, aching to get out.

I want this girl. I want her here, now, immediately.

I want her like I've never wanted a woman before. I want to kiss her and fuck her and eat her alive.

She can see it in my face. Her eyes are wide and unblinking. She's rooted to the spot.

I grab a handful of her sweaty hair and tilt her head back, exposing that long pale throat.

I run my tongue up the side of her neck, licking up her sweat. It's clear and salty, explosive on my tongue. Better than caviar. I swallow it down.

Then I kiss her. Her lips are parched from dancing. I lick those lips, tasting the salty skin. I thrust my tongue into her mouth and lick every part of that, too—teeth, tongue, palate. I inhale her scent and her taste. I fuck her mouth with my tongue.

For a moment she's frozen in my arms, tense and tight. Then,

shockingly, she responds to me. She's kissing me back, without skill or style but with a hunger that almost matches my own.

We're locked together, my fingers digging into her flesh, her hands gripping the material of my shirt.

How long it goes on, I have no idea.

We break apart, staring at each other, equally confused about what the fuck just happened.

There's blood on her lip. I can taste it in my mouth. I don't know if she bit me or I bit her.

She touches her lip before gazing at the bright spot of blood on her fingertip. Then she turns and runs, sprinting out of the room like I'm snapping at her heels.

I'm not following her. I'm too stunned to do it.

I kissed her. Why the fuck did I kiss her?

I had no intention of kissing Nessa or touching her at all.

Of all the evil things I've done in my life, and they are legion, I've never forced myself on a woman. It's the one thing I won't do.

So why did I kiss her?

She's beautiful. But there are thousands of beautiful women in the world.

She's innocent. But I fucking hate innocence.

She's talented. But what good is dancing in a world full of killers and thieves?

I pull out my phone, compelled to check on her as I've been doing more and more often.

I access the camera in her bedroom. There's only the one, pointed at the bed. I don't watch her in the toilet or the shower; I'm not that depraved.

Sure enough, she's lying on the bed facedown. But she's not sobbing as I expect her to be.

Oh, no. What she's doing is completely different.

She has her hand between her thighs, and she's touching herself. She's stroking that sweet little pussy with her fingers, while grinding her hips into the bed. She's still wearing her bodysuit. I can see the round muscles of her buttocks flexing with every roll of her hips.

Jesus Christ. My heart is racing. I can't take my eyes off the screen. The image is in black and white but totally clear.

I watch as she pulls a pillow between her legs and sits upright, grinding on the pillow instead of her hand. She clenches it between her thighs, grasping handfuls of the sheet, riding the pillow as if it were a man underneath her.

Without even realizing it, I've taken my cock out of my pants. I'm gripping it in one hand, the phone in the other. My eyes are locked on the screen. I couldn't look away if my life depended on it.

I watch Nessa ride the pillow, every muscle rigid down the length of her slim body—shoulders, chest, ass, thighs, all clenching as hard as they can. Her head is thrown back; her eyes are closed. Even in black and white, I can see the flush on her cheeks.

Her mouth opens as she starts to come. I see the long silent cry.

I explode into my hand at the same time. Shot after shot of come, timed to the motion of Nessa's hips. I didn't even have to stroke myself.

My knees buckle under me. I squeeze my cock hard, trying not to groan. The orgasm is wrenching. It drains the life out of me.

Still I'm staring at the screen, at Nessa's delicate features, her slender frame. She's finally relaxing, falling facedown on the bed once more.

I can't take my eyes off her. Every line of her body is burned into my retinas, from the strands of sweat-soaked hair, to the birdlike shoulder blades, to the long lines of her legs.

I can't look away.

16
NESSA

I WAKE IN THE MORNING, STICKY AND SWEATY AND FLOODED WITH shame.

The memories swirling around in my brain are nightmares. They must be.

There's no way on god's green earth that my very first kiss was with my kidnapper.

I could not possibly be that stupid.

And then to touch myself afterward!

My face burns with humiliation as I remember. I ran back to my room, intending to hide. But I was flustered, throbbing, aching for something. And when I put my hand there just for a second, it felt meltingly good. It felt like pleasure and relief and desperation to keep going all at once.

And that orgasm...

Oh my god. You could take every time I touched myself before, grind it in a blender, crank it up by a factor of ten, and it wouldn't even approach what I just experienced.

It's insane and impossible, so there's no way it actually happened.

I keep telling myself that while I stumble into the shower, stripping off my nasty bodysuit and soaping myself for what feels like an hour. I scrub every inch of my skin, trying to rid myself of the sensations that keep popping up—the way his hands felt when he was yanking my hair. The way his mouth tasted, like salt and cigarettes and citrus and blood. The surprising warmth of his lips. And the way his tongue slid up my neck, igniting each neuron in my brain like a string of firecrackers.

No, no, NO!

I hated that. I didn't like any of it. It was awful and crazy, and it's never happening again.

I step out of the shower before wrapping a towel around my body and swiping my palm across the foggy mirror. My own startled face looks back at me, my lips swollen and my eyes guilty.

I grab my toothbrush and scrub my mouth viciously, trying to remove the taste of him.

When I come out of the bathroom, Klara is standing by my bed. I give a little shriek.

"*Dzień dobry!*" she says cheerfully.

"Hey," I say dully, too depressed to respond in kind.

She purses her lips, looking me over. After we created the perfect little dance studio just yesterday, she likely expected to find me cheerful. "*Popatrz!*" she says, pointing to the bed. *Look!*

She's already made the bed, pulling the covers tight and tucking them in as always. She's spread a dozen pieces of dance wear across the coverlet: leotards, tights, warm-ups, socks, and two pairs of brand-new pointe shoes.

This isn't just any dance wear—it's Yumiko bodysuits and Grishko shoes. The warm-ups are some of the newest pieces from Elevé. These clothes are better than what I have in my own closet at home. Picking up the pointe shoes, I see they're the exact right size.

"Where did this come from?" I ask Klara weakly. "Did you buy this?"

She just shrugs, smiling.

She might have picked it up, but I don't think she paid for it. Not that I'd want her to—I doubt she makes much money. But the alternative is worse. Did Mikolaj tell her to get all this? Because I let him kiss me?

It makes me shudder. I want to pull it all off the bed and throw it in the trash.

I can't do that, though. Klara looks too pleased, too hopeful.

She thought I'd be thrilled to have something better to wear than my one increasingly tattered bodysuit.

"Thanks, Klara," I say, trying to force a smile.

Meanwhile, my stomach clenches in a knot.

I'm so confused. One minute I think the Beast is going to kill me, and the next, he's buying me gifts. I don't know which is worse.

Klara gestures for me to put on one of the outfits.

God, I really don't want to.

"*Tutaj*," she says, picking one for me.

It's a backless lavender leotard with knitted gray leg warmers and a matching crop top. It's really lovely. And just the right size.

I pull it on, appreciating the fine, stretchy material, how new and well fitting it all is.

Klara stands back, smiling with satisfaction.

"Thank you," I tell her again, more sincerely this time.

"*Oczywiście*," she says. *Of course.*

She's brought me breakfast—oatmeal, strawberries, and Greek yogurt. Coffee and tea as well. When I'm done eating, I head straight to my studio to get back to work.

I've never felt so compelled to work on a project before. Far from ruining it with his interruption, Mikolaj gave me more ideas than ever. I don't want to say that he inspired me, but he certainly stirred up some emotions I can pour into my work. Fear, confusion, angst, and maybe…a little arousal.

I'm not attracted to him. I'm absolutely not. He's a monster, and not in the way of a normal gangster. My family members may be criminals, but they're not violent, not unless they have to be. We do what we do to get ahead in the world, not to hurt people. Mikolaj takes pleasure in making me suffer. He's bitter and vengeful. He wants to kill everyone I love.

I could never be attracted to a man like that.

What happened last night was just the result of being locked up for weeks at a time. It was some sort of twisted Stockholm Syndrome.

When I get a boyfriend someday—when I have time, when I meet somebody nice—he'll be sweet and complimentary. He'll bring me flowers and hold the door for me. He won't scare the wits out of me and attack me with a kiss that makes me feel like I'm being eaten alive.

That's what I'm thinking as I put the record back on the turntable and set the needle in place.

But as soon as that eerie, gothic music starts up again, my mind drifts in a different direction.

I picture a girl wandering in the forest. She comes to a castle. She opens the door and creeps inside.

She's very, very hungry. So, when she finds a dining room with the table all set, she sits down to eat.

But she's not alone at the table.

She's sitting across from a creature.

A creature with patterned skin. Sharp teeth and claws. And pale eyes, like chips of arctic ice…

He's a wolf and a man all at once. And he's horribly hungry. But not for anything on the table…

I work all morning and straight through lunch. Klara sets a tray down inside my new studio. I forget to look at it until the chicken soup is stone-cold.

After lunch, I spend some time studying my copy of *Lalka*, and then I plan to take a walk around the garden. As I cross the main level of the house, I hear the unmistakable sound of Mikolaj's voice.

It sends a current through my body.

Before I know what I'm doing, I'm slowing to listen. He's walking down the hallway toward me, but he hasn't spotted me yet. It's Mikolaj and the dark-haired one with the pleasant smile—Marcel.

I'm understanding more and more of what they say. In fact, their next sentences are so simple that I understand them perfectly:

"*Rosjanie są szczęśliwi,*" Marcel says. *The Russians are happy.*

"*Oczywiście że są,*" Mikolaj replies. "*Dwie rzeczy sprawiają, że Rosjanie są szczęśliwi. Pieniądze i wódka.*" *Of course they are. Two things make Russians happy—money and vodka.*

Mikolaj spots me and stops short. His eyes sweep over my new clothes. I think I see the hint of a smile on his lips. I dislike it immensely.

"Finished your work for the day?" he says politely.

"Yes."

"Now let me guess…a walk in the garden."

I'm annoyed that he thinks I'm so predictable. He thinks he knows me.

I'd like to ask him what money he gave the Russians, just to see the look on his face. I want to show him he doesn't know everything inside my head.

But that would be very foolish. Learning their language in secret is one of the only weapons I have. I can't squander it like that. I have to use it at the right moment, when it counts.

So I force a smile onto my face. "That's right."

As the two men are about to pass me, I add, "Thank you for the new clothes, Mikolaj."

I see the flicker of surprise on Marcel's face. He's just as shocked as I was that my captor is buying me presents.

The Beast doesn't give a damn what either of us thinks.

He just shrugs. "Your old ones were filthy."

Then he sweeps past me like I don't exist.

Good. I don't care if he ignores me. Just as long as he keeps his hands to himself.

17
MIKO

IT'S A STRANGE THING, STUDYING THE MEN YOU WISH TO KILL.

You watch them, follow them, learn all about them.

In some ways you become closer to them than their own family.

You learn things about them that not even their family knows. You see their gambling habits, their mistresses, their illegitimate children, their love for feeding the pigeons in Lincoln Park.

Dante Gallo isn't easy to follow or to learn about.

As the oldest Gallo child, he's had the longest time to learn from Enzo Gallo. He's a classic eldest son—a leader, disciplined and responsible.

He's also wary as a cat. He seems to sense when anything is out of place, when anybody has eyes on him. Must be his military training. They say he served six years in Iraq—unusual for a mafioso. They're not patriots. Their loyalty is to their family, not their country.

Maybe Enzo wanted him to become the perfect soldier. Or maybe it was youthful rebellion on Dante's part. All I know is that it makes it damn hard to find his weak points.

He follows no set schedule. He rarely goes anywhere alone. And as far as I can tell, he's completely lacking in vices.

Of course, that can't actually be true. Nobody is that regimented.

He certainly has a soft spot for his siblings. If he's not working, he's catering to them.

He does the lion's share of the labor running his father's businesses. He manages to keep Nero Gallo out of serious trouble—a Sisyphean task that seems as varied as it is unending, since Nero seems equal parts creative and deranged. In one week, Nero gets in a knife fight outside Prysm, crashes his vintage Bel Air on Grand Avenue, and seduces the wife of an extremely nasty Vietnamese gangster.

Dante smooths over every one of these indiscretions, while visiting his youngest brother at school and his sister, Aida, at the alderman's office.

What a busy boy, our Dante.

He barely has time to drink a pint at a pub. He doesn't seem to have a girlfriend, a boyfriend, or a favorite whore.

His only hobby is the shooting range. He goes there three times a week to practice the marksmanship that apparently accounted for sixty-seven kills from Fallujah to Mosul.

I suppose that's how he hit Tymon with three shots to the chest. Practice makes perfect.

Now that I've killed two birds with one stone, extorting money from the Griffins and paying it to the Russians, I'd like to do the same with Dante. I'd like to fuck him up royally, while ridding myself of another enemy at the same time.

So, the next time Dante makes his visit to the shooting range, I have Andrei steal Dante's Beretta right out of his bag. It's his old service weapon, one of the few I can be certain was legally purchased and registered to his name.

The next part is a bit tricky. Dante is too clever to lure into an ambush. So I have to bring the ambush to him.

I may not be chummy with the police commissioner like Fergus Griffin, but I have two beat cops on my payroll: Officers Hernandez and O'Malley. One never covers the spread on the Cubs; the other owes child support to three different women.

I tell them to park their patrol car a block away from the Gallo house, right in the center of Old Town. They wait there every night, all week long. Until finally there's an evening when Enzo and Nero are out, and Dante is home all alone.

Now I bring in the second bird.

Walton Miller is the head of the BACP in Chicago—which means he's the fellow who hands out liquor licenses. Or rescinds them, when his chubby little palm isn't crossed with a bribe that suits his fancy.

He's been getting greedier and greedier by the year, extorting me for five separate payments for my bars and strip clubs.

Miller has beef with the Gallos. The Gallos own two Italian restaurants, and Dante hasn't paid up for either, despite selling enough wine to fill Lake Michigan.

I give Miller a nice, hefty payment for my liquor licenses. Then I give him a briefcase full of evidence against Dante Gallo—a bunch of photoshopped shit that looks like illegal tax returns from the restaurant.

Like the fool he is, Miller goes scurrying over to the Gallo house, thinking he's going to twist Dante's arm.

Under the normal course of events, Dante would literally twist Miller's arm in return—twist it until it fucking breaks, set his evidence on fire, and send Miller slinking back home with his tail between his legs and a better appreciation for why nobody else in the city of Chicago would be stupid enough to try to blackmail Dante Gallo.

That's what would usually happen.

But at 10:04 p.m., Miller knocks on the door.

At 10:05, Dante lets him inside.

At 10:06, an anonymous caller dials 911, reporting shots fired at 1540 North Wieland Street.

At 10:08, officers Hernandez and O'Malley are sent to investigate, as the closest squad car to the scene.

At 10:09, they stand where Miller stood, hammering on the door of the Gallo residence. Dante opens up. He tries to refuse entry without a warrant, but the officers have probable cause. Reluctantly, he lets them in the house.

The rest is relayed to me via Officer Hernandez himself, later that night, in his usual colorful manner:

"So we go in the house, and we start poking around while Gallo's standing there all sulky, arms crossed. He says, 'See, no firefight going on. So get the fuck out.' Miller is lurking in the dining room, looking squirrelly as fuck. So I say, 'Can you come out here please, sir,' like I have no idea who he is. He comes out in the hallway, eyes kinda darting back and forth, not knowing what the hell is going on. Nervous as can be. Gallo is cool as a cucumber, not giving anything away.

"O'Malley says, 'What are you two gentlemen up to?' And Gallo says, 'None of your fucking business.' And Miller tries to make some excuse, and Gallo cuts him off and says, 'Don't answer any of their questions.' Then I say, 'Do you have any weapons on you, sir?' And Gallo says, 'No.' So I say, 'Good,' and I pull my gun on him.

"Gallo says, 'Better watch yourself, Officer. I'm not some kid outside a 7-Eleven. You don't get to put eight in my chest and call it self-defense.' Then O'Malley says, 'Don't worry, we're not here for you.' And he pulls the Beretta and empties half the clip into Miller.

"Miller goes down without a peep, just a dumb fucking look on his face. He didn't even see it comin'. O'Malley kicks his leg to make sure he's dead, and sure enough, Miller is an insta-corpse.

"I'm watching Gallo the whole time. He's like a rock, man—he doesn't flinch. But as soon as he sees the Beretta, he recognizes it. His eyes get wide 'cause he knows he's fucked. He looks at me, and I can see his brain workin'. I think he's gonna run at me.

"O'Malley says, 'Don't even think about it. I've got four shots left.' He turns his gun on Gallo. I've got mine pointed right in his face.

"Cold as a Popsicle, Gallo says, 'How much you getting paid for this?' Which of course I don't entertain at all, boss. I say, 'None ya fuckin' business. You ain't gettin' out of this one.'

"So we cuff that son of a bitch, and O'Malley puts him in the squad car. I wipe down the Beretta, and then I shove it into Gallo's hands while they're cuffed behind his back to get some prints on the gun and some residue on his hands. I make sure the scene looks nice and pretty, and then I call it in. It all went down peachy, boss. Just like we planned."

Just like *I* planned. Those two idiots could barely fill out a McDonald's application without help.

"Where is he now?" I ask.

"Miller?"

"*No*," I say through gritted teeth. "I assume Miller's at the morgue. I'm asking about Dante Gallo."

"Oh. He's down at the station. Gallo called Riona Griffin down there the same hour, and she tried to get a quick dismissal, but it's Judge Pitz running cases this week and he said no fuckin' way, and no bail either. He's not a fan of the Gallos. So Dante gets to sit in jail for the foreseeable future while we investigate this thing, nice and slow."

I smile, picturing Dante in a crisp set of prison blues, crammed in a cell barely big enough to fit his burly body. And his siblings, all too eager to run wild without their older brother keeping them in check. Enzo's getting old—Dante is the lynchpin holding the Gallos together. They'll fall to pieces without him.

"You want me to figure out who's in the cell with him, boss?" Hernandez asks. "I can get a nice rusty shank put between his ribs anytime you like."

"No."

Dante is going to rot in there, miserable and furious.

When I decide it's time for him to die, I won't be delegating the task to a moron like Hernandez.

I like that Riona Griffin is defending Gallo. That gives me plenty of opportunity to dirty her hands as well—not that anybody was under the impression she got her legal degree to uphold the law.

It's all falling into place beautifully.

Of course, I'm expecting some pushback from my enemies. They're not going to take hits like this lying down.

Sure enough, the very next day, the Griffins' men confiscate a warehouse full of blow belonging to the Russians, shooting two of their soldiers in the process.

Meanwhile, on the opposite side of town, Nero Gallo inciner- ates my most profitable strip club. Luckily, it was 3:00 a.m., after all my girls had gone home. But it's still infuriating, watching the footage of Nero setting it all alight.

It's no more than I expected—less, actually. Those are weak reprisals from two families that usually rule this city with an iron fist. They're shaken and scattered, just as I hoped. Lacking in purpose and plan.

All this action is almost enough to distract me from the girl living in my house. The one who works on her ballet day and night, the scratchy strains of music from her dusty turntable drifting down the stairs.

I watch her more than I would ever admit. There's a camera in her studio, the same as every room in the east wing. I can spy on her through my phone anytime I like. She's in my pocket constantly. The compulsion to pull out that phone is omnipresent.

But I want more.

I want to see her in person again.

So, about a week after I successfully frame Dante Gallo, I track her down in the little library in the east wing.

She's wearing one of the outfits I ordered Klara to buy for her: a blue floral bodysuit and a chiffon skirt over cream-colored tights, the heels and toes cut so bits of her bare feet show through.

Those feet hang over the arm of an overstuffed leather chair. Nessa has fallen asleep reading. The book is open on her chest—*The Doll* by Bolesław Prus. Well, well...Nessa is trying to absorb a little of our culture. Klara probably recommended it.

Nessa has another book pressed between her thigh and the chair. Something old with a worn leather cover. I'm about to pull it free when she startles awake.

"Oh!" she gasps, stuffing the books out of sight beneath a cushion. "What are you doing in here?"

"It's my house," I remind her.

"I know," she says. "But you never come up here. Or not much anyway." She colors, likely remembering what happened the last time I came to the east wing.

She doesn't have to worry. That won't be happening again.

"You don't have to hide the books," I tell her. "You're allowed to read."

"Yes," she says, not quite meeting my eyes. "Right. Well…did you need something?"

Many things. None of which Nessa can give me.

"Actually, I came to ask you the same question."

It's not what I planned to say. But I find myself asking it all the same.

"No!" She shakes her head violently. "I don't need anything else."

She doesn't want any more gifts from me. I hadn't planned to give her any. But now I almost want to, just to deepen the pretty pink flush of her cheeks.

"Are you sure?" I press her. "I don't want you creeping around in my attic trying to scrounge up what you need."

She bites her lip, embarrassed that I found out about that. I know everything that happens in my house. She'd do well to remember that.

She hesitates. There is something she wants. She's scared to ask me.

"Now that you mention the attic…" she murmurs, "there's a dress up there…"

"What kind of dress?"

"An old one. In a box with a bunch of other fancy clothes."

I frown. "What about it?"

She takes a deep breath, twisting her hands together in her lap. "Could I take it? And do whatever I like with it?"

What an odd request. She hasn't asked me for a single thing since she came, and now she wants some moth-eaten old dress? "What for?"

"I just…like it," she says lamely.

She likes it? She has dozens of dresses in the wardrobe in her room. Designer dresses, new and in exactly her size. Maybe she wants an old gown for her ballet.

"Fine," I say.

"Really?" Her face lights up, her mouth open with surprise and happiness.

Kurwa, if that's all it takes to get her excited, I'd hate to see her reaction to an actual favor. Or maybe I'd love to see it. I don't even know anymore.

The peace offering seems to relax her. She sits up in the chair and actually leans toward me instead of cringing away.

"Did you just come in from the garden?" she says.

"Yes," I admit. "Did you see me out the window before you fell asleep?"

"No." She shakes her head. "I can smell the katsura on your clothes."

"The kat—What?"

She flushes. She didn't mean to make conversation. "It's a tree. You have it in the garden. When the leaves change color, they smell like brown sugar."

She glances at my arms, bare beneath the sleeves of my T-shirt. Those expressive eyebrows of hers draw together, and her lashes sweep up and down like fans as she examines me.

"Irish mobsters have tattoos, don't they? Or have the Griffins evolved beyond that?"

"We have plenty of tattoos," she says, unoffended.

"Not you, though."

"Actually, I do." She tucks a lock of hair behind her ear, turning her head so I can see. Sure enough, she has a tiny crescent moon tattooed behind her right ear. I never noticed it before.

"Why a moon?"

She shrugs. "I like the moon. It changes all the time. But it also stays the same."

Now she's looking at my arms again, no doubt trying to decipher the meaning of my tattoos. She won't understand them. They're dense, convoluted, and have meaning only to me.

Which is why I'm shocked when she says, "Is that from the map in *The Hobbit*?"

She's pointing at a tiny symbol concealed within the swirling patterns on my left forearm. It's a small delta, next to the barest suggestion of a line. Camouflaged by all the ink around it.

Nessa's bright green eyes are scouring my skin, darting from place to place.

"That's the edge of the mountain." She points. "So that's the river. And a tree. Oh, and there's the corner of the spider's web!"

She's like a child hunting clues, so pleased with herself that she's failing to see the outrage on my face. I feel exposed as I never have before. How fucking dare she spot the things I hid so carefully?

Worse still, she keeps going.

"Oh, that's from *The Snow Queen*." She points to a tiny snowflake. "That's from *Alice in Wonderland*." A medicine bottle. "And that's… oh, that's *The Little Prince*!" A rose.

It's only when she looks up at me, likely expecting me to be likewise impressed with her observation, that she sees the shock and bitterness in my face.

"You must like to read…" she says.

The symbols from those books are tiny and obscure. I took only the smallest and least-recognizable parts of the illustrations, hiding them inside the larger work that means nothing at all.

No one ever noticed them before, let alone guessed what they meant.

It's violating. Nessa has no idea how she's blundered. I could strangle her right now, just to stop her from speaking another word.

But she has no intention of saying anything else. Her face is pale and frightened once more. She sees that she's offended me, without knowing why.

"I'm sorry," she whispers.

"How did you see that?" I demand.

"I don't know." She shakes her head. "I'm good at picking out patterns. It's why I can learn dances so quickly. And lang—" She breaks off, not finishing that sentence.

My skin is burning. Every tattoo she named feels like it's on fire.

I'm not used to being unnerved. Especially not by a girl who's barely an adult. Not even a fucking adult, in the American sense of the word. She's only nineteen. She can't buy a beer or rent a car. She can barely vote!

"I'm sorry," Nessa says again. "I didn't realize they were a secret. That they were just for you."

What the fuck is happening?

How does she know that? How did she know what they meant?

The last person who could guess the thoughts in my head was Anna. She was the only one who could ever do it.

Anna was clever. Good at remembering things. A lover of books. No one has ever reminded me of her.

Nessa doesn't either. They don't look alike or sound alike. They don't have much in common. Except in this one thing…

To change the subject, I say abruptly, "Are you almost done with your ballet?"

"Yes." Nessa bites her lips nervously. "Well, halfway through anyway."

"Is it a whole show?"

"Yes."

"Have you ever made one before?"

"Well..." She frowns. "I choreographed four dances for this ballet called *Bliss*. It was supposed to premiere...well, right now, I guess. But the director, his name's Jackson Wright, said my dances were shit. So he didn't put my name in the program..." She sighs. "I know that sounds silly. It mattered to me at the time. It hurt my feelings. I kind of felt like he stole my work. But he might have been right. Now that I'm working on this other thing, I think what I did before was stupid. And not very good."

"Good enough for him to use."

"Yeah," she says. "Parts of it anyway."

She wraps her thin arms around her legs, hugging her thighs against her chest. Her flexibility is unnerving. So is her fragility. No wonder so many people take advantage of her. Her family. This director. And me, of course.

Nothing about Nessa exudes strength.

She's not intimidating. But she is...intriguing.

She's a piece of music that gets stuck in your head, repeating over and over. The more you hear it, the more it lodges in your brain.

Most people become predictable, the longer you watch them. Nessa Griffin is the opposite. I thought I knew exactly who she was—a sheltered little princess. A dancer living in a fantasy world.

But she's much cleverer than I gave her credit for. She's creative, perceptive.

And genuinely kind.

I learn that the next day when I spy on her yet again. I see her slip back up to the attic to retrieve this mysterious dress on which she's so fixated.

It's black and silver, definitely old-fashioned. Maybe from one of those Gilded Age costume balls like the Vanderbilts used to throw. I didn't know the dress existed. The attic is packed with boxes, more added by every family that lived in this house and almost none ever removed.

I watch Nessa bring the dress back to her room. She airs it out, making sure it's clean of every speck of dust.

Then she lays it out on the bed and waits.

When Klara comes in with the dinner tray, Nessa rushes over to her.

There's no sound from the camera, but I can see the expressions on their faces clearly enough.

Klara shakes her head, not wanting to get in trouble.

Nessa assures her it's all right, that I've given permission.

Still not believing, Klara touches the skirt of the dress. Then she hugs Nessa.

Out of all the things Nessa could have asked me for, she wanted that dress. But not for herself. She wanted to give it as a gift.

I should fire Klara. It's obvious the two girls have grown close. It's too risky for Nessa's jailer to be her friend.

But as I watch them laughing and talking, gently touching the dress, I don't want to do it.

Maybe later. Not today.

18
NESSA

I'm losing track of how long I've been at Mikolaj's house.

Days slip by so fast when you don't have a schedule or anything planned.

I have no idea what's going on in the real world. I don't have a TV, a phone, or a computer. World War III could have started, and I'd have no idea.

I'm in a place without dates or times. It could be 1890 or 2020 or something in between.

You'd think I'd obsess about my family constantly. At first, I was—I knew they'd be looking for me. Worried, terrified, thinking I was dead. I missed them. God, I missed them. I'd never gone that long without speaking to my mom, not to mention Riona, Callum, and Dad. Aida, too! We usually texted twenty times a day, even if it was just cat memes.

Now I feel like I've slipped into another world. They're much farther away than the other side of the city.

I'm not dreaming about them at night anymore.

My dreams are much darker than that. I wake in the morning flushed and sweating. Too embarrassed to even admit where my mind wandered in the night…

In the day I think about the strangers living in this house with me. I wonder about Klara, what her life was like in Poland. What her family's like. I wonder about the rest of the men in this house—why

Andrei spends so much time roaming the grounds and whether Marcel has a crush on Klara as I suspect he does.

The only person I don't wonder about is Jonas because I find him deeply creepy. I hate the way he watches me whenever we cross paths in the house. He's worse than Mikolaj because at least Mikolaj is genuine—he genuinely hates me. Jonas pretends to be friendly. He's always smiling and trying to make conversation. His smiles are as fake as his cologne.

Today he corners me in the kitchen. I'm looking for Klara, but she's not there.

"What do you need?" Jonas says, leaning against the fridge so I can't pass.

"Nothing."

"Come on." He grins. "You must need something, or else why would you come in here? What is it? What's your favorite treat? You want cookies? Milk?"

"I was just looking for Klara," I tell him, trying to sneak by on his right side.

He straightens, stepping in front of me to block my path. "I know how to cook, too. You know Klara's my cousin? Anything she can do, I can do better…"

I try not to let my face show how disgusted I feel. Jonas always makes everything sound like a sexual innuendo. Even if I don't understand his meaning, I can tell he's trying to provoke me.

"Let me pass, please," I say quietly.

"To go where?" Jonas says in a low voice. "Do you have some hiding spot I don't know about?"

"Jonas," someone barks from the doorway.

Jonas whips around even quicker than I do. We both recognize Mikolaj's voice.

"Hey, boss," Jonas says, trying to recover his casual tone.

There's nothing casual in Mikolaj's expression. His eyes are narrowed to slits, his lips bone pale.

"*Odejdź od niej,*" he hisses. *Get away from her.*

"*Tak, szefie,*" Jonas says, with a little bow of his head. *Yes, boss.*

Jonas hurries out of the kitchen. Mikolaj doesn't move to let him pass, so Jonas has to turn sideways before scurrying away.

Under Mikolaj's blazing stare, I feel like I've done something wrong, too. I can't look him in the eye.

"Don't talk to him," Mikolaj orders, low and furious.

"I don't want to talk to him!" I cry, outraged. "He's the one bothering me! I hate him!"

"Good," Mikolaj says.

He has the strangest look on his face. I can't understand it at all. If I didn't know better, I'd almost think he was jealous.

I expect him to say something else. Instead, he turns and stalks away without another word. I hear him exit through the conservatory door, and when I peer out through the window, I see him striding off across the lawn to the far end of the grounds.

I'm confused and infuriated.

Of all the people in this house, I think about Mikolaj the most.

I don't want to. But I can't help it. When he's in the house, I feel like I'm trapped inside a tiger's cage with the tiger roaming around. I can't ignore him; I have to keep track of where he is, what he's doing, so he can't creep up behind me.

But when he's out, it's even worse because I know he's doing something awful, probably to the people I love most.

I don't think he's killed any of them yet. I don't believe he has. I'd hear his men talking about it. Or he'd tell me himself, just to gloat.

But I can feel the wheels turning, rushing us down the track to this destination he's set. The train keeps chugging on.

Which is why I should hate him more than I hate Jonas.

It should be the easiest thing in the world to despise him. He kidnapped me. He ripped me away from everything I love and locked me in this house.

Yet, when I examine the bubbling mixture of emotions swirling in my guts, I find fear, confusion, anxiety...but also a strange sense of respect. And sometimes, even arousal...

I want to know more about my captor. I tell myself it's only so I can stand up to him. Or maybe escape.

But there's more to it than that. I'm curious about him. He was so angry about those tattoos—I want to know why. I want to know exactly what they mean to him.

Once I know he's out on the grounds, I get a very stupid idea in my head.

I want to see what's in the west wing. He told me not to go there, in no uncertain terms.

What's he hiding there? Weapons? Money? Evidence of his dastardly plan?

There's no door to keep me out. Just a wide curved staircase, the twin of the one that leads to my own rooms.

It's so easy to run up those steps, to the long hallway that leads west instead of east.

I expect the forbidden wing to be even darker and creepier than my own, but the opposite is true—this part of the house is the most modern. I see a lounge with a fully stocked bar and a huge study. This must be Mikolaj's office. I see his safe, his desk, his computer. If I actually care about his plans, this is where I should snoop around.

Instead, I find myself continuing down the hall to the largest room at the end. The main suite.

It's modern and masculine. As soon as I slip through the door, I'm hit with the distinctive scent of my captor. He smells like cedarwood, cigarettes, scotch, fresh orange rind, shoe polish, and that rich, heady musk that belongs only to him. The scent is so unadulterated that I doubt any other person has stepped foot in this room, not even Klara to clean it.

Unlike the rest of the house, this room isn't dark and moody at all. The furniture is dark, but the space is light. That's because it's one of the highest points in the house, and the far wall is one gigantic window. It runs from floor to ceiling, the whole length of the room.

While my window faces east into the tree-stuffed grounds, Mikolaj's window looks out over the Chicago skyline. The whole city is laid out before him. This is where he stands when he imagines taking it all under his control.

I know exactly where I am now. I could almost point to my own house situated on the rim of the lake. If I searched, I could find it, picking out its gray-shingled roof from the other mansions along the Gold Coast.

Instead, my eyes are drawn back inside by the irresistible temptation of this private space. Looking through Mikolaj's room is like looking inside his brain. In the rest of the house, I only see what he wants me to see. This is where I'll find everything hidden.

He might keep his keys in here. I could steal the key to the front door and escape some night when everyone's asleep.

I tell myself that's what I'm looking for.

Meanwhile, I'm trailing my fingers over his unmade sheets, releasing the heady scent of his skin. I can still see the indent where his body lay. It's hard to imagine him unconscious and vulnerable. He doesn't seem like someone who eats or sleeps, laughs or cries.

Yet here's the evidence right in front of me. I lay my palm down in that indent, as if I'll still feel the heat of his body. My skin prickles, and my blood runs faster, until I snatch my hand back again.

His bed is surrounded by built-in bookshelves. I draw close to read the spines.

Sure enough, I find exactly what I expected: weathered copies of *The Hobbit*, *The Snow Queen*, *Alice in Wonderland*, *Through the Looking Glass*, and *The Little Prince*, mixed in with *Persuasion*, *Anna Karenina*, and dozens more, some in English, some in Polish.

I pull *Through the Looking Glass* off the shelf, cracking the spine carefully because the book is so soft and fragile that I'm afraid some of the pages will come loose.

On the very first page, written in pencil, is a name: Anna.

I let out a sigh.

I knew it.

He was so angry when I spotted the illustrations in his tattoos. I knew they meant something, that they were tied to someone he loved.

That's why he was angry. To brutal men, love is a liability. I discovered his weakness.

Who was Anna? Most of the books are for children or young adults. Was she his daughter?

No, the books are too old. Even if they were purchased second-hand, the handwriting doesn't look childish.

What, then, a wife?

No, when I took that jab at him about not being married, he didn't flinch. He's no widower.

Anna is his sister. That must be it.

Right as I realize it, a hand grips my wrist and jerks me around.

The book flies out of my fingers. Just as I feared, the glue holding the binding together is too old to withstand this kind of treatment. As I spin around, a dozen pages tear free, floating through the air like falling leaves.

"What the fuck are you doing in my room?"

Mikolaj's teeth are bared, his fingers digging into my wrist. He's run up here so fast that his pale blond hair has fallen over his left eye. He swipes it back furiously, not looking away from me for a second.

"I'm sorry!" I gasp.

He grabs my shoulders, gives me a hard shake. "I said what the fuck are you doing!" he shouts.

While I may have seen him angry before, I've never seen him out of control. Those times that he sneered at me or taunted me, he was fully restrained. Now there's no restraint, no self-control. He's raging.

"Mikolaj!" I cry. "Please…"

When I say his name, he lets go of me like my skin burned his hands. He takes a step back, grimacing.

It's all the opportunity I need. Abandoning the book torn on the ground, I run away from him as fast as I can.

I flee the west wing, back down the stairs and across the main floor. I run out the back door into the garden, and then I hide in the very farthest corner of the grounds, in the shelter of a willow tree where the boughs hang all the way down to the grass.

I hide there until it's night, too afraid to go back inside the house.

19
MIKO

KURWA, WHAT AM I DOING?

As I pick the old copy of *Through the Looking Glass* off the ground, I feel like I, too, have passed through a mirror into some bizarre, backward sort of world.

Nessa Griffin is getting under my skin.

First the tattoos, then sneaking into my room…

I feel like she's peeling back my layers one by one. She's peering into crevices nobody should see.

I've kept myself closed off from everyone for ten years. From my family back in Poland, from my own brothers in the *Braterstwo*, even from Tymon. They knew me, but they only knew the adult version. What I became after my sister died.

They didn't know the boy before.

I thought he was dead. I thought he'd died at the same time as Anna. We came into the world together, and I thought we'd left it together. All that remained was this husk, this man who felt nothing. Who could never be hurt.

Now Nessa is digging into me. Unearthing the remains of what I thought could never be resurrected.

She's making me feel things I never thought I'd feel again.

I don't want to feel them.

I don't want to think about some young, vulnerable girl. I don't want to worry about her.

I don't want to walk into the kitchen and see Jonas leaning over her, and I don't want to feel a furious spike of jealousy that makes me want to rip my own brother's head off his shoulders. And then, after I've banished him to the opposite corner of the house, I don't want my brain stewing with thoughts of what he might do if he ever got Nessa alone…

These are distractions.

They weaken my plans and my resolve.

After I shout at Nessa, she runs out and hides in the garden for hours. Of course, I know exactly where she is. I can track the location of her ankle monitor within a couple of feet.

It gets dark and cold. We're midway through the autumn now, at the point of the season when some days seem like an endless summer, only with more color in the leaves, while other days are bitter, windy, and rainy, with the promise of worse to come.

I sit in my office staring at my phone, at the little pin representing Nessa Griffin huddled against the far wall. I thought she would come back inside, but either I terrified her more than I knew, or she has more grit in her than I would have guessed.

My thoughts swirl around and around.

I'm in the perfect position to strike again. I bled out a large portion of the liquid cash of the Griffins. I have a solid alliance with the Russians via Kolya Kristoff—in fact, he nags me daily as to our next move. Dante Gallo is trapped in a holding cell while Riona Griffin burns every bridge she has at the DA's office trying to get him out.

My next target should be Callum Griffin. Nessa's beloved older brother.

He was the spark that lit this conflict.

He was the one who spat in Tymon's face when we offered him friendship.

He has to die, or at the very least he has to be cut off at the knees, brought low in abject humility. I know him—I know he'll never accept that. I saw his face when Tymon plunged his knife into Callum's side. There wasn't a hint of surrender.

Nessa's tracking device sends me a warning. It's not reading her pulse through the skin. She might be fucking with it, trying to get it off.

Before I can check, the screen switches over to an incoming call—Kristoff again.

I pick it up.

"*Dobryy vecher, moy drug*," Kristoff says smoothly. *Good evening, my friend.*

"*Dobry wieczór*," I reply in Polish.

Kristoff chuckles softly.

Poland and Russia have a long and stormy history. As long as our countries have been in existence, we've struggled for control of the same lands. We've fought wars against each other. In the 1600s the Poles captured Moscow. In the nineteenth and twentieth century, the Russians enveloped us in the smothering embrace of communism.

Our Mafias likewise grew in tandem. They call it the *Bratva*, we call it the *Braterstwo*—in either case, it means "the Brotherhood." We swear oaths to our brothers. We keep a history of our accomplishments on our skin. They wear eight-pointed stars as a badge of leadership on their shoulders. We mark our military ranks on our arms.

We're two sides of the same coin. Our blood has mixed—our language and traditions, too.

And yet we are not the same. We thrust our hands into the same clay, and we built something different from it. To give you a small example, consider the many "false friends" in our language—words with the same origin that have come to convey opposite meanings. In Russian, Kristoff would say *zapominat*, meaning "to memorize," while to me, *zapomniec* means "to forget."

So while Kristoff and I may be allies in this moment, I can never forget that what he wants and what I want may run parallel, but they will never be the same. He can become my enemy again as easily as he became my friend.

He's a dangerous enemy. Because he knows me better than most.

"I enjoyed our trick on the Irish," Kristoff says. "I'm enjoying spending their money even more."

"Nothing tastes as sweet as the fruits of others' labor."

"I think we agree on many things," Kristoff says. "I see many similarities between us, Mikolaj. Both unexpectedly ascending to our positions at a young age. Both risen from the lowest ranks of our organization. I'm not from a wealthy or connected family either. No royal blood in these veins."

I grunt. I know part of Kristoff's history—he wasn't *Bratva* to begin with. Quite the opposite. He trained with the Russian military. He was an assassin, plain and simple. How he moved from military operative to underworld kingpin, I have no idea. His men trust him. I'm not as willing to do the same.

"They say Zajac was your father," Kristoff says. "You were his natural son?"

He's asking if I'm Tymon's bastard. Tymon was never married, but he did father a son on his favorite whore—that son is Jonas. People assume, because I succeeded Tymon, that I must be another bastard son.

"What's the point of these questions?" I say impatiently.

I have no interest in trying to explain to Kristoff that Tymon and I had a bond of respect and understanding, not of blood. Jonas knew it. All the men knew it. Tymon selected the best leader from our ranks. He wanted the man with the will to lead, not the genetics.

"Just making conversation," Kristoff says pleasantly.

"Do you know the saying '*Rosjanin sika z celem*'? It means 'a Russian takes a piss with purpose.'"

Kristoff laughs, unoffended. "I think I like one of your other sayings better—'*Nie dziel skóry na niedźwiedziu.*'"

It means "don't divide the skin while it's still on the bear."

Kristoff wants to divide Chicago. But first we have to kill the bear. "You want to plan the hunt," I say.

"That's right."

I sigh, glancing at the dark, moonless night outside my window. Nessa is still out in the garden, refusing to come back inside. The first few drops of rain break against the glass.

"When?" I say.

"Tomorrow night."

"Where?"

"Come to my house in Lincoln Park."

"Fine."

As I'm about to hang up, Kristoff adds, "Bring the girl."

Nessa hasn't left the house once since I captured her. Taking her anywhere is a risk, let alone right into the Russians' lair. "Why?"

"I was disappointed that I didn't get to see her in the flesh during our last operation. She's one of our most valuable chess pieces, and she cost me a warehouse of product the other day. I want to see for myself this girl who has the whole city in an uproar."

I don't like this at all. I don't trust Kristoff, and I don't like the idea of him gloating over Nessa like she's a prisoner of war.

This is the trouble with alliances. They demand compromises.

"I'll bring her with me," I say. "Understanding that no one lays a hand on her. She stays right next to me, every second."

"Of course," Kristoff says easily.

"*Do jutra*." I hang up the phone. *Until tomorrow.*

As the rain starts coming down in earnest, I send Klara out to the garden to retrieve the little runaway.

Klara heads out through the conservatory carrying a heavy knit blanket from the library. When she returns, Nessa is wrapped in that blanket, pale and shivering. I can see the monitor still firmly in place around her ankle. It looks scuffed like she tried to bash it off with a rock. Her leg is scraped, too. Klara's arm is around her shoulders, Nessa's head down, her cheeks streaked with rain and tears.

She must have cried a bathtub of tears since I brought her here.

At first, I didn't care in the slightest. In fact, I saw those tears as my due. They were the salt that would season my revenge.

But now I feel that most dangerous emotion of all—guilt. The emotion that drains you, that makes you regret even the most necessary actions.

Those girls are growing too close.

And I'm growing too soft.

Nessa is obviously exhausted, half-frozen in her flimsy dance wear. I'm sure Klara will feed her and bathe her and put her to bed.

Meanwhile, I won't be going to sleep for hours yet. If I'm going to meet with the Russians tomorrow, I need to speak with my men tonight. I want our strategy decided before we throw Kristoff in the mix.

I call them all into the billiard room. It's one of the largest and most central rooms on the main floor, with plenty of seating, I like to talk and play at the same time. It makes everyone more relaxed and more honest. Plus, it reminds my men that I can whip their asses at pool anytime I please.

We've had a hotly contested tournament since the day we moved into this house. Sometimes Marcel is second in the rankings; sometimes Jonas is. I'm always at the top.

Marcel racks the balls while Jonas and I square off for the first game.

Jonas makes a show out of chalking the tip of his cue, sending blue powder drifting onto the black hairs on his forearm. He hasn't shaved yet today, so his dark stubble is halfway to a beard.

"You want to put money on the line, boss?" he says.

"Sure. I'm feeling lucky today—how about five?"

The standard bet is two hundred dollars a game. I'm starting at five hundred to fuck with Jonas's head and to let him know I haven't forgotten about his little stunt with Nessa in the kitchen. I've told him before to stay the fuck away from her. I know how he is with women, constantly hounding the girls at our clubs. The more they turn him down, the more interested he becomes.

Jonas wins the coin toss and breaks first. He makes a nice, clean break, dropping two striped balls into corner pockets. He grins, thinking he's got the advantage. He hasn't bothered to look at the placement of the rest of the balls, so he doesn't see how jammed up his twelve and fourteen are, over by the eight ball.

"So," I say in Polish, leaning on my cue. "We meet with the Russians tomorrow. They want to discuss our endgame."

Jonas sinks the nine and the eleven, still confident and grinning.

"Before I haggle over the details, I want to hear ideas. If you've got something to say, say it now."

"Why don't we kill the girl?" Andrei says. He's sitting over by the bar, drinking a Heineken. He has a square, blocky head, very little neck, and ginger-tinged hair. He looks surly and malcontent tonight. He hates the Russians and hates that we're working with them. Understandable, since both his brothers were killed by *Bratva*—one in prison in Wroclaw, one right here in Chicago.

Andrei takes a long pull of his beer, then sets it down on the bar. "We got rid of Miller and framed Dante Gallo. We should do the same with the girl. Make it look like Nero killed her, or Enzo. That will blow up the alliance between the Irish and the Italians quicker than anything else we could do."

He's not wrong. When I first kidnapped Nessa Griffin, that was my plan. Her disappearance was intended to cause chaos. Her death would split the two families apart.

A wedding bound them together in the first place. Death is stronger than marriage.

But now I want to take my pool cue and break it over Andrei's thick skull just for suggesting it. The idea of him walking up to her room and wrapping those ugly calloused hands around her throat…I won't allow it. I won't even consider it. He's not fucking touching her, and neither is anybody else.

Nessa isn't a blank-faced pawn to be shuffled around the board at will. She won't be sacrificed either.

She's worth more than that. She can be used to much greater effect.

Jonas misses his next shot. I sink the one, the four, and the five in quick succession while I reply.

"We're not killing her. She's the best leverage we have at the moment. Why do you think the Griffins and the Gallos haven't attacked us directly?"

"They did!" Marcel says. "They raided the Russian's warehouse and torched Exotica."

I snort, sinking the three ball as well. "You think that was the best they could do? It was fucking weak. Why do you think they haven't firebombed this house?"

Jonas and Andrei exchange a glance in which no information is shared because they're both equally stupid.

"Because they know she might be in here," Marcel says.

"That's right." I sink the two and the seven with one split shot. "As long as they can't be certain where she is—here or with the Russians—all they can do is throw a few grenades. They can't rain down napalm on our heads. Nessa is our insurance, for now."

The green six is trapped behind Jonas's thirteen. I hit a bank shot to come at it from behind, sending the six rolling neatly into the side pocket. Jonas scowls.

"Why don't we kill the dons? They shot Zajac. We should kill Enzo and Fergus."

"What good would that do?" I say. "Their successors are already in place."

I sink the eight ball without even looking. Marcel snickers, and Jonas grips his pool cue so hard, his arm shakes. He looks like he wants to snap it in two.

"What then?" he demands. "What's the next step?"

"Callum," I say. "We took him once. We can take him again."

"You lost him last time," Jonas says, fixing me with his dark stare.

I walk over to him, leaning my pool cue against the table. We face off, nose to nose.

"That's right," I say softly. "You were there, too, Brother. If I remember correctly, you were the one in charge of his wife. Little Aida Gallo, the Italian wench. She made a proper fool out of you. Almost took the whole warehouse down. You still have the scar from that Molotov cocktail she chucked at your head, don't you?"

I know very well that Jonas has a nice long burn down his back. She ruined one of his favorite tattoos, and he's been sore about it ever since. Both literally and figuratively.

"We should take them both," Jonas growls. "Callum and Aida."

"Now you're thinking." I nod. "I hear the arranged marriage has become a love match. He'll do anything for her."

"Not if I snap her fucking neck," Jonas says.

"I don't want to blackmail those Irish fucks," Andrei says bitterly. "I want blood for blood."

"That's right," Marcel says quietly. "They killed Tymon. At the very least, we kill one from each family—a Griffin and a Gallo."

"Better to kill the son than the father," Jonas says. "Callum Griffin is the only son they've got. He's the heir—unless his wife is pregnant. Callum should die."

There are murmurs all around as Andrei and Marcel voice their agreement. I haven't agreed or disagreed. It's what I always planned. But I'm distracted by the choking sound outside the door. Something between a gasp and a sob.

I stride over to the door and wrench it open, expecting to see Klara outside. Instead, I see the hysterical face of Nessa Griffin. I seize her by the wrist before she can turn and flee. I drag her into the billiard room, while she kicks and fights.

"No!" she screams. "You can't kill my brother! I won't let you!"

"Everyone out," I bark at my men.

They hesitate, their faces frozen in confusion.

"*Out!*" I roar.

They scatter, closing the doors behind them.

I throw Nessa on the carpet at my feet. She leaps right back up again, flailing her arms in her mad attempts to hit me, scratch me, tear me to pieces.

"I won't let you!" she screams. "I swear to god, I'll kill every one of you!"

After my initial surprise at seeing her when Klara should have locked her in her room for the night, I'm starting to realize something completely different.

We were speaking in Polish.

Yet Nessa understood every word we said.

"*Co robisz, szpiegując mnie,*" I hiss.

"I'll spy on you all I like!" Nessa shouts. She claps her hand over her mouth, realizing she's given herself away.

"*Kto nauczył cię polskiego?*" I say furiously. I already know the answer. It had to be Klara.

Nessa throws me off, standing as tall and dignified as possible, considering her hair is a tangled mess, her face is still puffy with tears, and she's wearing a nightgown. "*Nikt nie nauczył mnie polskiego,*" she says haughtily. *I learned it myself, in the library. I have a lot of time on my hands.*

I don't know if I've ever been struck dumb before.

Her pronunciation is shit, and her grammar is mediocre. But she really has learned a shocking amount.

That tricky little devil. I didn't give a damn about her sneaking around because I didn't think she could understand our conversations. Not that it matters—she can't do anything with the information. She's still my prisoner.

But…I'm impressed. Nessa is smarter than I guessed, and more daring.

Still, she's got another think coming if she thinks she's going to boss me around in my own house, in front of my own men. She doesn't give orders here—I do. I'm the master. She's the captive.

"What are you going to do about it?" I stare down into her face. "You think you can threaten me? Try to attack me? I could snap every bone in your body without even trying."

She shakes her head, more tears streaming down her face. When she cries, her eyes look greener than ever. Each tear is a refracting lens, clinging to those black lashes, magnifying every freckle on her cheeks.

"I know you're stronger than me. I know I'm nothing and nobody. But I love my brother. Can you understand that? I love him more than anyone in the world. Did you ever feel that way, before you got so cold and angry? Did you love somebody once? I know you did. I know about Anna."

Now I really do want to hit her.

How fucking dare she say that name.

She doesn't know anything, anything at all.

She thinks she can poke in my brain, trying to drag out the things I've successfully hidden.

She wants to make me as weak and emotional as her.

I seize her by the front of her nightgown and speak directly into her face. "*Don't you ever say her name again.*"

Nessa raises her hand. I think she's going to try to slap me. Instead, she rests her hand on top of mine, her slim little fingers clinging to my clenched fist.

She looks up into my eyes.

"Mikolaj, please," she begs. "My brother is a good man. I know this is a war and you're on opposite sides. I know he hurt you. But if you kill him, you won't be hurting him back. You'll be hurting me. And I never wronged you."

She's talking about fairness, justice. There is no fucking justice in this world. There are only debts that have to be paid.

But there's more than one kind of currency.

Nessa is standing in front of me—slender, delicate, trembling like a leaf. Tangles of light-brown hair in a cloud around her face and shoulders. Big tear-soaked eyes and soft-pink lips.

She's touching my hand. She's never touched me voluntarily before.

My hand is on fire, sending heat and warmth throughout my body. Making every part of me throb like frozen flesh finally coming back to life. Nerves burning.

The fire is everywhere in my veins. My cock pulses, hard enough to punch through a wall.

I look down into her tearstained face.

"Convince me, Nessa... Convince me I should spare your brother."

She looks up at me, uncomprehending at first. Then realization dawns.

I'm still holding the front of her nightgown. I feel her heart pounding against my clenched fingers. I let go of her, waiting to see what she'll do.

Her tongue darts out to moisten her lips. She says, "Sit down on the couch."

I take a seat on the low sofa. It's the first order I've obeyed in a very long time. I sit back against the cushions, my hands beside me, my legs slightly spread.

"Can I borrow your phone?" Nessa whispers.

I pass it to her silently.

She scrolls for a moment, then presses the screen. Music comes out of the speakers—a low, moody, insistent beat. It's not the usual music I hear my little ballerina playing. This is much darker.

Rain pounds against the windows. The beat of the raindrops mixes with the beat of the music. The light is dim and watery, the shadows distorted by the raindrops.

Nessa looks like she's underwater. Her skin is paler than ever. She stands in front of me, her hips curving to the music.

I've watched her dance countless times. But never like this. Never right in front of me. Never directed at me. Her eyes are fixed on mine. Her body sways sinuously.

The very first time I saw her at the club, she danced a little bit like this.

That was a peek through a keyhole. Now the door is flung wide open.

I'm seeing Nessa unleashed. Nessa when no one is watching her—no one but me.

She's rolling and swaying, her hips moving as I've never seen before, her eyes locked on mine. She bends all the way to the ground, then slides her hands up one long leg, pulling up the skirt of her nightgown to show her smooth, creamy thigh.

Then she spins the other way, so when she bends over, I can see the curve of her ass cheek beneath the hem of the nightie.

She's teasing me. She knows that my eyes are glued to her body, that her every movement is sending jolts down my spine, making my cock stiffen and swell until I have to shift in place, trying to find relief.

She turns around again to face me. Without breaking eye contact, she grabs the hem of her nightgown and slowly lifts it over her head, revealing her narrow hips, impossibly slim waist, and then her small round breasts. She wads up the thin cotton nightie and tosses it to the side.

She's naked now, except for her panties.

It's my first full view of her breasts. I've seen them through soaked material but never completely bare. They're hardly big enough to fill my hands, but they're fucking gorgeous, set high on her chest, the nipples pointing painfully in the air. They look sculpted out of marble, if marble could be soft and mobile and sensitive.

There's just enough flesh that her breasts bounce and move along with the rest of her body, as if every ounce of her is calling to me, enticing me, begging to be touched.

I've never seen a body like hers. No excess, just a perfect, lean frame that's been trained and sculpted to its purpose. She's strong, graceful, and the sexiest fucking thing imaginable.

The music is pounding. So is the rain.

The lyrics drill into my head.

🎵 *Blood in the Cut—K.Flay*

Nessa spins and drops, then crawls across the floor toward me, catlike and sinuous, a panther hunting its prey. I'm supposed to be the hunter. But I'm fixed in place, mesmerized by her green eyes looking up at me.

She crawls up my leg, her hands sliding up my thigh. I know she can see my cock straining against the crotch of my pants. When she turns around and grinds her body against mine, I know she can feel it, too, digging into her ass.

My cock leaks come. It's dying to get free, to feel that butter-soft skin instead of the constricting material of my pants. A wet spot appears where the head presses against my trousers, and there's an even bigger damp patch where Nessa grinds against me.

She turns and straddles my lap, gyrating her ass against my crotch. Her arms link around my neck, those beautiful breasts just millimeters from my face. God, I want to close my mouth around those stiff little nipples.

I'm waiting. I want to see what Nessa will do all on her own, without my interference.

It takes every bit of my willpower. I've never been so turned on in my life. My cock rages to be set free, to sink deep inside her tight little body. I don't just want it—I need it. I'll fucking explode without it.

I've never seen a woman move like this, and I own a fucking strip club. Nessa is as innocent as they come. I kissed her once—I know how fumbling and inexperienced she is.

But there's something inside her. Something darkly sensual, buried deep inside her. A black and bottomless well.

Dancing unleashes her.

She grinds against me, rubbing those soft little breasts and that aching pussy against my body. Begging me to touch her back, to respond in kind. Her lashes are heavy with lust, her face flushed, her lips parted.

She slides down my body once more until she's kneeling between my legs. Her fingers fumble at the button of my pants. She opens my trousers, setting my cock free. It springs up to meet her, thick and fully hard, one of the only places where the skin is pure, unmarked by tattoos.

She gives a little gasp of surprise. I'm almost certain that what I guessed is true—Nessa is a virgin. She's never even seen a cock before, let alone touched one.

Hesitantly, she puts out her hand and closes it around my cock. It fills her hand. When she squeezes the shaft, her fingers don't meet around it.

She looks up at me once more, nervous and wide-eyed.

Those pale pink lips part. Her open mouth is about to close around my cock.

Until I stop her.

Gently, I push her away, tucking my cock back inside my pants.

I want Nessa to suck my cock. Fucking hell, I want it so bad. But not like this. Not by coercion.

I don't want her to do it because she's scared, because she's trying to convince me not to hurt her brother.

I want her to do it because she craves me as badly as I want her.

That's not going to happen. She's my prisoner; I'm the monster keeping her here.

I have to lock her back in her bedroom before I lose my last shred of self-control.

20
NESSA

I'm lying in my bed in the dark. My heart races like I'm sprinting on a treadmill.

Oh my god, oh my god, oh my god.

Why did he bring me back here?

I know Mikolaj wants me. I could see it on his face.

He felt what I felt. The same desperation, the same lust. The same wildness telling me to ignore all rational thought, to take what I wanted and damn the consequences.

I wanted *him*.

I know it's insane. I know he's my enemy, that he wants to destroy everything I love.

But my body and my brain are two separate entities.

I've never even had a boyfriend! I've had crushes, boys I thought were cute. It was almost a game—something I liked to imagine without taking any action.

I never really wanted to be kissed, not badly enough to make it happen. There was nothing special about any of those boys. Nothing made them stand out. They were interchangeable in my fantasies.

I've never had a strong attraction to anybody.

Until now.

My attraction to Mikolaj is a compulsion. It's nothing as simple as lust. It's every emotion wrapped into one: fear, intimidation, arousal, fixation, and anguish. It's so intense that nothing as normal as a crush could hope to compare to it. It's a force of nature. A goddamned tsunami.

It takes control of me. The old Nessa is becoming as pale and transparent as a ghost. The new Nessa is something else entirely...a dark and terrifying creature who seems to take over my body more and more each day.

I know *he's* feeling it, too. But he pushed me away, then brought me back to my room and left me here.

Why?

One tiny corner of my brain is still thinking rationally. It tells me, *Because he knows this is doomed. He knows he's going to kill your brother, your parents, and even you. And the tiny shred of morality left inside him says that it's wrong to fuck you before he murders you.*

It's a sobering thought. One that should shake me out of this madness.

I roll over under the blankets, closing my eyes, trying to force myself to go to sleep.

I'm plagued by the throbbing between my thighs. The itching and burning of my skin. I wanted him to touch me so badly. Why didn't he run his hands down my body at least?

If he had just kissed me again, I could be satisfied. I could go to sleep thinking of that. But he refused to touch me at all.

It almost makes me angry. He told me to convince him. Then he sat there like a fucking robot.

Yeah, I'm definitely pissed.

I used to be a girl who would curl up and cry when she was disappointed. Well, not anymore. I'm tired of crying. I'm tired of doing what people say. I'm tired of being locked in this room.

I slip out from under the blanket and pad barefoot toward the door.

I'm still naked, other than my underwear. I never recovered the nightgown—it's probably still down in the billiard room.

I try the door handle. It turns silently under my palm.

I'm going to take that as a sign. Mikolaj didn't actually lock me in my room. He's not sloppy—either he did it on purpose, or subconsciously he wants this as badly as I do.

I creep out of my room and pad down the dark hallway.

I remember how terrified I was the first time I did this.

I've spent more than a month in this house now. I know its sounds as well as I know the sound of my own heartbeat and my own breath in my lungs. I know exactly how to avoid Andrei, who's supposed to be keeping watch tonight. I hear him in the kitchen, pouring himself a glass of milk. He always drinks milk, never water.

I cross the main floor.

Then I hear another sound up the staircase that leads to Klara's room. It's a low murmur like two people talking quietly, not wanting to be heard. I'd bet my arm it's Marcel. I've seen how he looks at Klara and how she looks at him when she thinks no one will notice.

They won't hear me. They're too wrapped up in their own whispered conversation.

That means I just have to watch out for Jonas.

I cross over to the west wing, the forbidden part of the house. It's only been nine hours since Mikolaj chased me out of here. He looked so angry, I thought he'd strangle me right then and there.

Before, I was propelled by simple curiosity. Now I'm driven by something stronger.

I climb the staircase, then creep silently down the long hallway. As I pass Mikolaj's office, I peek inside in case he stayed up working. His chair is empty.

I come to the main suite with its heavy double doors. I turn the latch and slip inside, thinking for certain he'll still be awake. It's only been an hour since he dropped me off at my room. I expect to hear his low, clear voice, demanding to know why I'm back here already. But the suite is dark and silent.

I cross over to the bed.

There he lies. My beast. My enemy. My captor.

He's nearly naked on top of the covers, wearing only a pair of boxer shorts. For the first time, I have a full view of his body.

Every inch of his skin is covered in tattoos except for his palms and face. His body is a living, breathing piece of art. It's a complete tapestry of patterns, images, and swirls in shades of gray, blue, and oxblood.

Beneath the tattoos, planes of lean, hard muscle. He's more ripped than a male dancer. I see the deep cuts of his abs, then his hip bones, then the waistband of his boxer shorts barely covering his cock.

My mouth waters. I have to swallow hard.

Earlier, I almost put that cock in my mouth.

I don't know how in the hell I got the courage to do it. I unbuttoned his pants, and it jumped out like a snake, twice as big as I expected. It was terrifying, and I had no idea what to do with it.

At the same time, I was fascinated by that smooth, bare skin. It looked like the softest skin on his whole body. When I held his cock in my hand, it felt like it had a life of its own, twitching and throbbing against my palm.

I expect him to wake up any second with me standing over him. He'll probably be furious.

Right now, his face is totally relaxed.

I've never seen it like that.

It makes me realize how beautiful Mikolaj is. His features are so sharply defined, they're almost godly. What would he look like if he were happy, if he actually smiled?

It would be too much. I don't think I could stand it.

I stare at his face for a long time.

I'm looking at the man he could have been. A man without anger or bitterness. A man without pain.

Now my heart is hurting, and I don't know why. Why should I have sympathy for the Beast?

But I do. Some bizarre connection has grown between us, without either of us wanting it.

I slip into his bed, expecting him to wake any second.

He'll wake up now that I'm lying next to him.

Now that I've rested my hand on his stomach.

Now that I'm sliding it into his shorts…

He sighs—a long, slow masculine sigh. It makes my thighs squeeze together.

I have his cock in my hand. It's warm, half-hard, getting harder by the moment.

Then I bend over and take it in my mouth.

I can smell his skin, warm and musky with sleep. And I can taste his cock, which has a flavor all its own—rich, salty, and compelling. It floods my mouth with saliva. My tongue slides easily over his smooth flesh, the head of his cock filling my mouth.

The harder he gets, the wider I have to open my jaw.

I have no clue how to give a blow job properly. I'm just trying things out as I go—sometimes licking, sometimes sucking, sometimes just sliding my lips and tongue around on it.

Really, I'm just doing whatever feels good to me. It seems to work well enough because his cock has gotten equally as hard as it was in the billiard room when I danced for him.

Mikolaj's hands thrust into my hair, holding my head on both sides.

I glance upward and see he's fully awake, looking down at me.

I thought he'd be angry or annoyed. Those are the only two options I was expecting. Instead, I see an expression I can hardly understand. It almost looks like gratitude.

He's holding my head, rolling his hips so his cock slides in and out of my mouth in a steady rhythm. I keep licking and sucking the best I can. His breath is coming quicker, and he's making little sounds, something like a sigh and a groan mixed together.

He starts thrusting harder, and his cock goes too deep, hitting the back of my throat. I gag.

"Sorry." He pants.

Mikolaj has never apologized for anything before. It sounds so odd that I almost laugh.

I keep my eyes open, enthralled by the sight of him. His body looks insanely sexy, his arms tensed, every muscle on his chest and stomach flexing.

He keeps pumping his cock in and out. My jaw is starting to hurt, but I don't want to stop. He's looking down at me, and I'm looking up at him. We're locked together in this thing that is intimate, intense, and impossible to stop.

He closes his eyes, tilting his head back on the pillow. His cock starts to pulse in my mouth. He lets out a long low cry. Then my mouth is flooded with warmth, slippery and salty but not unpleasant.

His cock is still pulsing, so I keep sucking, not wanting to stop too soon.

When it's finally done, he lets go of my head and grabs my arms instead, pulling me up on the bed so he can roll on top of me.

He kisses me, not caring if the taste of his come is still in my mouth.

This kiss is nothing like the one in the ballroom. Mikolaj is still warm and heavy with sleep. His lips are softer than snowfall.

"What are you doing, little ballerina?" he growls.

"I couldn't sleep."

"I know why."

Now he's the one sliding down the length of my body. He stops at my breasts, taking each one into his mouth in turn. He sucks on the nipple until it's fully hard, and then he gently rolls and squeezes it between his fingers while he sucks on the other.

He slips farther down, all the way between my thighs.

I have the impulse to push him away. I'm nervous that I may taste or smell bad. I wish I would have checked before I came in here.

But Mikolaj doesn't seem any more concerned with the state of my lady bits than he was with my mouth. He buries his face between my thighs, licking my pussy in long wet strokes.

Oh my god, I never imagined anything could feel that good.

I've touched myself before, plenty of times. But a tongue is so very different from fingers. It's warm and wet, and it seems to awaken nerve endings I never knew existed.

It sends a flood of moisture out of me, so much that I worry for a second that I've wet myself. Mikolaj is still licking and kissing me down there, totally unconcerned.

He moistens one of his fingers and slides it inside me. I gasp, thinking it's going to hurt. I don't usually put anything in there, not toys or my own fingers, because it's painfully tight.

Even though Mikolaj's finger is much larger than mine, it seems to fit perfectly inside me. Probably because I'm more aroused than I've ever been before.

Actually, it feels much better than tolerable. It feels incredible.

His finger gives me something to grip while his tongue laps steadily at my clit. It seems to increase the sensation, so I squeeze on his finger while grinding my clit against his tongue.

That familiar sensation starts to build—the start of a climax. But god, oh god, it feels so much better on his tongue than on my pillow. It feels like a warm bath and a massage and the sexiest dream imaginable, all rolled into one.

The pleasure builds and builds until I'm almost afraid.

The orgasm rushes through me, flooding like a waterfall.

I'm bucking my hips against his face, trying to smother my cries in the pillow. I'm embarrassed to be this loud, but I also can't give a damn because it just feels so good.

I shout and squirm. Then it's all over, and I'm lying there panting and sweating, thinking about how crazy this is.

Mikolaj has given me the most pleasurable moment of my life.

We're looking at each other across the pillow. I think he's as lost as I am. He doesn't know what to do.

He kisses me once more, softly on the lips.

Then he says, "Go back to your room, little ballerina. Don't let anyone see you."

Quietly, I slip out of the bed and run back the way I came, my body weak with pleasure and my head spinning 'round and 'round.

21
MIKO

The next morning, everything is as usual.

When I come down to the main floor, I hear Nessa practicing up in her studio with a new record playing on the turntable. She must have finished choreographing one dance and started the next.

The house looks the same as always. My face looked the same in the mirror, after I showered and dressed.

And yet I feel completely different.

For one thing, I'm actually hungry.

I go into the kitchen where Klara is clearing the remains of the breakfast she made for Nessa.

She looks startled to see me. Usually, I only drink coffee in the morning.

"Is there any bacon left?"

"Oh!" she says, bustling around with the fry pans. "Just two pieces—but give me a moment, I'll make more!"

"No need," I tell her. "I'll eat this."

I grab the bacon out of the pan before eating it where I stand, leaning against the island. It's crispy and salty and slightly burned. It tastes phenomenal.

"I can make more!" Klara says, flustered. "It will only take a minute. That's probably cold."

"It's perfect," I say, snatching the last sausage from the pan, too.

Klara looks alarmed, either from the fact I've come into the kitchen, which I never do, or the fact I'm in a cheerful mood, which also never happens.

"Is Nessa in her studio?" I say to Klara, already knowing the answer.

"Yes," she says cautiously.

"She likes to work. I hear her in there constantly."

"That's right."

Klara probably respects that. She has a highly developed work ethic herself, doing the job of at least three people with all the cooking and cleaning and errands she runs for us.

I pay her well. But she drives a twenty-year-old Kia and carries a canvas tote as a purse. She sends all her money back to Poland, to her parents and grandparents. Jonas shares those same grandparents. He doesn't send anything back, despite making a lot more than Klara.

"You've taken good care of our little prisoner."

Klara sets the pans to soak in the sink, running the water and not looking up at me. "Yes," she says quietly.

"You two have grown close."

She squirts dish soap onto the fry pans. Her hand trembles slightly, and some of the soap lands on the faucet. She wipes it off hastily with the sponge.

"She's a good girl," Klara says. "She has a kind heart." There's a note of reproach in her voice.

"Did you know she learned to speak Polish?"

Klara stiffens, and her eyes fly guiltily to my face. "I didn't mean to teach her anything!" She gulps. "She picked it up so quick—I thought she'd learn the word for spoon or cup, just as entertainment. The next thing I knew, she was saying sentences..."

Klara's explanation comes tumbling out, her cheeks flaming with anxiety. She doesn't have to convince me—I've seen for myself have clever Nessa is, how perceptive. She looks like an innocent little faun, but her mind is always working a thousand miles a minute.

"Please don't be angry with her," Klara adds. "It wasn't her fault."

I thought Klara was pleading for herself, not wanting to be punished. Now I realize it's Nessa she's worried about.

This is worse than I thought. They've become friends. Close friends.

I should fire Klara. Or, at the very least, keep her away from Nessa.

But who would I trust to guard her? Fucking nobody. Nessa could worm her way into the heart of a rabid badger.

So I stare silently at Klara until she stops speaking, biting her lip and wiping her wet hands convulsively on her apron.

"I'm concerned about where your loyalties lie."

She tugs on her apron with her chapped hands. "I would never betray the *Braterstwo*."

"Nessa Griffin is not a pet. She's an asset—a very valuable asset."

"I know," Klara whispers.

"If you had some idea of setting her free—"

"I would never!"

"Just remember that I know where your family lives in Boleslawiec. Your mother, your uncle, your little nieces, your grand-parents... They aren't safe just because they're connected to Jonas, too. Jonas would put a bullet in your mother's skull if I told him to."

"I know," Klara breathes. "I know he would."

"Just remember that. You're raising a lamb for the slaughter. However sweet that lamb may be."

Klara nods, her eyes cast down to the floor.

I pour myself a cup of coffee and leave the kitchen.

It was a good speech I gave her. I wonder if it was actually for Klara or if I was trying to convince myself.

I keep thinking about last night. It felt like a dream. Yet it was realer than my usual daily life. I keep thinking of the taste of Nessa's pussy in my mouth, the feel of her skin against mine. I could go upstairs this minute and take it again...

No. Not happening. I've got to prepare for my meeting with Kristoff tonight.

I spend the bulk of the day with my men, planning our final assault on the Griffins. By this point, we have a clear picture of Callum and Aida's schedule. The alderman and his wife will be going to the opening of a new library in Englewood in six days' time. It's the perfect opportunity to take them both.

We'll execute Tymon's idea again, this time with proper planning. We'll leverage Aida against her husband, draining his remaining accounts at Hyde Park Bank and Madison Capital.

Meanwhile, we'll make a deal with the Gallos. They can sign over the Oak Street Tower in exchange for the safe return of Aida and the evidence against Dante Gallo disappearing. I'll let Dante walk free. Then, the second his feet touch the pavement, I'll shoot him in the fucking face.

That's the plan as it stands. I'll present it to Kristoff tonight.

I'd rather not bring Nessa along with me, but Kristoff was insistent.

While Klara gets Nessa ready, I dress myself, pulling on a thin gray cashmere sweater, slacks, and loafers.

I don't wear suits like most gangsters. They think it makes them look like businessmen. I think it's a fucking farce. Suit jackets are good for concealing a gun but otherwise are bulky and constricting. I'm not a businessman—I'm a predator. And I'm not going to shackle myself for fashion. I don't ever want to catch a bullet because I couldn't get out of the way in time.

It doesn't take me long to get ready. I wait at the bottom of the stairs, looking up to the east wing.

At last, Nessa appears at the top, posed against the window like a painting in a frame.

She's wearing a white chiffon gown with weightless layers that float around her like wings. Her hair is piled up on her head, with teardrop diamonds hanging from her ears. Her slender arms and shoulders are bare, glowing in the evening light.

As she descends the staircase, I'm rooted to the spot, staring up at her. Instead of walking down the stairs, I see her walking down an aisle toward me. Instead of an evening gown, I see her in a white wedding dress. I see what Nessa would look like if she were my bride.

It's like a vision. Time slows, sound fades, and all I can see is this girl—a little shy, a little nervous, but radiating a joy that can never be snuffed out of her. Because it doesn't come from circumstance or situation. It comes from the goodness inside her.

Nessa reaches the bottom of the stairs.

I blink, and the vision is gone.

She's not my bride; she's my prisoner. I'm taking her to a negotiating table where Kristoff and I will decide how to divide the carcass of her family's empire.

She glances up at me, warm and expectant, likely thinking I'll tell her how beautiful she looks.

Instead, I keep my expression stern. "Let's go. We're going to be late."

I turn away, trying to ignore the hurt on her face.

She follows me out to the car.

Nessa pauses as she steps out on the front steps. The sun is going down. It sends sheets of color across the blank canvas of her dress. Her skin glows gold, her eyes brighter than ever.

I get into the car, trying not to look at her.

Jonas takes her hand so she can gather her skirt and climb in without dirtying the dress. I'm irritated that he's touching her. I'm irritated that she's allowing it.

Once Nessa and I are seated in the back, with Jonas and Marcel in the front, we head out. The car speeds down the winding drive, then out through the gates. Nessa sits up a little taller, her forehead pressed against the window so she can look out.

It's been a long time since she was in a car. A long time since she saw anything besides the house and grounds. I can see her excitement at the streets and buildings, the people on the sidewalks, the vendors on the corners.

The windows are heavily tinted. Nobody can see in. Still, I feel anxious taking her out of the house. It's like releasing a songbird from its cage—if anything goes wrong, she'll fly away.

We drive a short way south to Lincoln Park, where Kolya Kristoff has his house. It's a sprawling compound, newly built and wildly modern. The main house looks like a lot of glass boxes stacked on one another. It seems like a terrible setup from a security standpoint. But Kristoff is flamboyant like that. He likes to show off, from his Maserati to his Zegna suits.

The interior is just as impractical. There's an artificial river running through the entryway floor, beneath a chandelier made of rotating orbs like a solar system.

When Kristoff comes to greet us, he's wearing a velvet smoking jacket and tasseled loafers. I want to cancel the alliance right now, just based off the fact I don't want to do business with someone who thinks he's Hugh Hefner reincarnated.

I'm edgy and irritable, and we haven't even started.

It doesn't help that the first thing Kristoff does is walk around Nessa like she's a sculpture on a plinth, his eyes roaming over every inch of her.

"My god, what a specimen," he says. "What have you been doing to her, Mikolaj? You kidnapped a girl and turned her into a goddess."

Nessa's eyes dart between us, her cheeks tinged with that hint of pink I know so well. She doesn't like this kind of attention, and she's looking to me for protection.

"She's the same as she always was," I snap.

I wish Klara hadn't dolled her up so much. I told her to make Nessa presentable, not to turn her into Princess Grace.

"I thought we Russians had the most beautiful women." Kristoff grins. "I guess I haven't sampled enough variety…"

Nessa is edging closer to me, away from Kristoff.

"Do the Irish train them, though?" Kristoff says, raising his dark eyebrows. "Russian girls learn to suck cock better than a porn star. They can blow you in the time it takes a kettle to boil. What do you say, Mikolaj…how does she compare?"

If Kristoff keeps talking, I'm going to rip his vocal cords out of his throat and strangle him with them.

Nessa looks close to tears. My stomach is clenched to the size of a walnut.

There's no good answer here. If I tell Kristoff I haven't fucked her, he won't believe me. If he knew the truth, it would be even worse. Nothing could be more dangerous to Nessa than the *Bratva* boss knowing he has the beautiful virginal daughter of his rival in his house.

"She wouldn't interest you," I say shortly. "No skills at all."

Nessa turns those big green eyes on me, stricken and hurt. I can't look at her. I can't even give her the smallest sign of sympathy.

I bark, "Let's get to it already. I haven't got all night."

"Of course." Kristoff grins.

He leads us into his formal dining room, where the table is piled with food. Kristoff sits on one side of the table, along with three of his top lieutenants. I sit on the other, with Nessa right beside me and Jonas and Marcel on either end.

Nessa is pale and silent, unwilling to touch her food.

"What's wrong?" Kristoff says. "You don't like pelmeni?"

"You know dancers," I tell him. "They don't eat."

Nessa reminds me of Persephone, kidnapped by Hades and forced to reign as queen of the dead. Persephone tried so hard not to eat Hades's food so that one day she could return to the sunlit realms.

But Nessa has already eaten my food. Just like Persephone, who grew so hungry that she lost her resolve, consuming six tiny pomegranate seeds.

Kristoff looks offended. Russians are sensitive about their

dishes. Luckily, Jonas and Marcel are shoveling enough food into their mouths to make up for it.

"*Davayte pristupim k delu*," I say. *Let's get down to business.*

Kristoff is surprised I'm speaking Russian. I know it perfectly well, but I usually refuse to speak it to him. English is our lingua franca. However, I don't want Nessa to have to sit through a lengthy discussion of how we're going to destroy her family. It's bad enough that she's got me on one side and Jonas on the other, with Kristoff leering at her from across the table. The least I can do is keep her ignorant of the coming events.

She's too smart to be ignorant, however. As we go over our plans, with some argument and plenty of debate, she catches the subject without understanding the details. Her expression grows more and more miserable, her shoulders slumped.

Finally, Kristoff and I reach an agreement. We'll attack Callum Griffin at the library opening and take Aida at the same time. It's a small event. His security will be sparse.

With that decided, Kristoff leans back in his chair, sipping his wine. "And what do you intend to do with her?" he says, jerking his head toward Nessa.

"She stays with me for the present."

Nessa casts a quick glance in my direction. She knows we're talking about her.

"You ought to put a baby in her belly," Kristoff says. "They killed your father. She can give you a son."

I can't say I haven't thought about it.

The Griffins and the Gallos made their alliance by marriage. I could do the same.

But I'm not looking for an alliance. I never have been. I'm looking for total and complete domination. I don't want to share the city; I want to own it. I don't want recompense—I want revenge.

"To victory," Kristoff says, raising his glass one last time.

"*Nostrovia*," I say, clinking my glass against his.

When we're ready to leave, Kristoff walks us back to the entry-way. He shakes my hand slowly to seal our agreement.

Then he spies the monitor on Nessa's ankle.

"You should put a collar around her neck," he says. "I'd love to have a little kitten crawling around after me…"

He reaches out to touch Nessa's face.

Before I can think, I've caught his hand, locking my fingers around his wrist.

Kristoff's men jump to attention, two flanking me and one with his hand on his gun. Jonas and Marcel likewise tense, eyeing the Russian soldiers and readying themselves for a fight. The air is thick with anticipation; it's so silent that you can hear the artificial river running through the middle of the floor.

"Don't," I say.

"Be careful," Kristoff says softly. "Remember who's your friend in this room and who's your enemy."

"Remember what belongs to me if you want to remain friends." I let go of his wrist.

He steps back and his soldiers relax. Jonas and Marcel do the same—externally, at least. I'm sure their hearts are still racing as rapidly as mine.

"Thank you for dinner," I say stiffly.

"The first of many, I hope," Kristoff replies.

His eyes are cold. He looks at Nessa—not with lust this time but with resentment. "*Spokoynoy nochi malen'kaya, shlyukha*," he says. *Good night, little whore.*

I almost hit him in the mouth. My fist is clenched, my arm flexed to do it. I stop myself just in time.

If I attack Kristoff in his house, I doubt a single one of us will make it out alive. And that includes Nessa.

She doesn't understand the insult, but she knows the tone. She turns away from Kristoff without giving him the satisfaction of a response.

As we drive away from his house, Nessa stares out the window.

She's lost all the excitement from earlier in the night. She no longer seems to register the last of the falling leaves or the city lights. She looks tired. And defeated.

"I won't let him touch you," I promise her.

She glances at me for a moment, then sighs and stares out the window again without answering.

She's right to ignore me. She knows the *Bratva* and the *Braterstwo* have much worse plans for her family than anything Kristoff might do to her personally.

As we drive up Halsted Street, I say to Jonas, impulsively, "Turn here."

"Right here?"

"Yes."

He jerks the wheel hard to the left, and we turn in the opposite direction of my house, heading south instead. We drive down to the waterfront, with Jonas following my terse commands.

"Pull up here," I tell him. "Wait in the car."

Jonas parks in front of the Yard. I go inside for a minute before returning shortly for Nessa.

"What are we doing?" she says, bewildered.

"I want you to see something. But you have to promise not to make a scene or try to run away."

I'm pretty sure her ankle monitor is broken. If she gives me the slip, I'm fucked. But if she makes me a promise, I think she'll keep it.

"I… All right," she says.

"You promise me?"

She looks up at me with those clear green eyes, without a hint of a lie in them. "I promise, Mikolaj."

I lead her up the steps to the lobby. I've already bribed the usher. He sneaks us up a back staircase, all the way to the top box, usually reserved for major donors to the theater.

As soon as Nessa sees the performers on the stage, brightly lit directly below us, she gasps and claps her hands over her mouth.

"It's my show!"

This is the last night the Lake City Ballet will be perform- ing *Bliss*. We've missed half the show, but Nessa doesn't seem to care. Her eyes are glued to the stage, darting back and forth to follow each of the dancers in turn. She doesn't sit in the comfort- able recliners arranged in front of the glass—instead, she stands right against the window, trying to get as close as she can to see every detail.

"My friend Marnie made that set," she tells me. "She hand painted every one of those sunflowers. It took her weeks and weeks. She came in at night and listened to all the Jack Reacher books while she did it. Isabel sewed that dress. It's made from a curtain from the last show we did. And those two dancers there, they're brothers. I went to school with the younger one…"

She tells me everything, so excited that she forgets the discom- fort and humiliation she endured tonight. As the music pours through the speakers, I can see her keeping time with her fingertips against the glass. I can see how much she'd love to dance around the room, but she can't tear her eyes away from the stage.

As the next song begins, she claps her hands and says, "Oh, this is my favorite! I did this one!"

Four dancers cross the stage, dressed as butterflies: a monarch, a morpho, a swallowtail, and a papilio rumanzovia. They swirl around in formation, then break apart, then come back together again. Sometimes they're synchronized; sometimes they create intricate cascading patterns. It's a complicated dance, light and joyful. I don't know what any of the moves are called. I only know that what I'm watching is lovely.

"You choreographed all this?"

I already know she did. I see her fingerprints on it, like the bits and pieces of her work I've seen at my house.

"Yes!" Nessa says happily. "Look how well it turned out!"

I only intended to stay a short while, but I can't drag Nessa away.

We watch all the way to the end, Nessa's face and hands pressed against the glass.

When the show finishes, the audience cheers, and an athletic man with graying hair bounds up on the stage to take his bows.

"Is that the director?" I ask Nessa casually.

"Yes," she says. "That's Jackson."

"Let's get going," I tell her. "Before everyone comes out."

I can't risk anybody spotting Nessa as the crowd exits.

On the drive home, we're quiet—Nessa because she's swimming in the happiness of seeing her show live, seeing what she imagined brought to life on the stage. Me because I'm realizing more and more how brilliant this girl is. She channeled a portion of her own spirit, her own bliss, and she brought it to life for everyone else to see. She made me feel it. Me, who never feels happiness, let alone pure joy.

When we pull up to the house, Nessa gets out and waits for me, thinking we'll go inside together.

Instead, I tell Jonas to wait. Then I say to Marcel, "Take her up to her room. Make sure she has everything she needs."

"Where are you going?" Nessa asks me, her eyebrows drawn together in concern.

"A quick errand."

She gets up on tiptoe and kisses me softly on the cheek. "Thank you, Miko," she says. "Seeing that show was the best gift you could give me."

I feel Marcel's eyes on me—and Jonas's, too.

I nod stiffly. "Good night, Nessa."

Then I get back in the car.

"Where to?" Jonas asks.

"Back to the Yard."

We cruise through the silent streets. I'm sitting in the passenger seat now, right next to Jonas. I can see the tension in his shoulders, in his hands gripping the wheel.

"We're taking her on field trips now?" he says.

"I'll take her to fucking Mars if I feel like it."

Jonas is silent for a moment. Then he says, "Miko, you're my brother. Not just in the *Braterstwo* but in all things. You saved my life in Warsaw. I told you I'd never forget it, and I haven't. We've done a hundred jobs together. Came to this country together. Built an empire together. Promise me you won't destroy it all because you've had your head turned by a pretty girl."

My first impulse is to bite his head off for daring to question me. But I hear the sincerity in his words. Jonas truly has been a brother to me. We've suffered, learned, and triumphed by each other's sides. It's a bond only soldiers know.

"It's a heavy weight, taking Zajac's place," I tell him. "We owe a debt to our father. I don't want to sacrifice my brothers to pay it."

"I'm not afraid of the Italians or the Irish," Jonas says. "We're stronger than both. Especially with the Russians on our side."

"Words are not results," I say. It's something Zajac always told us.

"You don't believe in your own family anymore?" Jonas's voice is low and angry.

"I want to choose the battle I can win."

I could marry Nessa Griffin. She could bear my child. And I could take a piece of the empire without stepping over the bodies of everyone she loves. Without sacrificing the lives of my brothers. Because no matter what Jonas says, if we continue our assault on the Griffins and the Gallos, we won't win the war without casualties. Assuming we win at all.

We've reached the theater once more. I tell Jonas to stop out front. We watch the straggling train of dancers and theater employees who come through the doors as the show wraps up. Then, finally, Jackson Wright emerges, flanked by a plump curly-haired woman and a tall scrawny man.

They walk down the street together, laughing and talking over the success of the evening before turning left into the Whiskey Pub.

"Wait here," I tell Jonas.

I follow Jackson into the pub. I take a seat at a high top and watch him order a Guinness. He sits and chats with his friends for ten, twenty minutes. I already dislike him, even from a distance of twenty feet. I see his pompous expression, the way he dominates the conversation, talking over the plump lady whenever she tries to speak.

Eventually, the Guinness works its magic. Jackson heads toward the bathroom at the back of the bar.

It's a single stall. Perfect for my purposes.

As Jackson enters, before he can close the door behind him, I push my way inside.

"Hey!" he says in an irritated tone. "It's occupied, *obviously*."

I shut the door then dead bolt it from the inside.

Jackson looks at me through his horn-rimmed glasses, his eyebrows raised.

"I appreciate the enthusiasm, but not my gender and not my type, I'm afraid."

I cross the tiny room in one step, closing my hand around his throat. I lift him and slam his head against the tile wall.

Jackson lets out a terrified squeak, scrabbling at the hand choking him. His glasses have come askew. His feet kick helplessly in the air.

"I watched your show tonight," I say casually.

"*Can't…breathe…*" he rasps, his face turning a deep burgundy.

"It's funny…I recognized some of the choreography. Do you know Nessa Griffin? I saw her work in your show. But I didn't see her credited anywhere."

I lower him slightly, just enough that he can support his own weight on tiptoe but not enough for him to be comfortable. I relax my grip so he can speak.

"Wh-what are you talking about?" he sputters. "I don't know any—"

"Wrong answer," I say, hoisting him up again.

His fingernails claw at my hands and forearms. I could not give a shit about that. I keep choking him until he starts to pass out, and then I lower him again.

"Wakey, wakey." I slap the side of his face.

"Ow! Let go of me!" Jackson shrieks, coming to again.

"Let's try this again. You remember Nessa Griffin?"

A sullen silence. Then a resentful "yes."

"You remember how you stole her work and passed it off as your own?"

"I didn't—" Another slam of his head against the wall, and Jackson shrieks, "All right, all right! She did some work on the show."

"For which you failed to credit her."

He screws up his face like I'm forcing him to eat moldy porridge. Then he says, "Yes."

"I'm glad we agree."

I let him down. Before he can so much as blink, I grab his left arm and twist it behind his back. I already know from watching him drink his beer that he's a lefty. I wrench it all the way back until he's shrieking and sweating again.

"Stop! Stop!" he cries. "What do you expect me to do? The show's already over!"

"You make it up to her."

"How?"

"I'll leave that to you to figure out."

"But…but…"

"What?"

"Nessa's gone! People say she's dead."

"Nessa is alive and well. Don't worry about her—worry about yourself. Worry about what I'll do to you if I'm displeased with your solution."

"Fine! Whatever you want! Just let go of me." Jackson pants.

"I will. But first, there's a price to pay."

With one swift twist, I send a spiral fracture down his radius, clamping a hand over his mouth to stifle the scream. It's gross because snot and tears and saliva are getting all over my hand. Such is business.

I let go of Jackson. He slumps on the floor, moaning and sniveling.

"We'll talk soon," I tell him.

He cringes.

As I'm heading for the door, he croaks, "Do you work for her father?"

"No," I say. "Just a patron of the arts."

I leave him crying in the bathroom.

When I get back to the car, I grab Wet Wipes from the glove box to clean the mess off my hands. It looks like a tomcat attacked my arms.

"Everything go all right?" Jonas asks.

"Of course. He weighs less than your last girlfriend."

Jonas snorts. "I never had a girl I'd call a friend."

No, he hasn't. While the bond with my brothers is strong, they're not exactly what I'd call "good people." Especially Jonas.

But then, I'm not a good person either.

22
NESSA

MARCEL BRINGS ME INSIDE THE HOUSE, ALL THE WAY UP TO MY room as ordered. Klara was just turning down the sheets like they do in a fancy hotel. She doesn't leave a chocolate on the pillow, but I'm sure she would if I asked her to.

She straightens as I enter the room. Marcel is right behind me. When Klara sees him, she takes one quick breath, and I see her brush down the hem of her apron, trying to smooth away any wrinkles.

"Hello, Klara," Marcel says.

"Hello," she replies, looking at the ground.

You'd think they'd never met before. When I know for a fact they've worked here together for years.

"I'll help you get ready for bed," Klara says to me.

"Actually, would you mind making me tea, Klara? An herbal one? If you don't mind—I just need to wind down a little."

"Of course," Klara says.

She leaves the room. Marcel says, "Night," and hurries after her.

I don't actually need tea. I just wanted to give them time to talk if they wanted to. Mikolaj and Jonas are gone, so there's no one to catch them. No one except me.

I know this is awful, and I should stay put exactly where I am. But the curiosity is killing me. I have to know what's going on between those two. I've been making up all kinds of soap opera scenarios in my head.

I creep down the stairs, quiet as a mouse. Turns out I'm much more of a snoop than I realized. Or at least I become one after loneliness and boredom have preyed on me for a month. I never used to lie or eavesdrop. Dear god, my captors must be rubbing off on me.

Well, if they've been a bad influence, then they'll pay the price for it.

I stand just outside the kitchen, my back against the ancient green wallpaper, my ear almost at the edge of the wooden doorframe.

"It's only dinner, Klara," Marcel says in Polish. Marcel has a nice voice. He doesn't talk much, so I haven't heard it very often. It has a pleasant, soothing tone. Which he's trying to use to its greatest effect.

"I can make my own dinner," Klara says coolly.

I hear her filling the kettle and getting the cups out. It doesn't take long for her to make tea—Marcel better hurry up.

"When's the last time you ate a dinner you didn't have to make yourself?" Marcel says.

"Less time than it's been since you cooked anything. I doubt you even know how to use a toaster."

"Why don't you teach me?" Marcel says.

I can't resist peeking around the corner. Klara is setting the kettle on its stand. Marcel has come up behind her so close that they're almost touching down the length of their bodies, only an inch between them. They make a beautiful couple. A matching set—both tall, slim, and black-haired.

Marcel tries to put his hands on Klara's hips. She whips around. I have to duck back around the corner, so I don't see the slap, but I certainly hear it.

"Remember that I don't work at one of your clubs!" Klara shouts. "I won't be one of those girls who sucks your cock for coke and purses until you're tired of me."

"When have you ever seen me do that?" Marcel shouts back at her. "All I've done is ask for a chance, every day, for three fucking years."

"Not quite three," Klara replies.

"What?" Marcel says, bewildered.

"Two years and eleven months. Not three years yet."

"You're going to drive me insane, woman." Marcel's rapid footsteps sound like pacing. "I think you just like to torture me."

"I've got to take this up," Klara says.

I can hear her gathering the tea tray. I sprint back up the stairs before she can catch me.

I leap onto the bed and pull the covers over me, looking around wildly for a book.

When Klara comes in a moment later, she sets the tray next to the bed, then looks at me suspiciously.

"What are you doing?" she says in Polish.

"Nothing. Just waiting."

"Why are you breathing so hard?"

"Am I? Guess I was excited. About the tea coming."

Her eyebrows have disappeared under her bangs. She does not believe one word of this.

"Oh, thanks. Great tea!" I say hastily, gulping too much and burning my tongue.

Klara rolls her eyes and heads toward the door, taking the tray with her.

I drink all the tea, but I don't go to sleep.

I'm way too amped from the night I had. It started out promising since I actually got to leave the grounds for the first time in forever. But then I realized Mikolaj was taking me to meet some awful Russian gangster. I thought Jonas was bad, but this guy really made my skin crawl. Though I could understand barely anything they said during dinner, the callousness in his voice made it obvious exactly what kind of man he is.

Then he tried to touch me as we left—nothing gratuitous, not trying to grope me or anything. Mikolaj grabbed his arm like he was going to rip it right out of the socket. Instantly, we were in some kind of Mexican standoff, and I was pretty certain those were the last seconds of my life.

When we left, Mikolaj was like an ungrounded wire in the car, thrumming with electricity, fully capable of shocking me to death if I dared touch him.

Out of nowhere he directed us over to the Yard. I didn't even think about *Bliss* being there. I had almost forgotten the show even existed, living in the strange fantasy world of Mikolaj's mansion. But the moment I saw Marnie and Serena on the stage, I knew exactly where we were.

My god, seeing something I created brought to life…it was completely unlike performing in the ballet. More like watching my own dream, full and vibrant and real. I couldn't breathe.

I'd seen plenty of the rehearsals, but this was different, in full makeup and costume, with lighting and stage sets. I could have cried, I was so happy.

I should have been sitting right up front in the audience with my family around me. That's what would have happened opening night, if Mikolaj hadn't kidnapped me.

For a moment I was hit with a stab of anger. I remembered all the things I've lost out on these past weeks—my dancing, my father's birthday, my semester of school.

I looked at Mikolaj, so furious that I might have shouted something at him. But he wasn't looking at me at all—he was staring through the glass, watching the ballet. He had that look on his face, similar to when he was sleeping. The harshness and anger washed away. Calmness in its place.

And I remembered I hadn't actually missed out on dancing at his house. Actually, I'd been doing it more than ever. While creating something totally unlike anything I've done before. Not the product of the old Nessa but of the new Nessa, a girl in progress, one growing and changing by the moment in ways I never would have if I'd stayed at home.

My anger washed away. We finished watching the show and drove home. I thought Mikolaj might come upstairs with me. Instead, he rushed away somewhere else.

Now I'm lying here, unable to sleep until I hear his car in the drive. Because wherever gangsters go, it's never safe. There's always a chance this is the night they won't come home.

An hour passes. Maybe more. Finally, I hear the tires rolling over the loose stones in the driveway.

I jump out of my bed, shoving aside the dusty canopy curtains.

I run down the stairs, my legs bare beneath the hem of my nightgown. Klara stocked the wardrobe and drawers with so many beautiful pieces of clothing. The nighties are the one thing that makes me laugh. They're old-fashioned, like something a little girl from the Victorian era would wear. I'm a corporeal ghost running around this place.

When I'm halfway down the stairs, Mikolaj hears me. He turns around. I see long scratches running up his arms and across the back of his hands.

"What happened!" I gasp.

"It's nothing."

"Where did you go?" About to touch his arm to examine the injuries, I freeze in my tracks. The people most likely to have injured Mikolaj are members of my own family. Which means he might have done something awful to them in return.

My mouth hangs open, horrified.

Mikolaj sees it. He says, "No! I didn't… It's not…"

"Did you hurt someone I know?" I say, through numb lips.

"Well…I…"

I've never seen Mikolaj stutter before. My stomach rolls over. I think I'm going to be sick. I turn away from him, but Mikolaj grabs my shoulders, pulling me back.

"Wait," he says. "Let me explain."

He pulls me out of the entryway, over to the conservatory.

He leads me through the thick greenery. It's almost winter outside, but it's still warm and humid in here, the air rich with oxygen and chlorophyll. He pulls me down on the same little bench where he waited when I first woke up in his house.

He says, "I didn't kill anybody. I did hurt someone, but he fucking deserved it."

"Who?" I demand.

"That director."

I stare at him blankly for a second. This is so far outside what I expected him to say that I don't connect the dots.

"He's fine," Mikolaj says. "I just broke his arm."

A loose interpretation of the term *fine*, but much better than I feared.

"You broke Jackson Wright's arm," I say blankly.

"Yeah."

"Why?"

"Because he's a thieving shit."

I'm dumbfounded.

Mikolaj broke Jackson's arm…for me. It's the strangest favor anybody's ever done for me.

"I don't want you to hurt people on my behalf."

"People like that don't learn without consequences," Mikolaj says.

I'm not sure a jerk like Jackson is going to learn either way. But I don't care about him, not really. There's a different kind of dread swirling around inside me.

I've been completely cut off in Mikolaj's house. No contact with anyone I know and love. I've assumed nothing awful has happened while I've been gone. But I don't actually know if that's true.

"What is it?" Mikolaj says.

His light-blue eyes are fixed on my face, steady and clear.

It occurs to me that in all the time I've been here, Mikolaj has never lied to me. Not that I know of anyway. He's been harsh and aggressive at times. Hateful, even. But always honest.

"Miko," I say. "Is my family okay? Have you hurt any of them?"

I can see the thoughts running through his head as he decides whether to answer. His jaw flexes as he swallows. Then he says, "Yes. Jack Du Pont is dead."

My stomach clenches in a knot. Jack Du Pont is one of my brother's closest associates. They went to school together. He's worked at our house for years. He was my driver and bodyguard, and also a friend.

"Oh," I say.

I feel the tears sliding down my cheeks.

Mikolaj doesn't apologize or look away. His gaze is steady. "I've caused you pain."

"Is everyone else okay?" I ask him.

"Dante Gallo is in prison," he says. "Otherwise, yes."

I cover my face with my hands. My face is hot, my hands cool by comparison. Aida loves Dante the way I love Callum. She must be freaking out right now.

My whole family will be. Because I'm still missing. And Jack is dead. And they know more is coming.

I raise my face out of my hands, and I try to meet Mikolaj's gaze with an equal level of composure. "What's going to happen?"

When we first spoke in this room, he told me he was going to destroy everything I hold dear. I have to know if that's still his plan. If nothing has changed between us.

"Well," Mikolaj says, "that depends."

"On what?"

"On you, Nessa."

He runs his hand through his ash-blond hair, smoothing it back from his face. It falls again immediately. It's Mikolaj's only tell when he's nervous—otherwise you'd never know.

"Do you like this house?" he asks me.

What a bizarre question.

"Of course," I say hesitantly. "It's beautiful. In a spooky sort of way."

"What if you stayed here?" His ice-blue eyes cut into mine. "With me."

There's almost too much oxygen in this space. I feel a little dizzy, like I've taken a whiff of nitrous oxide.

Softly, I say, "I don't really have a choice about that, do I?"

"What if you did?" Mikolaj says. "Could you be happy here?"

"With you?" I repeat.

"Yes."

"You're talking about a marriage pact."

"Yes," he says. "If your family agrees."

The room spins around me. This is both the most terrifying thing I can imagine and the only thing that could give me hope.

This is nothing I ever pictured for myself. I'm familiar with the concept of Mafia marriages, obviously—my brother just married Aida under similar circumstances. But that seems so different.

My brother is a gangster. He's a politician and a businessman, too, but he was raised to this life. I wasn't. Not even a little bit.

I'm not like Callum and Aida. I'm not tough and resourceful. I'm not brave. I'm afraid of getting hurt. Physically and in a deeper, more lasting way.

I'm only now realizing how dangerous Mikolaj is for me. In the time I've been living in his house, he's dug his way under my skin, burrowed into my brain. I dream about him at night. I think about him all day while I'm composing my ballet. As my captor, he's taken me over completely.

How much worse would that be if he were my husband?

I always thought I'd fall in love in the normal way. With flirtation and romance and kindness and gentleness.

Instead, I've fallen into something so much darker.

Every time Mikolaj speaks to me, every time he even looks at me, he's throwing a tiny thread of spider silk around me. Each one is so thin and light, I don't notice them. Every dance, every kiss, every look my way…I had no idea how entangled I was becoming.

What frightens me is how much further this could go.

Everything that's happened so far between us has been by accident. What if I were to sink into this intentionally? How deep is this well? I feel like I could fall into it forever. So far that I'd never see the sun again.

I'm not looking at him because I can't. His gaze is so piercing, I feel like he'll be able to read every thought in my head.

Mikolaj takes my face in his hands and turns it toward him, forcing me to meet his eyes.

The first time I saw his face, I thought it was sharp and cruel. Now I think it's nothing short of devastating. It devastates my notions of what I thought was handsome before. I liked the clean-cut, boyish look. I liked sweet and conventional.

There's never been a man who looked quite like Mikolaj. He's the culmination of masculine and feminine beauty, all in one. His high cheekbones, sea-glass eyes, and white-blond hair combined with his razor-sharp jaw, thinly carved lips, and ruthless stare.

He's vicious and tender. His tattoos are a suit of armor he can never take off, with a few pale spots of vulnerability—his face and hands, the only bits of him that show what he was before.

I know he's just as multifaceted on the inside. He's a leader, a planner, a killer. But also someone who loves music and art. Someone loyal. Who has cared for people before—his sister, his adoptive father, his brothers…

And maybe, maybe…for me, too.

Mikolaj has embarrassed and frightened me. Taunted and tormented me. But I'm very aware of the lines he didn't cross.

I don't think he wanted this connection between us any more than I did. It happened all the same.

It's real. I don't think I could sever it if I wanted to.

What if he sent me home now?

It's what I wanted all this time.

I picture myself back in my bright modern house on the lake. Hugged and kissed and protected by my parents. Safe and secure.

I think of my room at home. Even in my mind, it looks childish now—ruffled bedspread. Fuzzy pillows. Pink curtains. My old teddy bear.

I cringe picturing it. Would I feel at home there now? Or would I lie in that ruffled narrow bed and think about the smell of stone and oil paint, dust and citrus, and the masculine scent of Mikolaj himself…

I know the truth already.

I'd miss this dark old house and the even darker man inside. I'd feel drawn back here like one of Dracula's victims, bitten and infected and compelled to come home.

Is it good to feel ensnared by a man? Probably not. This is likely sick and wrong on a hundred levels.

But it's powerful and real all the same. I can't fight it. I don't know if I even want to.

All this time he's been staring into my eyes, unblinking, infinitely patient. Waiting for me to make my choice.

There's no choice to make.

It already happened without me knowing it.

He captured me, and there's no letting go.

I close my eyes, bringing my lips to his. I kiss him, gently at first. Then I taste his lips and his tongue, I breathe in his scent, and it's gasoline on an open flame. I'm the wood; he's the accelerant. No matter how much we burn, we're never used up.

I'm straddling his lap, my hands holding his face, his hands holding mine. We're kissing each other deeply, hungrily, like we could never be satisfied.

Then he's picking me up and carrying me out of the conservatory, across the main floor, and up the stairs to the west wing.

He carries me into his room like a bride across the threshold. Our lips are locked together all the time. Every breath I take comes out of his lungs.

He throws me down on the bed, and I'm terrified looking up at his wolfish face and gleaming eyes.

I want this. Just as badly as he does.

23
MIKO

I THROW NESSA DOWN ON THE BED, TELLING MYSELF TO GO SLOW, to be gentle with her.

But it's been weeks of waiting, weeks of longing. I've held myself back a thousand times. I can't do it anymore.

She's wearing one of those old-fashioned nightgowns—cream-colored lace, with a hundred tiny buttons down the front. I fumble with one button, then grab the fabric in both hands and tear it open, ripping the nightie from neck to waist, baring Nessa's delicate little breasts.

The lace is soft. Her breasts are a thousand times softer. I run my tongue up the curve of her chest, closing my mouth around her nipple. Her breasts are small enough that I can suck on much more than just the nipple—my mouth is full of her warm flesh. I suck hard, kneading her other breast with my hand.

Nessa gasps. Her soft startled cries are incredibly erotic. She's like an animal caught in a snare. The more she calls out, the more it ignites my hunger.

I run my tongue over her breasts and throat. I lick her lips and delve my tongue deeply into her mouth.

I slide down the length of her body, down to the place I've been dreaming about day and night. I put my face between her thighs and inhale her scent. Her pussy is sweet like honey, flavorful like the ripest berry. Every woman's scent is different. If Nessa's could be bottled, it would be the cure to limp dick in the world. There's not a straight man on the planet who could catch a whiff of it without his cock raging back to life.

Her scent is intoxicating, unforgettable, addictive. From the moment I put my tongue between her legs, I wanted more of it.

I eat her pussy like a wild animal. I lick and nibble and thrust my tongue inside her. Then I slide my fingers in, too, to see if she's really as tight as I remember.

God, even tighter. I tell myself again, *Be careful. Don't hurt her.*

I can hardly control my breathing. My heart is racing faster and faster. My pupils dilate, my skin burning. My cock begs to buried in that warm, velvety cunt.

I used to feel about sex like I felt about sleeping—necessary but a waste of time.

Now I want to fuck Nessa like it's my destiny. Like it is the one and only thing I was created to do.

I use my fingers and tongue to get her as ready as possible. I wait until she's soaking wet, until I can slide my index finger in and out of her with ease. I'm massaging her clit with my tongue, bringing her well on her way to climax.

Then I grab my cock. I rub it around in her wetness, lubricating the head. Even that exterior contact, the head of my cock sliding between her pussy lips, feels achingly good. My nerves are thrumming. I could explode right now, just from the sight of her slim little body, her pink pussy lips.

"Are you ready?" I say to Nessa, pausing at her entrance.

She looks up at me with those wide green eyes, those expressive brows that seem to have a mind of their own. For once they're still—her whole face is calm and expectant.

"Yes," she breathes.

I slide inside her in one long, slow motion.

Nessa gives a little gasp. I pause, my cock buried deep in her.

I look down into her face. We're as physically connected as two people can be. I'm fully within her, and she's wrapped tight around me, her arms around my neck, her thighs squeezing my hips. We're sharing the same breath; I'm breathing in her scent, and she's sunk in my bed, in the hollow where I sleep every night.

I look in her eyes. This girl is not the same one I stole from her home. A metamorphosis has taken place. What Nessa is now, I can't be certain. She's still changing, not fully formed.

What I see is beautiful. Some things are the same—her kindness, her creativity. She was a running stream, sparkling in the sunshine. But her water runs deeper by the day. She's becoming a lake and then an ocean.

I see her and she sees me.

I was death and she was life.

I thought I'd stolen her, brought her down to the underworld.

All the while she was waking me. Stirring the blood in my veins. Breathing air into my lungs.

I'm so struck by the sight of her, the connection between us, that I forget to move at all.

It's only when Nessa squeezes around me, gently shifting her hips, that I remember we were in the middle of fucking.

I thrust in and out of her, watching her face, making sure it's not too painful.

She winces a little, but I can tell by the flush in her face, by the heavy look in her eyes—dazed and floating—that it feels good, too.

I kiss her lips and her neck as I thrust into her, until she tilts her head back and moans, her pulse thudding against my tongue.

She starts to roll her hips in response, moving along with me, matching my pace. It's like dancing together all over again. We move in sync, our bodies aligned, even our breath in rhythm.

I've never had trouble "lasting" before. In fact, it was reaching climax that was the problem. I got bored and gave up more often than not.

Now I'm experiencing the other side of the coin. The extraordinary pleasure and desperate impulse to explode immediately, now, without waiting a second longer.

Nessa isn't quite there yet. She's breathing faster and faster, moving beneath me. I want her to come. I want to feel that tight little pussy clenching around me.

I thrust into her a little deeper. I wrap my arms around her and hold her tight. I bury my face in the side of her neck and bite her gently, right where her neck meets her shoulder.

Nessa tenses from the bite. That tips her over the edge. She grinds her body hard against mine, the rhythmic contraction of her pussy squeezing my cock.

"*Oh my god!*" she cries out.

My yell is much less articulate. I groan into her neck, long and low and guttural. My balls tighten, and I erupt inside her, a white-hot flow that seems to drain the soul out of my body. It goes on and on, me pouring into her and her clinging to me, until we're shaking with pleasure, every ounce of energy spent.

When it's done, we break apart to lie panting on the bed. There's a little blood on her thighs, a little more on the sheets, but not as much as I feared.

"Does it hurt?"

"It burns a little," she says.

I reach down between her thighs and touch her gently, rubbing my thumb over the swollen nub of her clit.

"Does that help or make it worse?"

"It helps," she says.

I touch her a little lower, where my own come is melting and dripping out of her. It makes my fingers slippery, making them glide easily over her clit.

"How about that?"

"Yes," she sighs, closing her eyes. "Even better."

I rub her clit in slow circles with my thumb. As the flush spreads from her cheeks down to her chest, I rub with my fingers, applying more pressure over a larger area.

"Oh, whoa," Nessa gasps. "It's happening again …"

"I know."

I'm watching her face so I know when to speed up, when to go harder. Soon her skin is on fire; she's shaking like she's got a fever. She's bucking her hips up against my hand, coming all over again. Even at this moment, she's graceful, her back arched, her body taut. Her every movement is beautiful; she can't help it.

I can't get enough of it. I want to do this to her over and over. And a thousand other things, too. I'm only just getting started.

As Nessa lets out the last little moans, I roll on top of her again, kissing her deeply.

I can taste her arousal. It's rich and heady, dark chocolate on her breath.

"You want more?"

"Please," she begs.

24
NESSA

The next morning, I wake to shouting.

The sound is distant, but my eyes pop open all the same.

I'm alone in the bed. Mikolaj is gone.

I don't feel abandoned. For one thing, he left me in his room, when only a few days ago, he chased me out of here in a rage. Things have changed between us.

I have no time to ponder that or to bask in pleasurable memories of the night before. I slip out of the bed before finding my panties and the nightgown. That's ripped past repairing, so I pull on Mikolaj's discarded shirt instead. It comes down to midthigh and smells like him—like cigarettes and mandarin oranges.

I hurry out of the room, down the hallway. The argument is already finished before I catch what it's about. I see the doors of the billiard room thrown open, Jonas and Andrei stalking off in one direction, Marcel walking away in another.

I don't see Mikolaj at all, but I'm guessing he's still inside.

I hurry down the stairs barefoot. I'm sure my hair is a tangled mess, and I haven't brushed my teeth. I don't care. I need to speak with him.

Something's happening. I can feel the tension in the air.

When I enter the billiards room, Mikolaj is standing with his back to me. He's holding one of the balls in his hand—the eight ball. Turning it over and over in his long flexible fingers.

"Do you play pool, Nessa?" he asks, without turning around.

"No."

"You win by sinking all your balls before your opponent can do the same. There's only one way to win. But there are several ways to lose. You can sink his last ball accidentally. Or sink the eight ball too soon. Or sink the eight and the cue ball at the same time."

He sets the ball down on the felt and turns to look at me. "Even right at the end, no matter how far ahead you may be, when you think your victory is assured, you can still lose. Sometimes because of the tiniest imperfection in the cloth. Or by your own fault. Because you got distracted."

I understand the metaphor. I'm not sure what point he's trying to make. Am I the distraction? Or am I the prize if we can make it all the way through the game?

"I heard shouting. Was it Jonas?"

Mikolaj sighs. "Come here," he says.

I pad over to him. He puts his hands around my waist. Then he lifts me to sit on the edge of the billiards table.

He takes the ankle monitor in his hands. With one swift jerk, he snaps the band. He drops the broken pieces on the floor.

"What are you doing?" I say in surprise.

"It stopped working that night in the garden. When you hit it with a rock."

"Oh." I blush. "I didn't realize that."

My leg feels strange without it. The skin feels every puff of air. I roll my foot around experimentally.

"You won't need it anymore. You're going home today."

I stare at him, shocked. "What do you mean?"

"Exactly what I said."

I can't read his face. He doesn't look angry—but he doesn't look happy either. His expression is deliberately blank.

Tentatively, I ask, "Did I do something wrong?"

He lets out an impatient laugh. "I thought you'd be happy."

I don't know if I'm happy. I know I should be, but all I seem to feel is sick confusion. "Did you change your mind?"

"About what?"

I look down at my knees, oddly embarrassed. "About…wanting to marry me."

"No."

My heart revives, soaring upward again.

Now I see the conflict on his face. The struggle between what he's doing and what he actually wants to do.

"Why are you sending me back, then?"

"A show of good faith," he says. "I'll send you home. I'll set up a meeting with your father. We can negotiate. And if you want to come back to me after that…"

He holds up his hand to stop me from speaking. "Don't say anything now, Nessa. Go home. Then see how you feel."

He thinks I only agreed last night because I'm trapped in his house. Because it was the only way to keep him from murdering my family.

There's so much more to it than that. But…maybe he's right. Maybe it's impossible to think clearly when I'm here, a prisoner, with Mikolaj right in front of my face. What he's offering me is impossibly generous—freedom and a clear head.

That's why his men are angry. He's giving up their bargaining piece and getting nothing in return.

"Pack up whatever you want to take," Mikolaj says. "Marcel will drive you home."

I feel like I'm made of paper and I'm tearing in two.

The desire to see my family again is bright and strong. But I don't actually want to leave.

Last night was the most incredible experience of my life. It was dark and wild and pleasurable beyond anything I'd ever imagined.

It's like mainlining heroin. In this house, I'm always intoxicated. I have to get away from it before I can look at anything with a sober mind.

So I nod, without really wanting to.

"All right," I say. "I'll go and pack."

Mikolaj turns away again, his shoulders straight and broad, a barrier I can't cross.

As I leave the billiard room, I see Jonas and Andrei down at the end of the hall, talking in low voices with their heads together. They stop when they see me, Jonas giving me the fakest of fake smiles, Andrei glaring at me coldly.

I hurry up the stairs to the east wing. I'm relieved to see Klara in my room. Less relieved to see the suitcase she's laid on my bed.

"I thought you'd like to take some of your new clothes with you," she says.

"Is Jonas angry that I'm leaving?" I ask her. "He looks pissed."

"The men will do what Mikolaj says," Klara says, without quite answering my question. "He's the boss."

I'm not so sure. They trusted him completely when he was the coldhearted mercenary they expected. But even I know that what he's doing right now isn't for the good of the *Braterstwo*. It's for me.

"I don't know if I should go."

Klara is throwing things into the suitcase without her usual perfectionism. "It's not up to you," she tells me flatly. "Mikolaj has decided. And besides, Nessa—it's not safe for you here."

Her voice is low, her body tense. I realize that whatever Klara might say, she's frightened. She doesn't know what's going to happen either.

"Is it safe for you here?" I ask her.

"Of course it is." Klara's dark eyes are steady and firm. "I'm just the maid."

"You're not a maid. You're my friend."

I throw my arms around her and hug her tight. Klara stiffens for a moment, then relaxes, dropping the bodysuit she was holding so she can hug me back.

"Thank you for taking care of me."

"Thank you for not being a little shit," she says.

"Most of the time," I say, remembering all the meals I refused to eat.

"Yes." She laughs. "Mostly."

Klara smells nice, like soap and bleach and vanilla. Hugging her is comforting because she's so capable and always seems to know what to do.

"I'll see you again soon," I tell her.

"I hope so," she says, without really sounding like she believes it.

I shower and brush my teeth, then put on a pair of clean leggings and a soft, slouchy sweatshirt. I don't know where my original clothes got to, the jeans and hoodie I was wearing when Jonas snatched me. They disappeared.

Klara blow-dries my hair one last time before pulling it up in a high ponytail.

As she packs my toiletries in the suitcase, I stand at the window, looking down into the garden. I see two of Mikolaj's men crossing the grounds, walking rapidly with their heads down. I recognize one of them—he's a bouncer at Jungle. The other, I've never seen before.

I know Mikolaj has more soldiers other than the ones who live at the house. He doesn't usually let them come here. Klara said they used to, but nobody was supposed to see me. Or as few people as possible. I guess it doesn't matter anymore now that I'm leaving.

"Come on," Klara says. "No sense moping around."

The house is unusually silent as I descend the curving staircase. The quiet unnerves me. Usually, there's some kind of noise—the clinking of plates in the kitchen or of pool balls in the billiard room. A TV playing somewhere or somebody laughing.

Marcel is waiting for me by the front door. He's got the car pulled up—the same Land Rover that brought me here. Or maybe they have a whole fleet. I don't really know the nuts and bolts of this place, not really.

I thought Mikolaj would be waiting, too.

His absence hurts me. It's a sharp pang that only seems to grow stronger as Marcel opens the door for me, as I realize he's really not coming to say goodbye.

What is wrong with me? Why am I blinking back tears when I'm about to go home? I should be skipping over to the car.

Instead, I march over like a condemned prisoner while Marcel lifts my suitcase into the trunk. When I look back at the massive old mansion, only Klara stands in the doorway, her arms crossed over the chest of her apron, her face solemn.

I press my palm against the glass.

She lifts a hand in farewell. Marcel drives me away.

It's a dark and gloomy day. The sky is as flat and gray as a chalkboard, the air bitingly cold. The wind blows the last of the dried leaves and bits of trash across the street. The season changed. It's winter now.

I look over at Marcel, his handsome profile and his troubled expression.

"Klara likes you," I tell him in Polish.

He gives a little laugh. "I know."

He's silent for a minute, and I don't think he's going to talk to me any more than he usually does. Then he seems to change his mind. He actually looks at me, maybe for the first time. I see his eyes are lighter than I thought—more of a honey color than a deep brown.

"Klara's father was a drunk. Her uncles are shit," he says. "Especially Jonas's father. She only knows one kind of man. But it doesn't matter. I'm just as stubborn as she is. Persistent, too."

"Oh," I say. "That's good."

"Yeah." He smiles and looks back at the road. "I'm not worried."

We're getting closer and closer to the Gold Coast. I know these streets. I've driven them a hundred times.

I should be getting more excited with every mile. In just a few minutes, I'm going to walk through the doors of my house and see my family. They're going to be so surprised, they just might have a heart attack. In fact, I should probably have the guards at the gate call ahead to warn them.

Instead of my excitement building, my sense of unease grows. I didn't like the look Jonas gave me in the hallway. It was just another one of his stupid smirks, but there was something else behind it. A new brand of maliciousness.

"Why did those men come to the house?" I ask Marcel.

"What?" he says, taking one of the last turns before my street.

"I saw one of the bouncers from Jungle in the backyard. And another guy."

"I don't know," Marcel says blankly. "I didn't hear anything about it."

"Stop the car," I say.

"What are you—"

"STOP THE CAR!"

Marcel slams on the brakes, pulling over to the side of the road, while a white minivan honks in irritation, swerving around us.

He stares at me, the engine still running. "I've got to take you home. Mikolaj's orders."

"Something's wrong, Marcel. Jonas is going to do something, I know it."

"He's just a blowhard," Marcel says dismissively. "Mikolaj is the boss."

"Please," I beg him. "Please go back, just for a minute. Or call Miko, at least."

Marcel looks at me, considering.

"I'll call him," he says at last.

He hits the number, holding the phone to his ear with an expression that plainly says he's only humoring me.

The phone rings without answer.

After the sixth or seventh ring, Marcel's smile fades, and he pulls the car away from the curb.

"Are you going back to check?" I ask him.

"Yeah," he says. "I'll check."

25
MIKO

♫ *Someone You Loved—Lewis Capaldi*

WATCHING THE LAND ROVER LEAVE THE YARD, CARRYING NESSA back to her house, is like watching the sun sink below the horizon. The light fades, and all that's left in its place is darkness and cold.

The house is silent. No music coming from Nessa's little studio. No hint of her gentle laugh or her questions to Klara.

Actually, there's no noise at all. The men are silent, too. They're angry with me.

From a strategic perspective, what I'm doing is insane. Handing Nessa over to the Griffins without any exchange, without even an agreement in place, is the epitome of foolishness.

I don't care.

I lay awake all night watching her sleep.

In the early hours of the morning, when the light turned from gray to gold, her face glowed like a Caravaggio portrait. I thought that out of all the sights I'd ever seen, Nessa was the most beautiful.

I knew I didn't deserve to have her in my bed. Nessa is a pearl, and I'm just the mud at the bottom of the ocean. She's flawless and pure, talented and smart, while I'm an uneducated criminal. A monster who's done horrible things.

Strangely, I may be the best person to truly appreciate her. Because I've seen the ugliest parts of the world, I know how rare her goodness is.

In that moment, watching her sleep, I realized that I love her.

Love is the one thing you can't steal. You can't create it either. It either exists or it doesn't. And if it exists, you can't take it by force.

If I coerce Nessa into marrying me, I'll never know if she loves me. She'll never know either.

I have to give her the chance to make her choice. Free and unencumbered.

If she loves me, she'll come back.

But I don't expect her to.

As I watch the car drive away, I doubt I'll ever see her again.

She'll go home to her mother, father, sister, and brother. They'll wrap her in their arms, tears will be shed, joy shared. She'll be happy and relieved. And what happened here between us will start to feel like madness to her. It will be like a fever dream—real in the moment but fading in the light of day.

I know I've lost her.

My emptiness swallows me whole.

I don't care that my brothers are angry. I don't care what the Russians will do. I don't care about anything at all.

I walk down to the main level of the house, then out to the back garden.

It's not much of a garden at the moment. The leaves have fallen and moldered. Only bare black branches break up a slate-gray sky. The rosebushes are nothing but thorns. The fountains are silent, drained of water.

Everything looks dead in winter. Chicago winters are cold and brutal—just as bad as in Poland. Maybe I'd be a different man if I'd lived somewhere warmer. Or maybe fate decrees that bitter souls be born in frozen climes.

Boots scuff over dry ground.

Jonas stands beside me, his face somber. "Alone again," he says.

"Not alone," I reply dully.

There are still four people living in the house besides me. I command two dozen soldiers and many more employees, a small army at my disposal. I'm only as "alone" as I was before Nessa came. Which is to say, completely.

"Have you spoken to Kristoff yet?" Jonas asks.

"No."

"How do you think he'll take the change in plans?"

I look at Jonas, my eyes narrowed and my voice cold. "That's not your concern. I'll handle the Russians like I handle everything else."

"Of course you will. That's why you're the boss," Jonas says. He smiles. Jonas always smiles, no matter his mood. He has smiles of anger, smiles of mockery, and smiles of deceit. This one is difficult to read. It almost looks sad.

Jonas lets out a long whistle, like a sigh. Then he claps his left hand on my shoulder, squeezing tight. "And that's why I love you, Brother."

We've known each other a long time. Long enough for me to know when he's lying.

The knife cuts through the air between us, driving straight toward my liver.

Jonas is fast, but I'm faster. I twist away, just enough that his knife slices into my side instead, right below the ribs.

It's a shallow wound, one that burns but doesn't debilitate.

It's the next one that really gets me.

Another blade comes whistling at me from behind, plunging into my back. It sinks hilt-deep into my right shoulder blade.

I twist out of Jonas's grip, turning to face my new attacker. Andrei, that treacherous fuck. I should have guessed. Whatever Jonas does, Andrei follows. He's not smart enough to come up with plans on his own. Right next to him are Simon and Franciszek, two more of my "loyal" soldiers.

Their knives swing at me from all directions. I dodge Simon's, knocking his arm to the side and striking him hard across the jaw with my fist. While I'm doing this, Franciszek buries his blade in my belly.

Being stabbed hurts worse than being shot. A bullet is small and quick; a knife is huge. It tears through you, embedding in your body like a flaming brand. You go into shock. You start sweating like crazy. Your knees want to stiffen and collapse beneath you. Your brain demands for you to lie down, to lessen the loss of blood. If I do that, I'm dead.

Jonas wrenches Andrei's knife out of my back, intending to stab me again. It hurts worse coming out than it did going in. I almost black out from that alone.

I know exactly what's happening to me. This is the *Braterstwo* version of a vote of nonconfidence. It's a long tradition, going back to Caesar. The assassination is done this way so no man will know whose knife struck the killing blow. No single man is the traitor—the death belongs to the group.

They're rushing at me all at once, their knives raised. I can't fight them all.

A voice screams, "*Stop!*"

Klara sprints across the lawn, waving her arms like she's trying to scare off a flock of crows.

"Get back in the house," Jonas snarls at her.

"What are you doing?" she cries. "This isn't right!"

"Ignore her," Jonas says to the others.

"No!"

Klara has pulled a pistol out of her apron pocket. With shaking hands, she points it at Jonas.

"All of you stop," she says.

I can tell she's terrified. She can barely keep the gun steady, even with both hands. Someone's taught her how to hold it, though, and how to aim it. I'm guessing that was Marcel.

"Deal with her," Jonas mutters to Simon.

Simon starts stalking toward her, his fists clenched.

"Stay back!" she cries.

When he keeps coming, she pulls the trigger. The shot goes wide, hitting him in the shoulder. Roaring like a bull, Simon charges at her.

I take the opportunity to jump at Franciszek, wrenching his knife out of his hand. When Andrei swings at me, I block his knife, taking a slash across the forearm as I cut him across the belly. He stumbles back, clasping his hand over the wound. Blood seeps through his fingers.

Jonas and Franciszek charge me from opposite sides. I take another cut down the arm from Jonas, and Franciszek knocks me to the ground. I'm not as fast as usual—I've lost too much blood. My right arm is going numb.

I hear two more shots—I hope that was Klara putting Simon down, not Simon wrenching the gun out of her hands and turning it on her instead. I'm tussling with Franciszek, both of us wrestling for control of his knife. Jonas is coming around the other side, trying to stab me the next time I'm on top.

A bellow of rage splits the air, followed by Klara's gasp of surprise.

"Marcel!" she cries.

Jonas stabs me again, right above the collarbone.

I hear four shots that sound like Marcel's Sig Sauer.

"Should I shoot him?" Franciszek mutters to Jonas. I don't know if he's talking about me or Marcel.

Jonas looks down at me. His eyes are black and expressionless—no hint of pity or remorse. "Fuck it," he growls to Franciszek. "He's done, let's go."

Franciszek scrambles off me, and they beat a retreat, dragging Andrei along with them.

I try to roll over to see what the fuck is happening, but I seem to be stuck on my side, my whole body throbbing with pain. If I even try to move my head, the sky and the grass spin around, swapping positions rapidly.

I feel a hand on my shoulder, turning me over. Then the face of an angel hovers over mine.

"*Miko!*" Nessa cries.

Her hands are gentle on my face. Every other part of me is in agony. At first, I was on fire, but now I'm getting cold. I've lost too much blood.

"*Help him!*" Nessa screams.

Footsteps seem to take forever to reach me…

I gaze up at Nessa. Her wide green eyes and dark brows are more concerned than I've ever seen them. Her tears rain down on my face. It's the only warmth I can feel. My blood drains out onto the half-frozen ground.

She's so, so beautiful.

If this is the last thing I ever see, I can die peacefully.

"Nessa," I wheeze. "You came back."

She clutches my hand, squeezing it tight. "You're going to be okay," she promises me.

Probably not, but I won't argue. I have to tell her something while I still have time.

"Do you know why I sent you away?"

"Yes." She sobs. "Because you love me."

"That's right." I sigh.

Marcel is kneeling beside me, clamping his hand over the worst of the wounds on my stomach. Klara does the same on my shoulder. She's got a nasty cut on her cheek but otherwise looks all right.

"Call an ambulance," Klara says to Nessa.

"No time," Marcel tells them.

I wish Nessa would lay her head on my chest. That would keep me warm. But I can't lift my arms to pull her close.

Marcel is saying something I can't hear. His voice fades, along with the gray sky and Nessa's lovely face.

26
NESSA

WE TAKE MIKOLAJ TO A SAFE HOUSE IN EDGEWATER. KLARA drives, while Marcel shouts directions and rips open a medical kit with his teeth. He tears into a little packet containing a long tube and a syringe.

Mikolaj is sprawled across the back seat. His eyes are closed, and his skin looks gray. He doesn't respond when I squeeze his hand. I'm trying to hold a cloth tight against his stomach, but it's difficult with how wildly Klara is driving and how soaked the cloth has gotten already.

"What's your blood type?" Marcel barks at me.

"What? I—"

"Your blood type!"

"Uh…O positive, I think," I say. I've donated a few times during the blood drives at school.

"Good," he says, relieved. "I'm AB, which won't work." He shoves the needle into Mikolaj's arm, then says, "Give me yours."

He makes me stand half crouching in the speeding car so my arm is higher than Mikolaj's.

"How do you know how to do this?"

"I was in medical school in Warsaw," he says, his speech muffled because he's wrapping a long rubber band around my arm while holding one end in his mouth. "Got myself in trouble popping pills to stay awake. Started selling them, too. That's how I met Miko."

He jams the other end of the cannula into my vein.

Dark blood speeds down the tube into Mikolaj's arm. I can't feel it draining out of me, but I pray to god it's moving fast because Mikolaj needs it badly. I'm not even sure he's still alive.

After a minute I think a little color has come back into his cheeks. Maybe that's only wishful thinking.

It's funny to think of my blood in his veins. I've already had a bit of him inside me. Now he has me inside him.

"Left here," Marcel says to Klara.

Klara is intently focused on the road, her hands rigid on the steering wheel. "How is he?" she says, unable to look back at us.

"Don't know yet," Marcel replies.

We pull up in front of a building that looks deserted. The windows are dark, some smashed and some covered with cardboard. Marcel stops the blood transfusion, taking the needle out of my arm. He says, "Help me with his feet."

We haul Mikolaj into the building, trying not to jostle him.

As soon as we're through the door, Marcel shouts, "Cyrus! *Cyruuuus!*"

A little man appears in the hallway—short, balding, with deeply-tanned skin and a white goatee.

"You didn't call to tell me you were coming," he rasps.

"Yes I did!" Marcel says. "Twice!"

"Ah," Cyrus says. "I forgot to switch on my hearing aid." He fumbles with the device nestled in his right ear.

"We should take him to a hospital," I murmur to Marcel, highly concerned.

"This is closer," Marcel says. "No one will take better care of Mikolaj, I promise you. Cyrus is a wizard. He could stitch up Swiss cheese."

We carry Mikolaj into a tiny room filled by what looks like a dentist's chair and a couple of medical-supply cabinets. It's a jumble of mismatched items, old and older, most of it rust speckled or dented. I'm becoming more worried by the minute.

Once we've deposited Mikolaj on the chair, Marcel shoves Klara and me out.

"We have this," he says. "Go and wait—I'll call you if I need anything."

He closes the door in our faces.

Klara and I retreat to a little room with an ancient TV, a fridge, and an assortment of couches and chairs. Klara sinks into an overstuffed armchair, exhausted.

"Do you think he'll be okay?" I ask her.

"I don't know," she says, shaking her head. Then, seeing the misery on my face, she adds, "He's probably survived worse."

I try sitting on the couch, then pace the room for a minute, then sit down again. I'm anxious, but I've given out too much blood to keep up the pacing.

"That fucking backstabbing Judas," I hiss, furious at Jonas.

Klara raises her eyebrows. I don't usually talk like that. She's never seen me riled up like this. "He's trash," she agrees calmly.

"Isn't he your cousin?"

"Yeah," she sighs, pushing back her bangs, which are dark with sweat. "I never liked him, though. Mikolaj always treated me well. He was fair. Didn't let the men put their hands on me. And he gave me money for my mother when she got sick. Jonas didn't send her anything. She's his father's sister—he still didn't give a damn."

I could stab Jonas myself if he were standing here now.

I've never felt that kind of violent anger before. I don't lose my temper. I don't have murderous thoughts. I don't even kill spiders when I find them in the house. But if Mikolaj dies...I won't be a pacifist anymore.

"Marcel will take care of him, won't he?" I ask Klara.

"Yes," she says firmly. "He knows what he's doing."

She's quiet a minute. Then she says, "Marcel was from a wealthy family in Poland. That's why he sounds so posh. His father was a surgeon, as was his grandfather. He could have done the same." She laughs softly. "He never would have looked twice at me in Warsaw."

"Yes, he would!" I contradict. "He looks at you about a hundred times a day here. He can't pay attention to anything else when you're in the room."

Klara flushes. She doesn't smile, but her dark eyes look pleased.

"He shot Simon," she says, still shocked. "Simon was choking me..." She touches her throat, where bruises are already blooming.

"This is so insane." I shake my head. "Everyone's gone mad."

"We all have to choose where our loyalties lie," Klara says. "Mikolaj chose you."

Yes, he did.

And I chose him, too.

I was only minutes away from my family's house.

I turned around and ran back to him.

I knew he was in danger because of me. I had to help him.

Will I make the same choice once he's safe?

I don't know what a future with Mikolaj would look like. He has a darkness inside him that terrifies me. I know he's done awful things. And his resentment toward my family still burns.

On the other hand, I know he cares about me. He understands me in a different way than my mother or father or siblings. I'm not just a sweet, simple girl. I feel things deeply. I have a well of passion inside me—for things that are beautiful and for things that are broken...

Mikolaj brings out that other side of me. He lets me be so much more than innocent.

We're only just scratching the surface of this bond between us. I want to dive all the way in. I want to lose myself in him and find myself all over again—the real me. The complete Nessa.

And I want to know the real Miko: passionate, loyal, unbreakable. I see it. I see who he is.

I'm more than good, and he's more than bad.

We're opposites and yet made for each other.

This is what I'm thinking about while the hours drag by. The time seems horribly long. Klara is quiet, too. I'm sure she's thinking of Marcel—wishing she could help him with more than just thoughts.

Finally, the door cracks open. Marcel emerges from the makeshift operating room. His clothes are bloodstained, and he looks exhausted. But there's a grin on his handsome face.

"He's all right," he says to us.

The relief that washes over me is indescribable. I leap to my feet. "Can I see him?"

"Yeah," Marcel says. "He's awake now."

I run into the cramped room. Cyrus is still washing his hands in the sink, next to a pile of bloodstained gauze.

"Careful," he croaks. "Don't hug him too hard."

Mikolaj is lying in the dentist's chair, half reclining, half propped up. His color is still awful. His shirt has been cut away, so I can see the many places where Cyrus and Marcel stitched and taped and bandaged him.

His eyes are open. They look as clear and blue as ever. They find me at once, pulling me over to him.

"Miko," I whisper, taking his hand and raising it to my lips.

"You were right," he says.

"About what?"

"You said I wouldn't die. I thought I would. But you're always right…" He winces, still in pain.

"We don't have to talk now," I tell him.

"Yes, we do," he says, grimacing. "Listen, Nessa…Jonas, Andrei, and the others…they're going after your brother. Not just them— the *Bratva*, too. Kolya Kristoff…"

"I'll call Callum. We'll warn him."

I can tell it's hard for him to speak because he's still so drained. But he's determined to make sure I understand the danger.

"They want to kill him."

Mikolaj wanted to kill my brother, too. Now he's doing his best to save him. For me. Completely for me.

He chose me over his desire for revenge.

He chose me over his brothers.

He chose me over his own life.

"Thank you, Miko."

I lean over him, careful not to press against his injured body, and kiss him softly on the lips. He tastes like blood, smoke, and oranges. Like our very first kiss.

"Come on," Marcel says from the doorway. "I'll take you to your brother."

"I'm not leaving you," I say to Mikolaj, clinging to his hand.

"We'll stay together," Miko agrees, trying to sit up.

"Are you crazy?" Cyrus shouts, hurrying over and trying to make him lie back again. "You'll rip out all your stitches."

"I'm fine," Mikolaj says impatiently.

He's not fine, but he seems determined to will it into reality.

"We can't hang around here. We've got too much to do," Miko says.

"You almost just died," Marcel reminds him.

Mikolaj totally ignores that, as if it's already in the distant past. He's pulling himself upright, grimacing, not thinking about the pain. His mind is working a million miles a minute, strategizing, formulating our next steps. Half his men may have turned on him, but he's still the same leader and planner. He's still the boss.

"We've got to go to the west side, to Cook County Jail."

"What are you talking about?" Marcel says, clearly thinking Mikolaj has lost his mind.

Miko groans, putting his feet on the ground and slowly hoisting himself up. "We're going to get Dante Gallo."

27
MIKO

I FEEL LIKE I'VE BEEN RUN OVER BY A GARBAGE TRUCK. THERE'S NOT a part of me not throbbing, burning, or immobile. Cyrus warns me that if I'm not careful, I'll tear open my wounds and start bleeding all over again.

I'd like to go to sleep for about a week. But there's no time for that.

Jonas and Kristoff have surely met up by now to plan their final assault against Callum Griffin. I don't know if they'll still try to attack him at the library opening or if they'll switch to something else.

What I know for certain is that the Griffins are going to need all the firepower they can get to fend them off. Which means I need to round up any of my men who are still loyal and free Dante as well. When it comes to strategic defense, you need your sniper.

As we drive over to the west side of the city, Nessa calls Callum from my phone. I can hear both sides of the conversation in the small confines of the car.

"Cal, it's me," Nessa says.

"Nessa!" he cries. I hear the intense relief in his voice. "Thank god! Are you all right? Where are you? I'll come get you!"

"I'm fine," she assures him. "Listen, I have to—"

"Where are you? I'm coming right now!"

"Cal," she says, "listen to me! The *Bratva* and the *Braterstwo* are coming for you. Maybe Aida, too. They might come to the library opening. They want to kill you."

He's silent for a beat, processing this. Then he says, "Are you talking about Mikolaj Wilk and Kolya Kristoff?"

"Kristoff, yes. But not Mikolaj. It's his lieutenant, Jonas, and some of his men."

A longer pause.

"Nessa, what's going on?"

"I'll explain it all to you," Nessa says. "In fact, I'll meet you at the house in…" She glances over at me. I hold up a finger. "One hour."

There's silence on the other end of the line. Callum is confused, trying to figure out what the fuck is going on right now. He's been looking for Nessa for weeks, and now she's calling him out of the blue, not acting like a hostage at all. He's wondering if this is a trap, if she's being forced to say this.

"I'm okay," Nessa assures him. "Just come meet me. Trust me, big brother."

"I always trust you," Callum says at once.

"See you soon, then."

"Love you."

Nessa ends the call.

I've already made a call of my own to Officer Hernandez. And he's not too fucking happy about it. But he's meeting us over by the Cook County Jail.

We've already armed ourselves from the stockpile at the safe house. As Marcel drives, I show Nessa how to load a Glock, how to chamber a round, and how to make sure the safety's off. I show her how to aim down the sight and how to gently squeeze the trigger.

"Like this?" she says, practicing with an empty chamber.

"Right," I say. "Don't hold it so close to your face, or it'll hit you on the recoil."

Nessa remembers the steps perfectly—it's a kind of choreography after all. But then she lays the gun in her lap and looks at me seriously. "I don't want to hurt anyone."

"I don't want you to either," I tell her. "This is just in case."

We drive over to La Villita Park, and then we wait.

After about forty minutes, a squad car pulls up next to us. A very irritated-looking Officer Hernandez gets out of the driver's seat. He glances around to make sure nobody will see him in this deserted corner of the lot, and then he opens his rear door so Dante Gallo can step out.

Dante is still wearing his prison uniform, which looks like a pair of tan doctor's scrubs with *Cook County DOC* stamped on the back. He doesn't have proper shoes, just socks and slippers. His hands are cuffed in front of him. The uniform is too small, making him look more enormous than ever. His shoulders strain against the material, and the cuffs pinch his wrists. His dark hair is buzzed off, his face unshaven.

I haul myself out of the Land Rover with a lot more difficulty. When Dante sees me, his black brows slam down like a guillotine, and his shoulders hunch up like he's about to charge me, cuffs be damned. That is, until Nessa steps between us. Then Dante looks like he's seen a ghost. "Nessa?"

"Don't be mad," Nessa pleads. "We're all on the same side now."

Dante doesn't look like he believes that at all.

Hernandez is equally wound up. "I had to forge the prisoner transfer paperwork," he hisses at me. "Do you know how much waist-deep shit I'm gonna be in? I can't just hand him over to you—I'll be fired! Prosecuted, too."

"Don't worry," I tell him. "You can say you did it all under duress."

"How in the fuck are they going to believe that?" Hernandez shouts, hitching up his pants below his paunchy belly. "I never agreed to this, I—"

I cut off his rant by shooting him in the leg.

Hernandez drops to the ground, wailing and moaning. "Awww, what the *fuck*! You fucking Polish bastard—"

"Shut your mouth, or I'll shoot you again."

He stops yelling but doesn't stop groaning. He's clutching his thigh, blubbering away even though I aimed for the muscle and didn't even hit any artery or bone. Really, he couldn't have asked for a cleaner shot.

Turning to Dante, I say, "The Russians and half my men are going after Callum Griffin. Can you help us?"

Dante looks at Officer Hernandez rolling around on the pavement, then back at me.

"Probably." He holds up his hands so the chain between the cuffs stretches tight. "Don't forget the keys."

I nod to Marcel. He kneels to take the keys off Hernandez's belt.

"Better put pressure on that wound," Marcel says to Hernandez conversationally.

We climb back into the Land Rover: Marcel and Dante in the front; Klara, Nessa, and me in the back.

"Those look comfy," Marcel says to Dante, nodding at his scrubs.

"They are," Dante agrees. "Food's fuckin' awful, though."

Now we're ready to drive back to Nessa's house on the lake. I'm leaving my world and stepping into hers. There's nothing to stop the Griffins from killing me the second I walk through their door.

That's not what I'm afraid of, however.

I'm afraid of losing my hold on Nessa.

Was she only bound to me because she was my captive?

Or will she want me still when she has every other option at her fingertips?

There's only one way to know.

28
NESSA

THERE'S A NOVEL CALLED *YOU CAN'T GO HOME AGAIN*. IT'S ABOUT A man who goes away for a time, and when he returns, so much has changed that he's not really returning to the same place.

Of course, the thing that changed the most is him.

When I finally see my parents' house again, it is both the most familiar and the most unfamiliar sight I've ever seen. I know its architecture like my own bones. But also, it looks brighter and flatter and simpler than I remember. It's a lovely house—it just doesn't have the spooky grandeur of Miko's mansion.

This same strangeness has taken hold of my parents. They're dressed the same as always in expensive, well-fitting clothes, their hair nicely cut and styled. But they look older than they did before. They look tired.

It makes me cry when they wrap their arms around me and hug me harder than they ever have before. I'm crying because I missed them so much. And I'm crying because they're so happy to have their daughter back. But I'm afraid they don't have her back—not the same one.

There's an explosion of outrage when they see Mikolaj. My father is shouting, his men are threatening to shoot Miko and Marcel. Mikolaj is silent, not defending himself at all, while I stand in front of him, yelling right back at these people I love, whom I've been waiting so long to see.

Then Callum and Aida come into the kitchen, and the hugging and crying starts all over again.

It's a long time before we've all calmed down enough to speak rationally.

My father is leaning against the kitchen island, his arms crossed. He's glaring murderously at Mikolaj, too angry to speak. My mother pours drinks for those who want them. Her hand trembles as she tries to pour a steady measure of whiskey in each of the glasses.

Cal is sitting closest to Mikolaj, the two across from each other at the kitchen table. He's angry, too, but he's listening as Mikolaj explains, briefly and without emotion, the current situation with the *Bratva* and the *Braterstwo* who have sided with Jonas.

It's funny—my father would usually sit in that seat. Cal is taking his place, bit by bit. I knew he would someday, but seeing it happen makes me realize we're all growing up. Things change. And they never go back again.

By this time, Nero and Sebastian have arrived, too. All three of Aida's brothers sit next to her on the barstools, the siblings lined up from youngest to oldest.

Sebastian is on her right side. He's the youngest of the brothers, and the tallest. He's got soft curly hair and a gentle face. He used to play basketball until Jack Du Pont stomped on his knee—one of the last ugly acts in the feud between our families. Sebastian still limps a little, though Aida tells me it's getting better. I'm surprised to see him here. He's a college student and usually stays on campus, not involving himself with this side of the family business. His presence shows how serious this is.

Next to Sebastian is Nero Gallo. I suppose you could say he's the most handsome of Aida's brothers—if it's possible for the devil to be handsome. Quite honestly, Nero terrifies me. He's wild and violent, his full lips always twisted up in a sneer. He's chaos incarnate. I can never be comfortable around him, not knowing what he'll say or do.

Then there's Dante. He's the oldest and the only one who can keep the others in line. I don't know if I've ever heard him say ten words in a row. He's built like a mountain and looks older than his real age. Unlike Sebastian, who has half the girls at his school in love with him, and Nero, who makes a sport out of seducing women, I've never seen Dante with a girl. Aida told me he was in love once, a long time ago. But the girl broke his heart.

Finally, Aida. She's the only person who doesn't look different at all. And the only one smiling unreservedly. She's delighted to have me back. Unlike everyone else who seems to want to murder Mikolaj, she's looking at him curiously, her keen gray eyes taking in every detail of his person, from his tattoos, to his bandaged arms, to his resigned expression.

Mikolaj looks out of place in my parents' house, more than anyone else. He belongs in his dark, gothic mansion. In this bright, clean space, he's an obvious outsider.

Everyone is arguing over what we should do about Jonas and Kristoff.

Dante wants to go on the offensive and attack the Russians now. "We can split their forces," he says. "We don't want to fight the *Braterstwo* and the *Bratva* at once."

My father thinks we should wait and gather information so we know what they have planned. "They've already combined forces, if what Mikolaj says is true," my father says, with an expression that means he doesn't at all take Miko's honesty as a given.

"Yeah," Nero says, "but we already shook that tree, and we didn't get any fucking apples. If we couldn't find Nessa after a month of looking, how many decades do you think it will take to find a good source?"

While they're all arguing, Aida and Callum murmur to each other. During a break in the conversation, Aida says to Mikolaj, "Your men think you're dead?"

"Yes." Miko nods.

"That's one advantage we have."

"They plan to attack me at the library opening?" Callum says.

"Yes."

"Then we should let them."

Nobody likes this idea, least of all my father. "You need to cancel the event and lie low," he says.

Callum shakes his head. "The Russians are good at killing people. You can't avoid every car bomb or drive-by shooting. We should pretend we know nothing to draw them out."

Aida presses her lips together, unhappy with this. But she doesn't argue with Cal—at least not in front of everybody else.

After another contemplative pause, Marcel says, "I might have an idea."

Everyone turns to look at him. This is the first time he's spoken. Klara sits next to him, about as close as you can get without actually touching.

The one thing I haven't told my family is that Marcel is the one who killed Jack Du Pont. We've got enough resentment in the room without adding that to the mix.

"What's your idea?" Nero Gallo says, suspiciously.

"Well…" Marcel looks at Dante. "I don't think you're going to like it…"

29
MIKO

It's 3:00 in the morning, and I'm driving over to Jungle, with Nero Gallo in the passenger seat next to me and Sebastian in the back. Aida wanted to come, too, but Dante wouldn't agree to it.

"I'm a better shot than Seb," she argued.

"I don't give a shit," Dante said bluntly. "You're not going into a firefight."

"Because I'm a girl?" Aida cried, furious.

"No," Dante said. "Because you're Papa's favorite. It'll kill him if something happens to you."

"Let them go," Callum said to her, laying his hand on her arm. "We have our own plans to make."

Aida tossed her head resentfully but didn't argue further.

As we drive over to the club, Nero watches me instead of the road.

"If you turn on my brother, the first bullet out of my gun goes right between your eyes."

"If I wanted to kill Dante, I could have done it this afternoon," I say.

"You could have tried," Nero sneers. "Dante's not so easy to kill."

"Neither am I," I say with a short laugh. I think I proved that today, if nothing else.

We come around Jungle on the back side.

The club is closed for the night, all the exterior lights turned off. Still, a dozen cars are parked in the back lot. I've been "dead" for less than a day, and Jonas is already making himself at home in my club.

Actually, I feel half dead. I may be bandaged up, but I'm stiff and aching. I know I'm not as fast as I was before. One good punch to the guts where Franciszek got me with his knife, and I'll be right back where I started.

No time to heal, though.

Marcel called Jonas from the Griffins' kitchen, pretending to reconcile. Jonas picked up after only one ring.

"Marcel," he said, his tone confident and taunting. "Having second thoughts about whose side you're on?"

"I didn't side with Mikolaj," Marcel said coldly. "I don't give a fuck about that traitor. What I do take offense to is anybody trying to put their hands on Klara."

"Klara interfered in our business."

"I don't give a fuck if she shot the Pope in the face," Marcel growled into the phone. "Klara belongs to me now, do you understand?"

He looked over at Klara, and their eyes locked. The jolt of energy that passed between them was palpable.

"Fine, all right. I don't want to hurt Klara. She is my cousin after all," Jonas said magnanimously. "But you did shoot Simon, and that's a problem."

"I have a peace offering," Marcel said. "Dante Gallo. I thought you might like to skin him alive before you put a knife in his heart."

"You have Dante Gallo?"

"He's in my trunk right now," Marcel said. "I intercepted his transfer this afternoon. Shot the cop and took the prisoner. I was gonna throw him in the river with his cuffs on, for Zajac. But I thought you might like to do the honors instead."

"That's very generous of you," Jonas said in the tone of a king accepting a tribute from a lord.

"Where do you want me to bring him?"

That's how we found out exactly where Jonas would be that night. Becoming boss hasn't made him any less sloppy. He's lazy and overconfident.

Marcel goes into Jungle first, through the front door, dragging along Dante Gallo, who consented to have his wrists cuffed in front of him once more and a bag put over his head.

His brothers didn't like that one bit.

"That's how it's got to be," Marcel told them sharply. "Jonas isn't a complete idiot."

While Marcel goes in the front, Nero and I sneak in the back door. Jonas hasn't changed the locks. Why would he? Only a ghost has the other key.

Sebastian stays outside, acting as our lookout.

Nero and I creep through the back offices, past the storeroom. Then we split up, Nero flanking to the left and me to the right.

As I enter the main space of the club, I see my men spread out among the booths, helping themselves to the top-shelf liquors. There are about fifteen soldiers in total. Out of those fifteen, I know for certain three betrayed me: Andrei, Franciszek, and Jonas. Simon, too, but he's dead.

I can't be certain where the loyalties of the other men lie.

All I know is they're enjoying the largesse of their new leader. Aleksy and Andrei look tipsy, while Olie is fully on his way to drunk. Nobody is keeping watch. Nobody is fully sober. Sloppy, sloppy, sloppy.

Jonas is drinking straight from a bottle of Redbreast. His slicked-back hair is disarrayed, his eyes bloodshot. He roars with pleasure when he sees Marcel shoving Dante Gallo into the center of the group. "There you are, my brother! And with such a gift!"

Marcel pulls the bag off Dante's head. Dante gazes stoically around at the group, not flinching while they all jeer at the sight of him.

"Here's the man who shot Zajac!" Jonas shouts. "From a distance. Like a fucking coward."

He's speaking in English so both the men and Dante himself will understand. Jonas lurches over to Dante until they're nose to nose. He's breathing whiskey fumes right into Dante's face. They're both burly men, but while Jonas has the soft bulk of a bear, Dante is as hard as a full-grown steer. His arms flex against the cuffs, looking like he might snap the steel without even trying.

"Take these cuffs off, and we'll see who's the coward," Dante says to Jonas, in his low even voice.

"I have a better idea," Jonas says. "You killed the Butcher. So I'm going to kill you the way the Butcher would have done—piece by tiny piece. I'm going to cut off your ears, your nose, your fingers, your feet. I'll take you apart, one pound of flesh at a time. And only then, when you're a sightless, soundless lump…only then will I let you die."

Jonas's black eyes glitter. His smile looks more than cruel—it's almost demented. Power is going to his head, amping up all his worst characteristics.

Jonas pulls his knife from his belt—the same one he stabbed me with earlier this morning. He holds it up in the dim light so the edge of the blade gleams. He's cleaned my blood off, at least.

I hear the rustle of Nero Gallo tensing, over on my left side. He's getting ready to move. He won't stay put while his brother suffers.

Neither will I.

"What do you say?" Jonas shouts to the men. "Which piece of Dante Gallo should I cut off first?"

"You should finish one job before you start another." I stride out into the light.

There's an audible stir among my men. Their eyes pinball between Jonas and me. The ones who are the most drunk look baffled, like they must be delirious.

Jonas whirls around, his face twisted in shock and irritation. "Mikolaj," he snarls.

"In the flesh."

"Or what's left of you," he sneers. "You aren't looking very well, Brother."

"Still twice the boss you'll ever be, Jonas."

His eyes darken. He switches his grip on the knife handle, from upward to downward. Tool to weapon. "You're not a boss anymore at all," he says.

"The boss is boss until death," I remind him. "I'm very much alive."

Another stir among the men. Olie, Patryk, and Bruno mutter to the others. They look the most startled to see me still alive and the most displeased with whatever story they were told. The others are less certain.

I'll have to put that uncertainty to rest.

I hold up my hand, a signal to Nero Gallo to stay put.

If Nero, Marcel, and I start shooting, my men will likely side with Jonas. But with the right push, they'll come back to me. We could all get out of this in one piece. Well…most of us.

"You betrayed us," Jonas spits out at me.

"That's funny, coming from the man who stabbed me in the back."

"You chose that Irish whore over us," Andrei hisses.

"I'm making an alliance with the Irish, and the Italians, too."

Jonas says, "You want us to lick their boots."

"I want us to get rich together," I correct him. "I want you all in Maseratis instead of caskets."

"This is bullshit!" Jonas shouts, saliva flying from his mouth. "He'll say anything to save his skin and protect that little bitch. He doesn't care about us. And he doesn't care about Zajac! They killed our father! Zajac deserves vengeance."

"I took Nessa from them," I say. "Better to keep her than to kill her. Better to share power with the Irish than to share a mausoleum with Zajac."

"Those are the words of a shivering dog," Jonas spits.

"You think I'm afraid?" My voice is as calm and cool as a glacier. "You think you can lead my men better than me? Then prove it, Jonas. Not with four men against one. Prove it just you and me. Man against man. Boss against boss."

Jonas grins, his black eyes gleaming manically. He clenches his knife all the tighter. I don't think he would have agreed to this yesterday. Yesterday I was the better fighter. Today I'm barely alive.

Jonas knows how badly I'm injured. He knows he has the advantage.

"If that's what you want, Brother," he says.

We circle each other in the open area of the club usually used for dancing. The only illumination is from the filtered green lights that give the appearance of tall grass and jungle foliage. Jonas and I circle like predators. Two wolves fighting for control of the pack.

In a brawl, Jonas might have the advantage because he's heavier than me. In a knife fight, I'm much faster. But I'm not fast right now. My right arm feels heavy and swollen; my body is exhausted. I try not to telegraph my injuries, but I know I'm not moving as smoothly as usual. Jonas smiles, scenting blood.

We weave around each other, Jonas making a couple of feints in my direction. The key to knife fighting is footwork. You have to keep the right distance from your opponent. This is tricky because Jonas's reach is longer than mine.

Imagine two boxers facing off in a ring. Then think about how many times Muhammad Ali got hit, even though he was the best in the world at dodging blows. You can't afford to take that many cuts from a knife.

So I keep a wide space between us. Jonas keeps trying to dart inside that circle, slashing at my face and body. I narrowly avoid his cuts, though I have to jerk aside to do it. I feel stitches opening on my belly and down my back.

I'm not trying to cut Jonas open. I'm aiming for something different—his knife hand.

Jonas slashes at me again. This time I'm too slow. He slices a long gash on my left forearm. The blood patters down on the dance floor. Now I have to avoid that, too, or risk slipping in it.

"Come on." Jonas grunts. "Quit ducking away. Come on and fight me, *suka*."

I pretend to lower my guard. This means I have to actually lower my guard for a moment. Jonas rushes in, slashing his knife right at my face. I duck, again just a little too slow. His blade cuts a burning wound down my right cheek. But Jonas has come close. I slice the back of his knife hand, cutting through muscle and tendon. We call that defanging the snake. The effect is immediate—he can no longer grip. His knife falls, and I catch it out of the air, so I'm now holding a blade in each hand.

Jonas stumbles backward, slipping in my blood. He goes down hard, and I jump on top of him, ready to cut his throat.

Andrei and Franciszek know what will happen if Jonas dies. They rush forward to help their fallen leader.

Dante Gallo intercepts Franciszek. He clasps his fists together, still cuffed, and sends his arm swinging upward like a hammer, crashing under Franciszek's chin. Franciszek's head snaps backward. He sails off in the opposite direction, smashing into one of the empty booths.

Andrei is still running at me, yanking his gun from his coat. I'm holding Jonas down. I've stabbed one knife into his shoulder to pin him in place, an insect on a mount. The other blade presses against his throat. I'll have to let him go to jump up and meet Andrei.

Before I can do that, I hear the crack of a shot.

Andrei stops running. His gun drops limply from his hand. He sinks to his knees and tumbles over.

I look back to where Nero Gallo was hiding, thinking he was the shooter. Nero is standing by the bar with his mouth open, his expression as dumbfounded as mine.

I turn in the opposite direction instead, to the front doorway.

Sebastian Gallo lowers his gun. He shot from all the way across the room and hit Andrei in the back of the head. I guess Aida was wrong about his aim.

My other men seem frozen, unsure of what to do. They don't know what's happening; there's no precedent for this.

I know one thing for certain.

There can only be one boss.

Jonas is still struggling and spitting beneath me, one arm useless from the knife in his shoulder, the other trying to swing a fist and hit every part of me he can reach.

"I should have been the boss," he snarls. "It was my right by blood…"

"You're nothing like Zajac," I tell him. "You don't have his brains or his honor."

"Go to hell!" he howls, writhing and struggling.

"I'll see you there, Brother."

I cut his throat from ear to ear.

The blood pours out in a sheet, dousing my hand. I wipe it off on Jonas's shirt and clean the blade of my knife as well.

Then I stand, refusing to wince.

My face is throbbing—my arm, too. Blood seeps through the front of my shirt where my stitches pulled out. I stand tall regardless. I can't let my men see weakness.

They stare at me, shocked and guilty. Unsure of what to do.

It's Marcel who acts first. He strides over and kneels in front of me. "Good to have you back, boss," he says.

Olie and Bruno follow close after him, kneeling in front of me, so Jonas's spreading blood soaks the knees of their pants.

"Forgive me, boss," Bruno says. "They told me you were dead."

The rest of my soldiers rush over to kneel. This is the position of penance. Whatever punishment I mete out, they'll accept.

If I were Zajac, I'd take a finger from each of them.

But I'm not Zajac. The guilty have already been punished.

"Uncuff Dante Gallo," I say to Marcel.

He unlocks the cuffs. Dante, Nero, and Sebastian stand at the edge of the dance floor, shoulder to shoulder. My men eye them with wary looks, some still angry.

"Our dispute with the Italians is over," I tell them. "The same with the Irish."

"What about Zajac?" Olie says quietly.

"I'll put a monument on his grave," Dante Gallo says in his rumbling voice. "In honor of the new friendship between our families."

Olie nods once.

"Get up," I say to the rest of my men. "Clean up this mess. You had your fun—it's time to get back to work."

As my men start putting the club back in order, I head back to my office with the Gallo brothers.

"What the fuck was that shot?" Nero says to Sebastian.

Sebastian shrugs. "I told you, I'm the athlete in the family. I've got the fastest reflexes."

"Like hell." Nero scoffs. "I just had a shit angle."

Dante puts a heavy hand on Sebastian's shoulder. "Are you all right?" he asks his brother.

"Yeah." Sebastian shrugs.

He looks troubled. I'm guessing that was the first man he ever killed.

I'm not happy about it either. I knew Andrei for six years. He lived in my house. We played pool together. Ate at the same table. Laughed at the same jokes.

But in our world, you're brothers or enemies. There is nothing in between.

Once we're inside my office, I call Kolya Kristoff. He answers after a few rings, his voice thick with sleep but his brain as sharp as ever.

"I didn't expect to see a dead man's name on my phone."

"You picked up to see what it's like on the other side?"

He laughs. "Enlighten me."

"You'd have to ask Jonas."

"Ah," he sighs. "His reign didn't last long."

"I've made peace with the Griffins and the Gallos."

Kristoff chuckles softly. "So little Nessa Griffin put the collar on your neck instead."

I won't rise to the bait.

"Our agreement is off," I tell him.

"An agreement by two can't be broken by one," Kristoff says.

"Do as you will. Just know that the Griffins are expecting you. If you try to take Callum and Aida, you'll be slaughtered."

"We'll see," Kristoff says. Then he hangs up the phone.

I look at the Gallo brothers.

"He's a cocky little shit, isn't he?" Nero says.

Dante scowls. "I'll be waiting at the library," he says. "If Kristoff is stupid enough to pop up his head, I'll blow it off his shoulders for him."

30
NESSA

MIKOLAJ RETURNS TO MY PARENTS' HOUSE IN THE EARLY HOURS OF the morning. He has a fresh slash down the right side of his cheek and another on his arm. Dark stains on the front and back of his shirt show that his wounds have reopened. I run into the yard to meet him. He's paler than I've ever seen him, almost falling into my arms.

"Oh my god!" I cry, holding his face in my hands. "What happened? Are you all right?"

"Yes," he says. "I'm all right."

I press my forehead against his, and then I kiss him, assuring myself that he's breathing still, that he smells and tastes the same as ever.

He wraps his arms around me, his heart beating against my chest. He nuzzles against my ear.

"Nessa!" My mother's sharp cry interrupts us.

I let go of Mikolaj.

She's standing in the doorway, staring at us with a horrified expression. "Get in the house," she hisses.

From long habits of obedience, I go back into the kitchen where my mother and father stand side by side, their arms crossed over their chests and forbidding expressions on their faces.

Mikolaj follows me in.

The Gallo brothers are with him; Marcel is as well.

As soon as Klara sees Marcel, she runs over to him. She kisses him as deeply as I did Mikolaj. When Marcel gets over his surprise, he picks her up and kisses her harder before setting her down again.

I'd like to celebrate that development, but unfortunately, I've got to turn my attention back to my furious parents.

"This is over," my father says sternly, pointing between Mikolaj and me.

"Whatever you've done to her," my mother shouts at Mikolaj, "however you've messed with her head—"

"I love him," I say.

My parents stare at me, stunned and disgusted.

"That's ridiculous," my mother says. "He abducted you, Nessa. Kept you prisoner for weeks. Do you know what we went through, not knowing if you were alive or dead?"

She turns her tear-streaked face on Mikolaj, her blue eyes full of rage.

"You took our daughter from us," she hisses. "I ought to have you castrated."

"He saved my life," I tell them. "They all wanted to kill me. The Russians, his own men… He risked everything for me."

"Only because he stole you in the first place!" my mother cries.

"You don't know men like this," my father says to me. "Violent. Cruel. Killers."

"Criminals?" I say, almost laughing at the irony. "Dad…I know what Mafia men are like."

"He's not like us," my father growls.

"You don't know what he's like!" I snap.

"Neither do you!" my mother cries. "He's manipulated you, Nessa. You're a child! You don't know what you're saying—"

"I'm not a child!" I shout back at her. "Maybe I was when I left, but I'm not anymore."

"Are you saying you want to be with this animal?" my father demands.

"Yes."

"Absolutely not!" he shouts. "I'll kill him with my bare hands first."

"It's not your choice," I tell them.

"The hell it's not," my father says.

"What, are you going to ground me?" I laugh bitterly. "Unless you want to lock me up all over again, you can't keep me away from him."

"Nessa," Mikolaj says. "Your parents are right."

I whirl around, stricken and outraged. "No, they're not!" I cry.

Mikolaj takes my hand gently, to calm me. He squeezes my fingers, his hand as warm and strong as ever.

Then he faces my parents, composed and firm.

"I apologize for the pain I caused you," he says. "I know this will be difficult for you to understand, but I love Nessa. I love her more than I love my own soul. I would never hurt her. And that includes tearing her away from her family again."

"Miko—"

He squeezes my hand, silently asking me to be patient. "I brought Nessa back to your house. All I'm asking is for your permission to continue seeing her. I want to marry her. But you're right— she's young. I can wait. There's plenty of time for you to know me. For you to see that I will cherish and protect your daughter forever."

He's so exhausted that his voice comes out in a rasp. Still, his sincerity is undeniable. Even my parents can hear it. Without wanting it, their anger fades. They exchange anxious glances.

"She stays here," my mother says.

"You visit her here," my father says.

"Agreed." Mikolaj nods.

It's not what I want, not really. I understand that he's trying to do this for me, to preserve my relationship with my family. And to give me time to grow up a little more. To be certain of what I want in the long term.

But I already know what I want.

I want Mikolaj. I want to go back to the house where every day with him is like a dream more vivid than reality.

I want to go home.

In the weeks that follow, I sink into a new routine. I'm sleeping in my old bedroom. It doesn't look the same as it did before. I got rid of the stuffed animals and the frilled pillows and the pink curtains. It's a much plainer space now.

I haven't gone back to Loyola. I missed too many classes this semester and realized I don't care. I was only getting that degree to make my parents happy. My real interests lie elsewhere.

Instead, every day, I go to Lake City Ballet. I've almost finished my magnum opus. I work for hours and hours in the open studios, sometimes alone and sometimes with the other dancers. Marnie is designing my sets, and Serena will be dancing one of the secondary roles. I'll be the lead. Not because I'm technically the best dancer but because this ballet is so personal to me that I couldn't bear to have anyone else perform it.

Jackson Wright has been so extraordinarily supportive that I'm almost afraid he's been kidnapped by aliens and replaced with a clone. The first time I saw him, he had a cast and sling on his arm, and he was so eager to welcome me back that he almost tripped over his own feet. He didn't look at all like his usual dapper self: his hair was a mess, and he was jumpy as hell, startling every time someone tapped him on the shoulder or slammed a door.

Obviously, he was sponsoring my ballet out of coercion. But as we continued working on it together, I think he actually got excited. He offered to direct it, unprompted, and he's given me genuinely helpful advice. After the latest rehearsal, he pulls me aside and says, "I can't believe this came out of you, Nessa. I always thought you were one-note. A pretty note, but not enough to make a whole song."

I snort. Trust Jackson to temper a compliment with an insult.

"Thanks, Jackson," I say. "You've been surprisingly helpful. Guess you're not completely an asshole after all."

He scowls, swallowing the retort he so clearly wants to give me.

Mikolaj comes to see me almost every night. We take walks along the lakeshore. He tells me about growing up in Warsaw, about his biological parents, and about Anna. He tells me all the places she wanted to visit. He asks me where I'd like to go, of all the places in the world.

"Well…" I think about it. "I always wanted to see the Taj Mahal."

He smiles. "So did Anna. I was going to take her once we had money."

"My parents never want to go because it's too hot."

"I like heat." Mikolaj smiles. "Much better than snow."

It's snowing right now. Big, heavy flakes that drift down in slow motion. They're catching in Mikolaj's hair, blanketing his shoulders. We had to bundle up for our walk. He's wearing a navy peacoat with the collar turned up. I've got on a white parka with a fringe of fur all around my face.

"What about this?" I ask him. "Isn't this pretty?"

"This is the first winter I haven't hated."

He kisses me. His lips are burning hot on my frozen face. The snow is so thick that I can't see the lake or my house. We could be the only two people in the world. We could be two figures inside a snow globe, suspended for all time.

I want to do so much more than kiss him. I unbutton his coat so I can slip my hands inside. Then I run my fingers over his hard warm torso beneath his shirt. He doesn't care that my fingers are cold. He pulls me closer, kissing me deeper.

I'm careful not to touch him in the places that are still healing. The bandages are gone, but the wounds were deep, and the stitches haven't been taken out yet.

Usually, my father's men are spying on us wherever we walk on the grounds. Today the snow is too thick. They won't be able to see us.

I slide my hand down the front of Miko's jeans, inside his underwear. His body has warmed my hand. He doesn't flinch when I take hold of his cock. He groans and gently bites my lip between his teeth.

"I want to be close to you again," I tell him.

"I'm supposed to be earning trust with your parents."

"That could take a hundred years." I moan. "Don't you miss me?"

"More than I ever thought I could miss anything."

He strips off his coat and spreads it over the snow. Then he lays me on top of it. He unbuttons my jeans and pulls them down just a little—the same with his own. Positioning himself on top of me, he slides his cock into the narrow space between my thighs and pushes it in.

Because I'm still wearing my jeans, my legs are close together. This makes the space for his cock smaller and tighter than ever. The friction is insane. He barely thrusts in and out of me. I'm squeezing him tight along every inch of his length.

At the very first thrust, he gasps like he might pass out.

"Good god, Nessa," he groans. "You're going to kill me."

"Why?"

"It's too much. It feels too good."

It does feel outrageously good. But it's so much more than that. I feel connected to him, like we're becoming one soul as well as one body of tangled flesh. I know he's feeling what I'm feeling. Thinking what I'm thinking. He's loving me as I'm loving him: insanely, without reason, without limit.

Even though our motion is constricted, it doesn't matter. We've both been pent up and aching for each other. The release is almost immediate. In less than a minute, I feel that blooming warmth and pleasure that builds and builds inside me until it overflows. I'm coming, clenching tighter than ever around his cock. Miko lets go, too, wrapping his arms so hard around me that my bones bend. He erupts with a strangled sound, trying not to shout too loudly.

We want to lie there longer, but it's too cold. My teeth are chattering. I stand, pulling up my jeans and buttoning them again. I can feel his come dripping out of me, soaking my underwear. I love that sensation, primal and raw. The surest mark that I belong to him, and him alone.

Once we're dressed, he kisses me again.

"I'll bring you home soon," he promises me.

He knows my parents' house isn't my home anymore.

Sometimes he brings Marcel and Klara to visit me. We watch movies down in the theater, with Polish subtitles for Klara because her English is still shit. I can tell it disturbs my parents, hearing us speak Polish together. They look at me like I'm a changeling.

They haven't adjusted to the differences in me. My mother wants to take me to do the things we used to do: shopping, brunch, shows. I go along with her, and I try to be cheerful, to be who she wants me to be. But I miss Miko terribly. There's a barrier between my mother and me. She doesn't want to talk about that month I was missing. She wants me to be exactly as I was before. I can't do that, no matter how hard I try.

Strangely, the person who seems the happiest to have me back is Riona. She was holed up at her law office the night I came home, working on briefs till the early morning hours. When she saw the message from my parents, she abandoned her folders and came speeding home before hugging me for about ten times the length she'd ever hugged me before. I might even have seen the tiniest of tears in her eye, though she never let one fall.

Since then, she's swung by Lake City Ballet several times to have lunch with me, something she never bothered to do before.

We never used to spend much time together, so she doesn't expect me to behave in any particular way. She just asks how the ballet is coming along and whether we have a date set for the first performance. She asks me which music I'm using and makes a playlist out of the songs for her drive to work. She even books pedicures for us both on a Saturday morning to ease my aching feet, though I can tell it's killing her to sit there for thirty-eight entire minutes without checking her email.

Stranger still is the friendship that's sprung up between Riona and Dante Gallo. She spent several weeks trying to get him released from jail the first time around, and then she had to spend several more after he was "abducted by a rival gang" during a fraudulent prisoner transfer. In the end, she used Officer Hernandez's shady history to get the murder charge dropped. It helped that Officer O'Malley agreed to testify against his ex-partner. I don't know who paid the bribe for that—Mikolaj or the Gallos—but I'm sure it wasn't cheap.

I guess Dante and Riona talked a lot while Riona visited him in prison. Dante is a very calming presence. Riona seems less brittle around him, less ready to bite somebody's head off at the slightest provocation.

I screw up my courage to ask her if she thinks he's handsome. She rolls her eyes at me.

"Not everything is a love match, Nessa," she says. "Sometimes men and women are just friends."

"I just thought you might be curious to see that particular *friend* with his shirt off…seeing as he's built like the Rock."

Riona snorts like she's above petty considerations like bulging biceps and six-pack abs.

My parents haven't exactly warmed up to Miko, but they're beginning to realize that what I feel for him is much more than a passing infatuation. Every day the bond between us grows stronger. I miss his house—the stone walls, the creaking roof, the dim light, the overgrown garden. The smell of dust, and oil paint, and Mikolaj himself. I miss wandering around that labyrinth, continually drawn toward the man at the center. The one who pulls me in like a magnet.

I know he's lonely there without me. Now that Jonas and Andrei are gone, it's just Miko, Marcel, and Klara. And even those two might be moving to their own apartment sometime soon.

Mikolaj keeps himself busy with work. Building his businesses, expanding his empire without directly clashing with my family or Aida's. We're all coexisting…for now.

The only hanging thread is the Russians. The afternoon of the library opening, we were all waiting: Miko's men, the Gallos, and my father's men, too. Dante was up on the roof of a neighboring building, rifle at the ready, keeping watch for any sign of Kristoff or any of his men.

But there was nothing. Not a *Bratva* to be seen. The event went perfectly.

Maybe they gave up, knowing they were outgunned and outmatched.

After all, it's a big city. Plenty of crime to go around.

31
MIKO

It's the night of Nessa's ballet.

I've been waiting for this almost as eagerly as Nessa herself. Maybe more so, because I'm simply excited to see it, while Nessa has become increasingly anxious the closer it's gotten.

I'm not worried. I already know she'll be brilliant.

The ballet is being performed at the Harris Theater. That fuckwad Jackson Wright is directing it. I planned to visit him a few more times if he gave Nessa any shit—just casually, of course. As a gentle reminder. No broken bones required, unless he annoyed me. It proved to be unnecessary—he got sucked into the project almost as much as Nessa herself.

Nessa saved tickets for all her friends and family, deliberately seating me right next to her parents. It's not the most comfortable position, but I have to take whatever opportunities I can to get to know them. I don't expect they'll ever like me. They may not even stop hating me. They have to accept me, however, because I'm not letting go of Nessa.

Truthfully, my patience is running thin. I thought I could take my time—but I overestimated my own resolve.

I want her back. I want her fully. I want her as my bride.

I'm sitting right next to Fergus Griffin. He's a tall, trim, intelligent-looking man, well-dressed, with handsome gray streaks in his hair and cultured manners. To the untrained eye, he looks like a wealthy Chicago businessman. I see him for what he really is—a chameleon who takes on the appearance that best suits his purposes. I have no doubt that when he was breaking knees as an enforcer, he looked like walking retribution. When he rose through the ranks of the Irish Mafia, I'm sure he dressed like a gangster. Now he behaves like he's lived all his life in the upper crust.

It's difficult to tell who he really is underneath all that. I can guess a few things: he must be intelligent and strategic, with a core of steel. You don't get to the top any other way. But he can't be your average criminal sociopath. Because he made Nessa. He raised her. That gentle heart and creative mind of hers must have come from somewhere.

Maybe from Imogen Griffin. She's sitting on her husband's opposite side. I feel her looking at me with those cool-blue eyes she passed down to her son.

"Are you a patron of the arts?" she asks me acerbically.

"No." After a moment of chilly silence, I add, "I do like dancing."

"You do?" Her frosty expression melts by the tiniest degree.

"My sister and I did folk dancing when we were young," I take a breath, trying to think of how normal people speak when they make conversation. "We won a prize once, for the polonaise. We hated dancing together because we always quarreled—Anna wanted to lead. She was better than me. I should have let her. We probably only won because we looked so alike, like a matched set. The judges thought it was cute."

The words come out faster once I get in the flow of it. It helps that Imogen and Nessa look a little alike. It helps ease the awkwardness.

Imogen smiles. "I danced ballroom with my brother Angus," she says. "We thought it was so embarrassing being paired up. We never won any prizes."

"You needed a better partner," Fergus says.

"I hope you're not talking about yourself." Imogen laughs. She tells me, "He broke my foot at our wedding. Stepped right on my toes."

Fergus scowls. "I had a lot on my mind."

"And you were drunk."

"Mildly inebriated."

"Completely sloshed."

They share an amused glance, until they remember that I'm sitting right next to them and they hate me.

"Anyway," Fergus says. "Nessa's talent comes from her mother."

I hear the pride in his voice. They love Nessa—that much is clear.

Before I can say anything else, the lights dim and the curtain rises.

The set is stunning, epic in size and scale. It looks like a bright verdant forest. The music is light and joyful, too. Three girls come out dressed in green, blue, and pink—Nessa, Marnie, and Serena.

I notice Serena Breglio kept the brown hair the Russians gave her. I guess she decided she liked it. I don't know how much Nessa told her about why she was abducted and then abruptly released again. I do know Serena is one of Nessa's best friends, and that hasn't changed. So, in a fit of guilt, I anonymously paid off the balance of Serena's student loans. It was forty-eight thousand. Less than I make in a week, but a fuckload of shifts at the coffee shop where Serena works to supplement her meager dancer's salary.

A few months ago, I would have said she was lucky we didn't cut her throat and toss her in a ditch. Now I'm Father Christmas. That's how soft I've gotten.

The three girls are dancing in a formation Nessa tells me is called a pas de trois. Their dresses are soft, not stiff like tutus. Every time they twirl, the skirts bell out in a shape like flower petals.

I've watched very little ballet, but the dances Nessa choreographs are mesmerizing. There's so much movement and interaction, patterns that shift and evolve with barely any repetition.

Nessa's parents are fascinated right from the start. They lean forward, their eyes locked on the stage. I can see from their surprised expressions that even they didn't realize how beautiful Nessa's work can be.

Toward the end of the dance, Nessa separates from the other two girls. They exit the stage on the left, while Nessa crosses in the opposite direction, wandering as if lost.

As she moves across the stage, the lighting changes. The forest that looked bright and welcoming now becomes dense and dark. The music alters, too, switching from cheerful to eerie.

Nessa comes to a castle. After some hesitation, she walks inside.

The castle set slides across the floor in sections, locking into place around her. It's incredibly detailed—Marnie's work. Huge leaded glass windows give the walls a cagelike feeling, and there's a tattered, aged, and neglected look to everything, down to the melted candlesticks in the chandeliers.

Inside the castle, Nessa meets the Beast.

The Beast is played by Charles Tremblay, one of the principal dancers at Lake City Ballet. Usually, he's tall, fit, and friendly looking, with a shaggy surfer's cut of strawberry-blond hair and a slight Southern drawl. Onstage he's unrecognizable. Makeup and prosthetics have turned him into a monster—half wolf, half human, like a werewolf partway through its transformation.

Everything about his movement has changed, too. Gone is the confident swagger. Now he darts around the stage with unnerving speed, low to the ground like an animal.

Nessa told me she chose him for exactly this reason—his ability to "act" as well as dance.

I know they've been rehearsing together for hours every day, something that would usually make me horrifically jealous. Except that every night when I visit her, Nessa runs to me like she hasn't seen me in a hundred years. Like she can't stand another second apart. So I know who she's been thinking about, even when she's dancing in another man's arms.

The Beast entices Nessa to dance with him.

The beguiling strains of "Satin Birds" begin to play. I let out a long sigh. I didn't know Nessa even remembered that song, let alone that she planned to use it in the ballet. It brings my own ballroom into view before my eyes and makes me vividly remember the first night I held Nessa in my arms.

The pair waltzes across the stage, reluctantly at first, then with greater speed and intensity.

I see Nessa recreating that moment between us. I don't mind that she's portrayed me as the Beast. Actually, it's fitting. I was a wild animal that night. I wanted to tear her to pieces and swallow her whole. I barely kept control of my desire for her.

What I didn't realize is how strong *her* desire already was in return. I see it now as she looks up into the Beast's face. I see how intrigued she is. How drawn to him, despite every natural inclination of self-preservation.

The ballet goes on.

It's the classic fairy tale of Beauty and the Beast. But it's also our story, Nessa's and mine. She's mixed in pieces of what happened between us.

I'm reliving it all.

I forget I'm sitting next to her parents. I forget there's anyone else in this theater. I just see her and me, how we broke apart and came back together again, over and over, neither of us able to resist the pull of attraction that lured us in and bound us tight. She's showing me our whole story, a dark fantasy retold through her eyes.

Finally, there's a duet between the Beast and Nessa that takes place on a stormy night. The stage lighting mimics the appearance of rain, punctuated by lightning.

At first, the duet is a vicious combat: violent and aggressive. The Beast drags Nessa, pulling her back when she tries to escape, even lifting her over his head and carrying her across the stage. But as the dance goes on, their motions sync. Their bodies lock tight together until they become perfectly aligned, even in the most outrageous formations.

Soon they're moving as one person, faster and faster. Nessa told me this is the most technically difficult dance. She was afraid she wouldn't be able to keep up with Charles.

She's more than keeping up. She's dancing better than I've ever seen before—swift, precise, passionate. She's fucking incredible.

I can't take my eyes off her. The theater is completely silent. No one wants to breathe in case they interrupt the pair whirling across the stage. It's erotic and ethereal, utterly mesmerizing.

When at last they stop, locked in place in the center of the stage, wrapped in a kiss, the crowd erupts. The applause is thunderous.

Imogen and Fergus Griffin are staring at each other. They're amazed by Nessa's performance. But it's more than that. They know what it means just as well as I do. They've seen how Nessa really feels. She's laid her heart out on the stage for everyone to see.

At the end of the show, the applause goes on and on. The cast comes out to take their bows. The audience gives them a standing ovation, except for one man who slips out of his seat and exits via the side door before Nessa comes to take her bow.

The man's movement catches my eye. As thrilled and pleased as I am for Nessa, I can't turn off that part of my brain. The part that's always looking for something out of place.

Nessa strides across the stage, blushing with pleasure as the crowd cheers louder than ever. She curtsies, then scans the crowd, looking for her family. When she catches sight of me, she blows me a kiss.

Jackson Wright grabs her hand and lifts it in triumph. He's gotten his cast off finally, which seems to have improved his spirits. He's grinning, looking genuinely proud.

As the dancers head backstage once more, we exit to the lobby to wait for Nessa. She's changing out of her costume, probably talking excitedly with her friends. They'll all be high on the wave of their success.

I wait next to Nessa's parents with Callum, Aida, and Riona. Imogen is quiet as if she has a lot on her mind. Aida's talking enough for everyone.

"That was the best ballet I've ever seen. It's the only ballet I've ever seen, but I'm sure if I watched others, I'd still think that."

"It was beautiful," Riona agrees.

"I felt like there was a metaphor in there somewhere..." Aida muses, casting her sly gray eyes in my direction.

Callum gives her a stern look to make her shut up.

She grins up at him, not chastened in the slightest. I see the corner of his mouth quirk up in return.

Waiters in tuxedos circulate through the lobby, carrying trays laden with bubbling champagne flutes. Fergus Griffin takes a drink off one of the trays and swigs it. He offers a glass to his wife, but she shakes her head.

My stomach is rumbling. I haven't eaten any dinner yet. I doubt Nessa has either. Maybe I could convince Fergus to let me take her somewhere to celebrate...

The cast comes out into the lobby. They've changed into street clothes but haven't washed off the heavy stage makeup, so they're far from blending in. Audience members swarm around to congratulate them. A sinuous line forms like a wedding reception. I curse how far away I am—I'll have to wait my turn to speak to Nessa.

There's a flow to crowd movement. People naturally fall into the line or move aside to get out of the way. Again, out of the corner of my eye, I see motion that doesn't quite fit the pattern. A man in a wool coat striding toward the cast members from the edge of the room.

He's got dark hair, his collar pulled up so I can't see his face. But I see his hand reaching inside his coat.

I look over at Nessa, directly in line with the man's trajectory. She's changed into leggings and a knit sweater, her face still made up from the stage with false lashes and pink cheeks. Her hair is pulled up in its tight bun, dusted with glitter. She's flushed and laughing, her eyes bright with pleasure.

As I watch, she glances up and meets my gaze. Her smile beams out, then falters when she sees the expression on my face.

I start sprinting toward her.

The man is pulling a gun out of his coat. He's thumbing off the safety, raising the barrel.

I plow through the crowd, slamming into a waiter, knocking the tray of champagne out of his hand. The glasses fly everywhere. I catch the silver tray out of the air and sprint forward, shouting "*Nessa!*"

In slow motion I see the man point the gun right at her face. Nessa sees it, too. She freezes in place, her eyes wide, her dark brows flying upward. The dancers on either side of her cringe away. She's all alone, unprotected, too startled to even put up her hands.

I leap forward, the tray outstretched.

The gun goes off like a cannon.

I feel the jolt as it hits me, simultaneous with the noise.

I collide with Nessa, knocking her to the ground and covering her with my body. I don't know where the first bullet hit. I expect to feel several more riddling my back.

There are three more shots, but I don't feel any pain. I smother Nessa, keeping her trapped beneath me so nothing can hurt her. All through the screaming and stampeding of people trying to get away, I cover her, keeping her safe.

When I open my eyes, I see the bloodied snarling face of Kolya Kristoff. He's lying on the ground in front of me. Completely dead.

Fergus Griffin stands over him, smoke still rising from the barrel of his gun. His face is contorted with rage, his green eyes glittering demonically behind the sensible frames of his glasses. Now I see it—the real fucking gangster behind the veneer of civility.

His eyes dart in my direction. I can read his thoughts as clearly as my own: he could move that gun an inch to the right and shoot me right now, solving the last of his problems.

Instead, he keeps it pointed right where it is and puts another bullet in Kristoff's back. Then he tucks the gun back inside his suit jacket.

Callum Griffin helps me up.

I pull Nessa up, too, frantically checking her for signs of damage. "Are you all right?"

She's shaking with shock, her teeth knocking together, but she doesn't seem hurt. "I'm fine." She clings to me, her arms around my neck.

Fergus's jaw twitches. Nessa is his baby girl—usually, she'd run to him for comfort.

Callum picks up the silver tray. It's got a dent the size of the softball, right in the center. "Holy fuck," he says. "How'd you know that would work?"

"I didn't."

Imogen throws her arms around Nessa, tears rolling down her face.

"Oh my god," she says between sobs. "I can't take much more of this."

"Callum," Fergus says sharply. "The police will be here in a minute. Take Aida and go home. You don't need your name attached to this."

Then he looks over at me. "I assume you don't have the cleanest record either."

"I'm not leaving without Nessa."

His expression softens ever so slightly. "I'll be here with her," he says. "We'll give a statement to the police. Then we can meet you back at the house."

"I'll stay with you," Riona says to him, folding her arms across her chest. "As legal counsel."

I hesitate. I don't want to leave Nessa, but Kristoff is dead. There's no point fighting with Fergus. Not when we're finally starting to get along.

I kiss Nessa softly on the lips. Her parents are watching. I don't give a damn.

"I'll see you at the house," I tell her. "You were unbelievable tonight, Nessa. Don't let this detract from that. You're a fucking star."

She kisses me again, not wanting to let go of me.

I hear sirens and gently unclasp her hands from around my neck.

"See you soon," I promise.

As I turn to leave, Fergus claps me on the shoulder. "Thank you," he says hoarsely. "You were quicker than me. I wouldn't have made it in time."

32
NESSA

It's Christmas Eve.

My mother loves Christmas. Usually, she throws a huge party. Or, if it's just our family, we do all the little Irish traditions like making a ring of holly for the door and putting a candle in the window. Then we cook our own fudge, pop popcorn in the fireplace, and open one present each, which is always pajamas.

Tonight I'm doing something different.

I'm going to the north end of the city, to Mikolaj's house.

I'll be back in the morning to make pancakes and open presents with my parents. But tonight it's Miko and me, all alone, for the first time in a long time.

I was amazed my parents agreed to it. I think they realized after the ballet that this is real and it's not going away.

After all, Miko saved my life. He spotted Kristoff before anybody else. He blocked the bullet headed right for my face. Then he shielded me with his own body. That's what gave my father time to shoot Kristoff in the back.

I guess the *Bratva* will be needing a new boss all over again.

Hopefully the new one won't hold the same grudge. The Russians don't take kindly to broken alliances.

Still, it was worth it if it finally proved to my parents that Mikolaj loves me. Really, truly loves me.

I'm driving to see him in a new Jeep, army green this time instead of white. It was an early Christmas present from the Gallos. Aida picked it out, and Nero worked his magic on it. It roars like a jet engine now, not to mention the giant A/T tires, winch, lift kit, and rock sliders he added. It looks like I could drive it over a mountain.

Really, I just cruise down to the studio most of the time. I'm already working on another ballet.

The tires are great in the snow. The wind blows in off the lake, forceful and wet.

I don't care. Not even a blizzard could keep me home tonight.

Miko's watching for me. He opens the gates automatically as I approach.

I drive up to the house, which looks taller and darker than ever under the blanket of white covering the roof.

The front door stands open. I leave the Jeep out front and run inside.

I step into the glow of hundreds and hundreds of candles. The whole entryway is filled with them—all different heights and sizes, glimmering in the dark. The candles are white, the light they cast, rich gold, filling the space with the scent of smoke and sweet beeswax. Mikolaj is welcoming me home.

I follow the path through the candles, across the main floor, out to the conservatory.

It's always summer in here. The plants are as thickly green as ever. Mikolaj waits for me on the bench as I knew he would. He stands when he sees me. He's dressed more formally than usual, in a button-up shirt and trousers, his hair carefully combed. I can smell his cologne, and beneath that, there's the heart-pounding scent of his skin.

I run into his arms before kissing him. The kiss goes on and on, neither of us wanting it to end. I'm so happy to be back here. I don't know how such a strange place could suit me so well, but it does. It was made for me a hundred years before I was even born. And Miko bought it for us before he knew I existed.

When we finally break apart, he brushes the last of the melting snow from my hair. "God, I missed you."

"I have something for you," I say. "It's something small."

I pull it out of my bag—wrapped, even though it's impossible to disguise a book.

Mikolaj rips off the paper. He smiles when he sees what's inside.

It's a first edition of *Through the Looking Glass*, to replace the one I ruined. It has a rich red cover stamped with a gold border and a cameo of the Queen of Hearts.

He opens to the first page—an illustration of a knight on horseback.

"You don't have that in a tattoo yet," I say, teasing him. "Do you have any blank space left? Maybe on the bottom of your foot?"

He kisses me again, squeezing me tight. "Thank you, Nessa. It's perfect."

"So," I say, "should we go upstairs? I've been missing your bedroom, too…"

"Don't you want your present?" Miko says.

I try to hide my grin without success. I've always loved gifts. Even the littlest ones make me happy. I love to be surprised.

I'm thinking Mikolaj probably got me a new record. He let me keep the old turntable and the box of vintage vinyl. He knows I've been using it for the new ballet, so I'm guessing he has an addition for my collection.

But Miko really does surprise me by dropping to one knee.

"It's not a gift exactly," he says, "since I didn't pay for it…"

He pulls a little box out of his pocket and opens it. Inside, I see the last thing in the world I was expecting: my grandmother's ring.

"What?" I gasp. "How did you—"

"I was a corpse when I met you, Nessa. No breath, no heart, no life. I felt nothing, cared about nothing. Then I saw you, and you woke me up inside. I was such a fool at first. I was so numb that I thought that spark must be hatred. If I were a normal person, I would have realized it was love. Love at first sight. From the second I laid eyes on you."

He takes the ring out of the box and holds it up. The diamond sparkles as brightly as ever in its antique setting.

"I wanted to hate you because that was easier. But as I watched you, it was impossible to ignore your kindness, your intelligence, your creativity. You're good Nessa, truly and intrinsically good in a way that most people could never dream of being. But you're so much more than that. You're talented, and beautiful, and the sexiest fucking woman in the world. Shit, I wasn't going to swear during this."

I laugh and give a little sob because I'm so, so happy. I want to speak, but I don't want to interrupt Mikolaj. I want to hear everything he has to say.

"I hated being apart from you these past few weeks. But when I got to know you, Nessa, I understood how important your family is to you. I stole you the first time. This time, I wanted their blessing."

His fingers tighten on the band of the ring.

"Your mother gave this to me. She knows I love you. I love you more than money or power or my own life. I stole you, Nessa. And you stole my heart. It's yours forever. I couldn't take it back if I wanted to. Will you marry me?"

"Yes!" I cry. "Of course, yes!"

He slips the ring on my finger.

It looks different on my hand. It looks like it belongs to me. Like it was made for me.

"Did they really give it to you?" I ask him in amazement.

"Grudgingly," he says.

I laugh. "That still counts."

He sweeps me up in his arms, kissing me over and over.

Then he does carry me up to his room.

There's a fire blazing in the grate. He sets me down in front of it, on the thick rug.

"Let me undress you," I say to Mikolaj.

He stands still, letting me unbutton the front of his shirt.

Inch by inch, I bare his broad flat chest, hard with muscle and dark with ink. I run my fingertips over his chest, down to the center-line of his navel. Mikolaj's skin is incredibly smooth for a man. It's one of those deceptive things about him. How he looks and how he feels never match up. He looks as pale as a vampire, yet he's always warm to the touch. He's so lean that every muscle looks like it could cut you, but his skin is butter soft. His eyes look like shattered glass, but they're not just a mirror, reflecting all the pain in the world—they see inside me, all the way down to my soul.

I strip off his shirt. Then I gently touch the scars on his stomach, shoulders, and arms. They're mostly healed now, the white ridges standing out against the dark tattoos. Every one of those marks is a cut he took for me.

I unbutton his pants and slide them down. His boxers, too. Now he's standing naked in front of the fire. The light dances across his skin. It animates his tattoos, making them seem as if they've come alive, moving across his flesh.

His eyes gleam in the flickering light. They roam over my face, my body. He's got that look of hunger on his features. The look that never fails to jolt my heart, making it beat at triple its normal pace. We're not even kissing yet, and already my skin is prickling, my nipples tightening, wetness soaking through my underwear.

I can't tear my eyes away from him. There's never been a man who could look so commanding without a stitch of clothing on. There's power in every ounce of those tensely coiled muscles. There's ferocity in his gaze.

Mikolaj would do anything for me. And anything *to* me. He has no limit, no line he won't cross. It's terrifying and incredibly arousing.

His cock lies heavily against his thigh. As soon as my eyes fall on it, it starts to thicken and stiffen.

Like everything about Mikolaj, his cock is insanely aesthetic. Thick, white, smooth, perfectly proportioned. The harder it gets, the smoother and tighter the skin stretches. I know how soft that skin is—the softest on his entire body. I want to touch it with my most sensitive parts. Starting with my lips and tongue.

I drop to my knees in front of him. I let the head of his cock rest heavily on my tongue. Then I tease the tip around the ridge between his head and shaft. A little drop of clear fluid forms on the slit of his cock, and I lick it up, tasting him. It tastes almost the same as his mouth—clean and rich and just a little salty.

I close my mouth over the whole head, sucking harder. More fluid seeps into my mouth like a reward. Mikolaj groans.

I bob my mouth up and down on his cock as far as I can go, coating it with my saliva. Then I use my hand to stroke his shaft while I lick and suck the head.

I've only done this a couple of times, but I already feel like I'm getting much better at it. I'm learning how to relax my jaw, how to use my mouth and hands in tandem. Mikolaj moans. I can tell what feels the best for him based off his breathing and the way he moves his hips.

After a minute he stops me.

"Don't you like that?"

"Of course I like it," he growls.

He strips off my clothes so we're both naked, then pulls me down on the rug in front of the fireplace. He pulls me on top of him so we're facing opposite directions, my thighs wrapped around his face and his cock back in my mouth.

It's a little more difficult doing this upside down, but I think I can handle it. Until he delves his tongue inside me at the same time.

Holy hell, that makes it hard to concentrate. While I'm sucking his cock, he's penetrating me with his tongue and rubbing my clit with his fingers. The angle is different than usual, and so is the sensation. There's something incredibly satisfying about his mouth on me and my mouth on him at the same time. It makes the feeling of his cock against my tongue all the more pleasurable.

My heart races faster and faster. The time since we were last alone together is so long. I'm anxiously, painfully aroused. I touch myself in bed at night thinking about him, but it's not the same as the taste and smell and sensation of Mikolaj himself. Nothing can satisfy but him.

I'm rocking my hips, grinding my pussy against his tongue. It feels so good, it must be illegal. I'm moaning around his cock, getting so distracted that I can't do my part of the job anymore.

Mikolaj doesn't care. He switches to penetrating me with his fingers, licking my clit with his tongue. He puts one finger inside me, then two. I'm moaning and riding his face, the waves of pleasure rolling through me closer and closer until there's no break in between, until it's one long rush…

The orgasm ends, but I'm greedy for more. I can't get enough of him. We've been apart for too long.

I flip around and climb on top of him instead, sliding his cock snugly inside me. The warmth of the fire caresses my skin. It burns against my face, my bare breasts, my belly. I'm incredibly sensitive after that climax. Every stroke up and down on Mikolaj's cock seems to awaken a hundred new receptors I never knew existed.

Before I know it, I'm building up again. On my way to another orgasm before the first one has properly ended. This time the sensation is deeper, concentrated inside me instead of on my clit. The head of his cock hits that second pleasure center, each stroke flint against steel, sending off sparks.

All at once the sparks catch, letting loose an inferno of pleasure. I cry out like I really am on fire, a gasp that turns into a scream. My whole body tenses. I collapse on top of Miko, limp and wrung out.

He flips me over so I'm down on all fours and enters me from behind. I groan as he slides inside. His cock is too big—from this angle, it's bottoming out, banging against my cervix.

I arch my back, and that helps a little. He grabs my hips in his hands, sinking his fingers into my flesh. I feel how strong he is. How much energy he still hasn't unleashed on me.

He's not going to wait any longer. He fucks me hard, slamming into me over and over. It's pleasure right on the edge of pain, but I like it. I love feeling how powerful he is. I love when he takes control. I love how he takes what he needs out of me.

He's grunting with every thrust, his voice deep and animalistic. The fire is so hot that we're starting to sweat. Droplets fall off his face and hair, pattering down onto my back. He pounds into me harder and harder. I can't get enough.

"Keep going..." I gasp.

There's no way he's going to stop. His body slams against mine, his cock thrusting in as deep as it can go. He gives one last push, holding his cock in its deepest position, then explodes inside me. I feel the come boiling out without any space to fill. When he pulls his cock out, it pulls the come out, too, making it drip down my thighs.

I sink onto the rug, lying on my side. Mikolaj lies behind me, spooning me. I fit perfectly in the hollow of his body. His arms lock around me, lean and strong.

"When should we get married?" I ask him.

"Immediately."

"Do you want to wait for summer?"

"No," he growls. "I don't want to wait another minute."

33
MIKO

I MEET GEO RUSSO OUTSIDE THE BRASS POLE TO HAND THE KEYS over. His payment hit my bank account this morning—he'll be the new owner of both my strip clubs (minus the one Nero Gallo burned down).

Russo pulls up in his Bentley. He's a short, stocky man—completely bald, with hands as puffy as cartoon gloves. He looks pleased and suspicious about our deal.

"Now that it's settled," he says, tucking the keys in his pocket, "why don't you tell me the real reason you wanted to sell? What is it? Have men lost their taste for titties?" He gives a wheezy laugh.

"No," I say stiffly. "I'm just moving in a different direction."

"By god." He shakes his head in amazement. "They said you'd gone crazy over some girl, but I—" He breaks off, seeing my expression. He swallows hard, his Adam's apple bobbing up and down.

"Are you going to finish that sentence?" I ask him coldly.

"No," he mutters, staring down at my shoes. "My apologies, Mikolaj."

"You can thank 'that girl' for putting me in such a good mood," I tell him. "Otherwise I'd snap your fucking neck."

I walk back to the car, where Olie is waiting to drive me over to Jungle.

"Trouble, boss?" he asks me as I slide into the back seat.

"No," I say. "Just people forgetting their place in the world. I may have to make an example out of somebody."

"Russo would be a good place to start." Olie grunts. "He snaps his gum."

"I noticed."

I'm not sorry to let the strip clubs go. There are too many other things to sell in this world—I don't have the same taste for trading women as a commodity.

I'm not getting rid of Jungle, though. That was the first place I ever laid eyes on Nessa. And I'm not so reformed that I'm above selling liquor. In fact, I've got plans to open six more clubs—here and in St. Louis. There's still room to expand in Chicago and in neighboring cities as of yet unclaimed.

I plan to renovate the house, too. Nessa doesn't want me to change it, but I tell her we should at least have proper heating.

"Why?" she says. "I don't care if it's cold. We can cuddle up together."

"That's fine for us. But what about children?"

She looks up at me, her green eyes wide. "Do you want children?" she asks quietly.

I never did before. But with Nessa, I want everything. I want every experience life has to offer, as long as it's with her.

"I can wait," I tell her. "But yes, eventually."

"I want that, too," she says.

"Are you sure?" I smile. "You know twins are hereditary."

She laughs. "Nothing with you is ever simple, is it?"

"No," I say. "It really isn't."

For our honeymoon, I planned to take her to Agra, to see the Taj Mahal. Nessa wants to go to Warsaw instead.

"I want to see where you grew up."

"It's ugly," I tell her. "And dangerous."

"The whole city isn't ugly!" Nessa protests. "There are palaces, and parks, and museums…"

"How do you know?"

"I looked it up on Tripadvisor!"

I shake my head, smiling at Nessa's endless optimism. She always finds the beautiful parts of anything. Why would Warsaw be any different?

"Come on!" she coaxes me. "I really want to see it. And I do speak Polish now…"

"Somewhat."

"What do you mean 'somewhat'?"

"Ehhh…" I shrug.

She puts her hands on her hips, frowning at me. "How good is my Polish? Tell me the truth."

I don't want to hurt her feelings, but I don't want to lie to her either.

"It's about as good as that of a fourth-grade child," I tell her.

"What!" she shrieks.

"A clever fourth-grade child," I hasten to add.

"That's not any better!"

"It's a little better," I say. "It's a very difficult language."

"How long did it take you to learn English?"

"Maybe a week." That's not true at all—she knows I'm teasing her.

She tries to give me a playful smack. I'm too quick—I grab her hand and kiss her palm instead before closing her fingers around it.

"Are we going to Poland or not?" she demands.

I kiss her again, on the mouth this time.

"You know I'll take you anywhere you want."

34
NESSA

It's my wedding day.

You picture that day from the time you're a little girl. You imagine what colors you'll use, what your favors will look like. You plan it down to the tiniest detail.

Now that it's here, I don't give a damn about any of that.

The only thing I'm picturing is the man waiting for me at the altar.

I'm already bound to him, mind, body, and soul. All that's left to do is say the words out loud.

My mother helps me get ready in the morning. She tries to put on a cheerful face, but I can tell she's still worried about all this.

"You're so young," she says, more than once.

"Grandma was younger than me when she got married," I remind her, holding up my left hand with its lovely old ring.

"I know." My mother sighs.

My grandmother was the baby of her family, just like me. She was wealthy, pampered, and tacitly betrothed to a banker twenty years her senior. Then she got a flat tire on her bicycle riding around down by the boardwalk. She wheeled it over to the closest garage. A young man pushed his way out from under a car—messy, sweaty, dressed in coveralls, and coated in grease.

That was my grandfather. They snuck out to see each other every chance they got. She said the first time they met up in the park, she wasn't even certain it was him because she hardly recognized him cleanly scrubbed.

Eventually, they were caught, and her father swore to cut her off without a dime if she ever saw that boy again. They ran away together the next night. The ring she wore on her wedding day was just a cheap nickel-plated band. My grandfather bought her the diamond ten years later, after he became an enforcer for the Callaghans.

My grandmother never spoke to her parents again.

My mother knows that. It's why she gave me the ring in the end. She doesn't want the same thing to happen to us.

She kisses me gently on the forehead. "You look beautiful, Nessa."

Riona brings me my bouquet of white roses. I didn't bother with bridesmaids, so she's wearing her usual style of sheath dress—tight and smooth, like armor. Her red hair is loose and bright around her shoulders.

"I like when you wear your hair like that," I tell her.

"I hate when it's in my face," she says. "But I wanted to look nice today."

She sets the roses down next to me on the dressing table. "When will your new ballet be done?" she asks.

"A few more months."

"Is it another fairy tale?"

"I don't know." I laugh. "I don't know what it is yet. I'm experimenting."

"That's good," Riona says, nodding. "I admire that."

"You do?" I say, surprised.

"You're finding your own way. That's a good thing."

"Riona," I say, feeling a pang of guilt. "Didn't you want Grandma's ring?"

"No." She frowns. "I told you—I'm never getting married."

"How can you be sure?"

She tosses her head. "I know what I'm like. I'm not a romantic. And I can barely stand living with my own family."

"You never know… You may be surprised who catches your eye someday."

Riona shakes her head at me. "You think that because you *are* a romantic."

Aida comes in to visit me last, bringing me a pair of her shoes—the ones she wore at her own wedding, not even a year ago. It seems like another lifetime.

"There you go," she says. She looks at my ring, my bouquet, and her shoes. "Now you have something old, something new, something borrowed, and…do you have anything blue?"

I blush. "My underwear is blue," I tell her.

She laughs. "Perfect!"

She helps me slip on the shoes and buckle them. It's hard for me to bend all the way over in my dress. It's bright white with fitted sleeves of transparent lace, an open back, and a full tulle skirt. When I look at myself in the mirror, I see a full-grown woman for the very first time. I see who I was meant to be.

"My parents aren't very happy," I say to Aida.

She shrugs. "They weren't happy on my wedding day either."

"At least it was their idea."

"It doesn't matter," Aida says fiercely. "Cal and I hated each other. You and Miko are crazy about each other. All that matters is passion. A marriage strangles and dies on apathy. Passion keeps it alive."

"So you don't think they were brilliant matchmakers?" I tease her.

"Hell no!" Aida laughs. "It was pure luck we didn't murder each other. Don't give your parents too much credit."

I smile. "I'm not getting cold feet. I've never been more sure of anything."

"I know," Aida says, hugging me. "Come on. Cal's got your coat."

I walk across the main floor toward the back door.

We're in Mikolaj's house. We're going to be married out in his garden. It doesn't matter that it's February—I couldn't marry him anywhere but here, under the dark bare branches, beneath a wide-open sky.

My brother wraps the thick white cloak around my shoulders. It trails behind me, as long as the train of my dress.

I step out into the garden and cross the grass.

I don't feel the cold at all. The snow is drifting down, thick and soft. It makes the garden utterly quiet, muffling any sounds from outside the high stone walls.

My family waits for me, along with a dozen of Mikolaj's men. I see Klara standing next to Marcel, smiling excitedly. She's wearing the black gown from the attic underneath a long coat, and she looks absolutely gorgeous.

Mikolaj waits for me beneath the archway of an empty trellis. He's wearing a simple black suit, his hair combed back. He looks slim and stark and impossibly handsome. My heart flutters at the sight of him.

As soon as I reach him, he takes my hands in his.

There's no priest or minister. My parents hate that we're not doing this in a Catholic Church, but Miko isn't religious, and I don't want anyone to say our vows but us. Mikolaj and I are marrying each other because we want to, for no other reason and under no one else's authority.

Miko holds my hands tight, looking down into my eyes. "Nessa, I'll love you every second of my life. I'll love you for exactly what you are and whatever you become. Anything you want, I'll make it happen for you. I'll never hold you back. I'll always tell you the truth. I'll keep you safe and happy, at any cost."

I swallow hard, not knowing if I can make myself speak. My throat is tight with too much emotion.

"Mikolaj, I love you with all my heart. I promise you'll be the only man in the world to me. I'll be your lover and your best friend. We'll do the hard things and the fun things. We'll make our choices together, for the good of us both. I'll always put you before anything else so nothing can come between us."

I give one last quick glance over at my parents. I'm letting go of their approval, their influence. I meant what I said—Mikolaj is my priority now.

Still, I'm glad to see they're smiling at me at least a little. They want me to be happy.

I look back at Mikolaj, and I am happy. Fully and completely.

He pulls me into a kiss, and the rest of the world disappears.

We're creating a new world now, with us at the center.

PATREON

Want to see uncensored NSFW art and stories too hot for the printed page? Check out my Patreon:

BRUTAL BIRTHRIGHT

Callum & Aida

Miko & Nessa

Nero & Camille

Dante & Simone

Raylan & Riona

Sebastian & Yelena

ABOUT THE AUTHOR

Sophie Lark writes intelligent and powerful characters who are allowed to be flawed. She lives in the mountain west with her husband and three children.

The Love Lark Letter: geni.us/lark-letter
The Love Lark Reader Group: geni.us/love-larks
Website: sophielark.com
Instagram: @Sophie_Lark_Author
TikTok: @sophielarkauthor
Exclusive Content: patreon.com/sophielark
Complete Works: geni.us/lark-amazon
Book Playlists: geni.us/lark-spotify